PAWNS

Price
of
LOYALTY

AMBER RENEE TURBA

ISBN:069282507X
ISBN-13:9780692825075

"Where the battle rages, there—and only there—the loyalty of the soldier is proven."

-Martin Luther

PROLOGUE

Pittsburgh, Pennsylvania
January 17, 2005

THE NIGHT WAS CALM. The streets, lined row after row with houses that all looked the same from a distance, were vacant. There was a thick layer of mid-winter snow blanketing the city, reflecting crystallized shadows across the dark windows. Every house on one particular block was devoid of light or motion—save for the last one.

The kitchen lights were bright, especially to his over heightened eight-year-old senses. His father sat in the chair across from him at a small wooden table while his mother prepared a fresh batch of cookies. She hummed softly as she baked, the soothing sound of her voice, paired with the lighthearted voice of his father as he talked, set the air with a peaceful mood.

"Hey dad, when are you going to teach *me* how to shoot?"

The father continued to clean the barrel of his gun, polishing it atop the kitchen table. He smirked. "How about tomorrow?"

The child beamed. From across the room, his mother sent them disapproving looks and said, "We're busy tomorrow."

Before the child could argue, he felt someone grab him by the ankle. Crawling underneath the stool, his little brother smiled at him and began to mumble small words before laughing. The older boy kicked his foot at the five-year-old, annoyed that he'd been interrupted.

"Michael Moiré!"

Michael slumped in his chair. "But Mom! Beau won't leave me alone."

"He's your brother and I won't have you kicking him," his mother said. "*Or* playing with guns."

"But—"

"You are too young." Her tone was final. "I won't have my son becoming a trigger-happy soldier like his father."

"You used to like trigger-happy soldiers once," Mr. Moiré said as he moved the gun between his fingers, drawing her attention. "Quite a bit, actually."

"That was before the boys, Alex."

"Yes, a little over nine months before each of them, if I recall correctly," Alexander said, his eyes alight as he smiled at his wife.

Michael heard his mother sigh, but he didn't see the playful smile on her lips, for his attention was entirely focused on the gun in his father's hands. He felt drawn to it. It was miraculous, and for some reason, it gripped every part of him. He wanted this weapon to be his. To follow his command. To do what he wanted it to do. To make himself powerful, in control.

"Dad, can I hold it?"

"Alex…"

"Sure you can, Mike," said Alexander, pretending not to see the disapproval etched across his young wife's face.

Michael almost fell off his stool from the overwhelming burst of excitement as his father handed him the gun and positioned it on his shoulder. He stroked the lengths of the barrel with his fingers, smiling widely.

That was when they heard a loud knock at the door.

"Sweetheart, would you see who that is? My hands are covered," Alexander said as he adjusted the gun so that it sat more comfortably on his son's shoulder. "How does that feel?"

"Perfect," Michael whispered in awe.

"Of course," Diane Moiré replied as she walked in her lithe step across the kitchen and towards the front hall. "It seems quite perfect until you actually—"

That was when the gut-wrenching sound of his mother's scream echoed in Michael's ear, committing itself to his memory where it would stay and haunt him forever. He looked over at the same time as his father, to see his mother fall to the floor, writhing in pain from what appeared to be a deep cut in her side.

"Diane!"

Michael did fall off his stool this time. He landed a few inches away from his little brother, who was watching him with a curious look in his eyes.

Dazed, Michael slid himself across the floor, still underneath the table, hidden from view. He could just barely see, but the picture in front of him was one he didn't want to watch anyway.

His father jumped up from the table and ran to the door. The man standing there with a knife walked into the house and slammed the door shut behind him. Michael's father clutched his fragile wife in his arms, blood dripping from her side.

"Who are you?" Alexander demanded. "What do you want?"

"I'm here to deliver a long-awaited sentence to Major Alexander Joseph Moiré."

Alexander slid down to his knees, his hands cradling his wife, his expression clearly too distraught to think about any type of defense for his life. Or, honestly, to care for one.

"You knew this was coming when you lied to Reeves about the boy," the man said, his tone emotionless. Though he added, with a touch of familiarity, "No one is invincible, Alex. Not even you."

"He sent you…didn't he?"

"He did." The man pulled a gun out of his pocket and aimed it at Michael's father.

Instinctively, Michael lifted the gun in his hands and set the barrel on the carpet, aimed at this man who was threatening his father. Eight-year-old Michael's fingers shook, his lips quivered.

Pull the trigger, he ordered himself. *Save my father!*

But he didn't. He couldn't.

"Listen to me," Alexander said softly. "Whatever

he told you—anything he's tried to get you to believe about me—is a lie. I'm not a traitor, and you don't want to do this. My son—"

"Orders are orders, Alex. You of anyone should know that." The man cocked the gun, now aimed at Michael's mother. "No one can outrun the past."

"Please," Alexander whispered. "Let her live. If I die, the truth dies with me. No one else has to suffer for my past, my mistakes. Please...kill me."

The man shifted the aim of his gun and fired it at Alexander's chest. Michael watched his father fall back with a shudder, sending his mother's body tumbling across the floor. She landed only feet away from where Michael and Beau were hiding. She opened her eyes, stared right at him and he could see that she was going to die, just by that one look.

The blood pouring from her body with each passing second only confirmed the horrible truth.

Michael felt tears in his eyes. He gripped the gun tighter, harder. His finger was inches from the trigger. His mother watched him do it; she shook her head ever so slightly, glanced at Beau, and Michael knew she didn't want him to shoot, to be a killer or endanger him and his brother. She knew it was too late for her, anyway.

Tears in her eyes, his mother mouthed: *run.*

But that wasn't what stopped Michael from pulling the trigger, or even what made him retreat. It wasn't her, and it wasn't anything.

He just couldn't do it.

Careful not to make a sound, Michael slid out from under the table and pulled his little brother along with him, cupping a hand over his mouth, and snuck out of the kitchen through the back. He stopped in the doorway for a moment, tears in his eyes, frozen.

The man walked over to where his mother was lying and picked her up with steady ease. "Where is the boy?" he demanded. She didn't respond. "The truth of what you've been running from has died with your husband. Alexander Moiré is the last of them, and there is no reason for you to die along with him." The man gripped her harder. "Tell me where his son is, and I will let you live."

Surprisingly, Diane Moiré smiled. It was a painful smile, yet a victorious one. "You're wrong."

"What?"

"Alex lied to you, the truth is out. And someday soon, you all will get," she whispered, "*exactly* what you deserve."

Michael watched the man's knife pierce through her back, and she let out a quiet, agonized scream before he released her. She fell to the floor, her heartbeat dying almost as quickly as that of her husband's.

Michael couldn't breathe. His parents were dead—murdered, right before his eyes—and yet, he'd done nothing.

He turned his tear-stained face to look at Beau. His little brother was staring at him, wide-eyed. And Michael could see the accusation in his eyes that was there, that would evolve and would always be there. He knew. And he would always know.

And Michael would always remember.

He ran. In his arms he carried his brother, and, strapped across his back, he carried his father's gun.

Twenty-three-year-old Michael Moiré stared out the window at the broken city of Ghazni. Watching nothing, and feeling even less.

PART ONE

ENEMIES AND ALLIES

"Death.
Out of every aspect of this world, it is the least I
understand and the most I find myself searching
for an answer to.
Losing my parents at such a young age, however,
led me to more questions about life than to
answers about death.
At eight years old, I often wondered if death is
actually a force, rather than an occurrence. Playing
its own games, choosing its own victims. Enjoying
the entertainment of men who struggle their entire
lives against an inevitable end that death, itself, has
created.

How, then, do we find the balance?"

January 1, 2019
Eight months after The Breach
Location: Ghazni
Entry: Eleven

AMBER RENEE TURBA

DESPERATION

Kandahar, Afghanistan
July 13th, 2020

THE WALLS AND THE room were silent, but not unoccupied. In the center of the six-by-seven-foot building, two small scavengers crept stealthily around the boxes and broken furniture, pillaging the area with a quiet but frenzied desperation.

The wooden door heaved against the rusted bolt lock, splintered around the edges and finally crashed down to the floor—sending the rats scampering in opposite directions.

Beau Moiré ducked through the door and stepped into the shack, his dark eyes scanning the room with cool calculation.

"Empty." His eyes passed over a rat, huddled in the corner behind an empty bag of what used to be grain. "Almost," he amended.

Justin Roland wrinkled his nose as he surveyed the surroundings just outside the door, his eyes also scanning—though Beau suspected they wouldn't find what they'd been searching for. Again.

"Damn rodents," he cursed, spitting through the dry air into a mix of sand and dirt that could fry an egg. "Always one step ahead of us."

"Just like everyone else," Beau murmured.

"Stop it." Justin cupped his hands over his eyes and glared into the distance. "There's another one. Northwest of this place, probably an hour's walk."

"Forget it. I have a feeling it'll strangely resemble this one." Beau picked up the sack of grain, its rotted contents spewing through two giant, decayed holes. His eyes passed over a few other sad supplies, also torn into and destroyed by either infestation or decay.

"Should we go back?"

Beau wanted to say: *Back to what?* Instead he replied, "Your call."

Justin surveyed the abandoned shack one final time, then nodded his head towards the road. Emotionlessly, Beau followed.

"Well?"

Justin tossed his pack onto the dirt beside his brother, his hazel eyes frustrated but not entirely discouraged. "We found three more shacks, but they were like the rest—abandoned, ransacked."

"Anything sustainable?" Matthew Roland asked hopefully, seated in the dirt, his knees bent tightly to his chest and his thin arms rested over them.

"Of course," Beau said dryly, disarming himself and then heading away from where they were sitting. "We found enough food to end world hunger and enough ammo to start it back up again."

"Someone's particularly bitter today."

Beau ignored Wes and pushed the door open, forcing himself not to gag at the rotten-wood smell that always seemed to loom inside the shack they'd commandeered. Truthfully, Beau hated the way he treated the others. They weren't his family, true—but they were the closest he was ever going to get. Justin and Matthew Roland, his cousins; Wesley and Luke Marshall, his brothers in every way except blood. They were four out of six of his only allies.

Raymond Roland, his uncle, was dead.

And Leah Venn, well…

Closing his eyes and his mind to the mere thought, Beau gritted his teeth and cleared his head, leaving nothing to dwell on. Emotionless. Numb. Closing himself off brought with it a sharp reminder of the hopeless wreck he'd been for over ten years after his parents' deaths. But it was the only way to dull his current pain.

Aimlessly, Beau walked into the small shack—a pitiful residence, but the best they could manage—and dug through his bag in his designated corner. He searched for over a minute, his hands raw and clumsy from the heat and exhaustion of traveling across the deserted landscape—in what, he knew, was a futile quest for supplies.

Finally, his tired hands gripped the communicator. He fingered the buttons, thinking, as he did every day, about his last conversation over the technological device. Michael's challenging mockery, his dangerous words. The shock and horror in Leah's voice as he taunted her with them. And—a question Beau had been wrestling with for four days now—how much of

Michael's accusations were true.

The idea that there existed a plot—*The Cataclysmic Effect*—to target, identify, infiltrate and control an entire governing nation. That, instead of ultimately controlling America like Beau and the others believed the organization Division-7-9 to be aiming for, they planned to destroy it. That Wes had known about the entire thing. And of course, that Beau had been hiding from Leah one of the darkest secrets imaginable— that Michael Moiré, D79 and the General's most valuable assassin, was his older brother.

That, at least, was true, no matter how painfully so.

And, as he did every day, Beau slid the communicator back into his bag and stepped away from it. He turned towards the other side of the room and fought the urge to go back and retrieve the device. To threaten Michael, to contact The General and threaten him, too. To retrieve every gun and ammunition cartridge they had left and walk until he found someone to shoot.

His anger boiled every time he looked at Luke, just as every feeling inside of him froze over as he really *looked* at him.

Eighteen-year-old Luke Marshall, the always spirited, ambitious youth, lay on his back, his body thin and frail and sickeningly ghost-like. He still wore the clothes he'd been wounded in: tan shorts and a grayish-black t-shirt that had been sliced open straight down the middle so Matt could access the stab wound in his stomach. It was patched and laced with gauzelike bandage; as was his left arm from where he'd been shot by Gabriel Schrader—before Beau had killed him, in the hotel ambush here in Kandahar, Afghanistan.

Luke was lying on a small cot—the only remote piece of furniture they could establish—eyes closed. His chest rose and fell consistently, but the twisted grimace on his face made it clear that he was awake.

"How do you feel today?"

Luke's eyes flitted open, groggily, as if it took a great effort. He stared at the roof for a moment before he lowered his gaze and found Beau, kneeling on the wooden floor beside him.

"Did you...find any food?"

"Yeah." Beau pulled out his last pack of dried meat and wedged it into Luke's hand. "We found a whole supply cache."

Luke studied Beau's face and then closed his eyes. "You're lying."

"Take it. You need it more than I do."

"But—"

"Luke." Beau pressed the food into Luke's palm and closed his fingers around it. "We'll manage."

Luke held it gratefully and returned his dead-eyed stare back up at the roof. His hands, Beau noticed, were trembling. "I thought...Ray left us enough money..."

"He did," Beau answered quietly. "But we're not close enough to the city to be able to spend it, and we can't risk traveling back into Kandahar—Wes swears it's being watched. We have to stick to the outskirts like this and wait for a chance. If they find us, we won't have enough ammo to protect us all. If they find us, we're dead."

"And if they don't, we're dead anyway." Luke's low, rough voice was a whisper. "Like a siege. Either way…"

Either way, they win.

"We'll do what we have to," Beau replied. "We'll survive."

"Beau?"

"Yeah?"

Luke's breathing slowed suddenly, his eyes drifted to a close. Beau stood up feeling instantaneously cold. Every visit with Luke was painful, but, other than Matt, who was trained for this, he was the only one who put himself though it. Justin hated seeing his sparring partner so broken and weak. And Wes…

As he reached the door, Luke's fragile voice caught up with him. "Do you hate me?"

Beau took a breath and held the door handle between his knuckles, which were stretched and turned white. "For?"

"Losing her."

Beau closed his eyes. He replied, his voice much more controlled than any other part of him, "You're my brother, Luke. And you did everything you could. None of it was your fault."

Luke didn't respond. Beau walked out of the shack and closed the door behind him.

It was mine.

"If we cross through this town here and board a bus, follow this road southwest and bypass the inner-city, we have a clear shot to the base in Zaranj without alerting anyone where we are or where we're headed."

Wes lowered the map onto the sand and shrugged. "I'd say it's the best, easiest and safest route we can take."

"I think we should nix the bus and walk," said Justin, his face hidden by the shadow cast over the side of the shack he was leaning against "We'd be too exposed that way and they'll be expecting us to dodge the innermost route through the city."

"You'd rather walk straight through?"

Justin nodded. "We know how to blend in, Wes. You know that. We've been doing it for years."

"Is that why we're on the FBI's Most Wanted?"

"We need supplies," Matt pointed out quickly, covering Wes's remark before Justin could respond. "Our food supply is dangerously low."

"And we won't find any until we get out of this desert and reach the southern border," Wes replied, "which could take us days if we travel by foot. I know this terrain," he said shortly. "We should have no trouble finding a market or supply shack on the outskirts where the refugee camps are."

"We'll need water," Justin said, conceding. "Not to mention a re-supply of weapons and ammo."

"All of which," Wes concluded, "lie waiting for us, in Zaranj."

"Except there's one problem."

Wes, Justin and Matt turned their heads. Beau crested the top of the nearby mound that served as cover for their encampment, his brown hair a twisted and curly mess, his army boots unlaced, his T-shirt worn and sandy, his expression utterly dead. He moved to stand before them. Beau never attended or took part in their discussions about where to go or what to do, but he always listened.

"Zaranj," he said sharply, "is in the opposite direction."

"From here?" Matt frowned, puzzled. "No, it isn't—"

"From Ghazni." Wes studied the faint glimpse of the moon overhead for a long second. Finally, he looked at Beau, eyes hard. "I know what you're thinking and you can consider it impossible."

"Nothing's impossible."

"This isn't an idealistic adventure, Beau. Changing course when we're this low on supplies is a guaranteed way to get us all killed. If we don't get somewhere, *quickly*, Luke will be dead in a week's time. Is that what you want?"

"Fine." Beau reached for his Ak-47. "I'll go by myself."

Matt snatched the gun first and tossed it to Justin. They all shared the same, stubborn look. The one that infuriated Beau and set his nerves on fire the way little else could.

"You can't ask me," Beau said quietly, "to turn my back on her."

"We're not," Justin replied. "We're asking you to trust us, and to trust that when the time allows for it, we'll do everything we can to get Leah back. But right now—"

"Right now we stick to the plan," Wes said. "We've discussed this many times over. Zaranj, *then* Ghazni. We need their supplies, and we have a straight shot from here. That was the whole point of landing in

Kandahar—middle ground. We can't turn back. We go forward."

"Leah will be all right, Beau," Matt said softly. "She's a fighter."

"And he's a *killer*."

They averted their eyes. No one challenged that.

Beau turned and walked away, frustrated as he always seemed to be anymore with so much on his mind and nothing to say. He circled the area, paced the uneven dunes until the sand he carved became too high to traverse. Beau was restless and had been for four days.

And he would be, every day, until he was far, far away from this place that Beau associated with Hell.

As he was alone in the night, he allowed all of the pain he'd been shielding himself from to sweep over him again and he sank to the ground from the weight of it. The guilt of Leah suffering because of his mistakes. The anger at Division-7-9 for separating them and at Michael for taking her. Frustration at Wesley, Justin and Matt for controlling him and keeping him bound like a caged animal. Pity, desperation and more shame for Luke's condition and the fact that there was nothing he could do to stop it from worsening.

Why did it always seem like the only ones hurt were those who were the least hurtful? Raymond, Leah, Luke, his late aunt Alyson, Wes's late fiancée Laci. All dead or dying or captured, all because of the people who actually deserved the pain, the men who'd added fuel to the fire of war and who were now watching the smoke rise from the ashes of the innocent.

The people who didn't know how to save, only how to destroy.

"People like me," Beau whispered, his words carried by the soft, almost unnoticeable wind that shifted sand over where he and the ex-soldiers of Yankee Two's footsteps had fallen.

Yet the path Beau had carved in the sand remained.

TENSION

Ghazni, Afghanistan
July 13th, 2020

I IMMEDIATELY JUMPED UP.

Ouch.

Every part of my body was all for sitting up and getting as far away from this place as humanly possible, except for my hands. I gritted my teeth as the coarse surface of the rope dug into my wrists further, for beneath the inescapable knots he'd tied, there were already two deep, bloody rifts.

Brilliant, Leah.

Blinking away sleep, I edged myself up into a sitting position, moving as slowly as my shaking limbs would allow. There was a deep ache in my lower back from the position I had somehow fallen asleep in. I scanned the tiny, bland room with a renewed sense of distaste. The air was damp, stuffy and humid from mid-July heat, and there wasn't much to look at—the room contained two dressers, a closet and a single bed. The mattress, at least, was comfortable.

The ropes tied from my wrists to the wooden

bed frame were a little less so.

My mind went back to the last four days: endlessly boring, increasingly frustrating. I'd been locked away in this room the entire time, not a word or visit from my captor aside from the small tin can of water I'd found sitting on the bedframe the day before. I'd barely been able to reach it with my bound hands, had chugged it in under a minute. The thought reminded me of the burning sensation in my scratchy throat and the hollowness in my stomach. How many days had it been since I'd eaten? I tried not to think about that.

I saw the edge of my necklace at the base of my vision, clinging to my skin with the new addition I'd snagged from home several days before arriving in Kandahar, and fought back a new wave of tears as I thought of the life I'd left behind in California.

Michael hadn't shown his face since the day he'd captured me—the day I'd found out about something called *The Cataclysmic Effect*, the day Michael had stabbed my friend, Luke, and also the day I found out my boyfriend, Beau, was keeping secrets from me.

And by *secrets*, I mean Michael, the enemy, traitor, assassin. And Beau's brother.

I still had trouble wrapping my mind around that one. The idea that Beau had a brother was shocking enough, but knowing that he had a brother who just so happened to be one of the most dangerous of his—and now *my*—enemies?

Angry and annoyed, I yanked at the ropes and clenched my fists and my teeth in a futile, yet desperate, attempt at freedom. Once I broke free I could run, though I wasn't exactly sure where my destination would be. Maybe to find Beau and confront him for all the lies he'd tossed me into, and then hold him in my arms just to prove that he was okay. Or maybe back to Kandahar to find Luke, to see if he were alive and apologize to him if he was—for risking his life to protect me, for taking a bullet that should have been mine.

Somehow, however, I knew I wouldn't end up in either of those places. I would be right here, in the city of Ghazni, searching for my cousin, Sean Collins, who'd been misled into fighting for the very same organization we were fighting against.

I pulled against the ropes until my wrists were dripping blood and I was forced to scream. From the pain, the anger, the frustration.

I screamed and screamed and screamed.

From everything.

THE CITY OF ZARANJ was exactly the way Beau remembered it.

His mind went soaring back to two-and-a-half years ago, eighteen months after he'd joined the United States Army under the alias of Joseph Locke. He was with a convoy on the outskirts of the city, near the border of Afghanistan and Iran. The place was bustling with soldiers—both enemy and ally.

Shots fired, grenades exploded, men shouted orders to other older, more experienced men while others screamed prayers up to the red and orange colored sunset sky.

The pressure that had been slowly building in the Middle East had finally become too much. The United States had only lit the fuse, though no one knew it at the time. Certainly not (then) eighteen-year-old Beau Moiré, who felt consumed by the chaos of cartridges and bombshells.

The scenario couldn't have been any more different from now.

The horizon creased the miles of endless, dead terrain and the pool of deep, shifting blue that was the pre-morning sky. Matt led the pack as they approached a shack eerily similar to the one they'd left behind in Kandahar—though it was slightly larger and less decayed. Thousands of these small shacks had popped up after the war began and the Middle East had become a warzone—Arabic tribes fighting both in and out of its borders; military compounds that supported the militia of the Middle Eastern Council and Army bases established by the U.S. Embassy. A mass of Afghan and Iraq civilians left behind the shacks in their exodus to safer lands, most of which had been killed and raided by the warring and increasingly political Muslim tribes that dominated the now deserted outskirts of the larger cities, like Zaranj had become in such a short length of time.

Matthew Roland carried with him three bags: one was Leah's, one was his medical kit and the other contained what little food remained. Wesley followed, carrying two duffel bags of clothes, a .44 Magnum and his laptop and tech case. Justin followed, carrying Luke in his arms and an M1 Garand slung across his back. Beau brought up the rear, his eyes alert with suspicion—he did not trust the area—carrying two Ak-47's, an M-16, a .9mm Glock, the 1911 Colt .45, and a bag filled with just enough ammunition to restock each gun twice.

"Looks empty," Matt said—the first words anyone had spoken in a while. The mood, as it had been since the day they'd all lost their guardian, Raymond, was solemn.

"Beau, scout out the area," Wes said, his own eyes scanning the mounds surrounding the shack. "This place has decent coverage—which could go either way at this point. Make sure we're alone."

Beau nodded absently and headed towards the shack.

"Matt," Wes continued, "you set up a place out here for a fire—a small, inconspicuous one to cook from."

Matt nodded. He turned to Justin. "Bring Luke here; I'll set up an area for him next to the fire. I think he'll appreciate the fresh air."

"As if he didn't get enough on the seventy-five-hour trip over," Beau mumbled, as Justin and Matt helped Luke onto the sand. Wes was within range of the remark, but he pretended not to hear.

Tired from travelling, Beau didn't bother with the rusty door handle. He kicked the door with his right foot, his steel-toed boot easily sending the wood splitting to the floor.

The shack was almost double the size of their last. There were three small rooms; each, Beau inspected. Two of them contained beds, the other a large cot. A wooden chair and a poorly upholstered couch crowded the small front room, which also included a rusted old sink, two bags of dried vegetables and meats in the corner, and a rat trap right in the very center. Beau found two smashed boxes of ammunition in one of the rooms, but otherwise, nothing they could use in terms of weapons.

The wall directly opposite the furniture was smeared heavily with dried blood.

Studying the shack, Beau felt a dark sense of anxiety that had stuck with him ever since the hotel ambush in Kandahar. Even looking at the dust on the floor and the blood of most likely an innocent on the wall, even knowing where The General was and where he couldn't be, Beau had the urge to let go. To let go of everything that kept him standing here, bolted in this place, miles from any chance he had at rescuing Leah and putting a bullet in every forehead of every treacherous soldier he came across that associated with the organization Division-7-9. All the hate, rage and thirst for vengeance coursed through him like a poison, attacking every part of his conscience until his blood ran thick with anger that consumed him, too.

He closed his eyes and saw his uncle Raymond die from the explosive that shook the very foundation of their team, their family.

He saw Michael, stabbing Luke until he had all but bled out, and probably torturing Leah in front of her cousin and in front of The General who would be smiling at her pain.

Beau leaned against the wall, clutching at his head, the bags slipping out of his grasp where they crashed against the floor. For some reason, his control waned. The memories, the pain, the posttraumatic sensory images hit him stronger than ever. This time, he didn't have Raymond to walk him through it. He couldn't just look outside and see the Pacific Ocean and know he was safe. This time, he was in the desert again, where all that was familiar was the ringing in his ears, smoke in his nostrils and red in his vision.

He reached in one of the bags, searching for his liquor flask, found it and threw it against the wall when it turned up bone-dry like the sand that continued on for miles and miles and miles...

Beau leaned his forehead against his arm on the wall and breathed, his heart pounding. At that moment, he thought of Leah. Her long, crazy, curly blonde hair and striking green eyes; the way her lips turned up only at the edges when she smiled as if she were too shy to show her teeth; the way she wrinkled her nose and twisted her fingers through her hair when she laughed, self-consciously but with a deep certainty that she had no idea she radiated. The way she could ignite a fire in him, at any given second, and could just as easily take it away, calming him down with one simple, soft touch.

Beau breathed, his heartbeat slowing, and straightened himself.

With a leveled stare, he turned and walked out of the shack, off to get a look at the area, fists still clenched to stop his shaking hands.

The night was silent, save for the crackling of the fire Matt had built just a few feet from the shack they'd taken up residence in. Beau lay with his arms crossed behind his head, staring up at the starless night—away from the others and their campfire. His eyes were open, because every time he closed them, the reminiscent state he was in forced a picture that stabbed straight through his heart.

"Have you ever been in love?" Leah's voice was quiet, thoughtful.

"Yes," Beau answered, surprising himself with his own honesty. "But it was a long time ago, and it wasn't real."

"How do you know if it's real or not?"

Beau had shrugged. "I guess you just have to wait. See if it works out."

"But what if it doesn't? What's the point in getting your heart broken when there's a possibility it's not even real?" Leah's eyes were fixated above, focused intently on the bright, shining stars that had filled the sky on that warm May evening in California. Beau remembered how confused she was; how desperate for an answer she had been. As if it would pass over the sky in the form of a shooting star, her eyes had never left the sky.

Just as his had never left her face.

"Because when it is real," he'd whispered, "then all of the heartache will have been worth it."

It was the memory that haunted him the most, because it was the first time in a long time that he'd remembered feeling something, anything at all. The first time he'd let someone in, unaware that she was the only one with the power to hurt him.

It was the night he'd fallen in love with her.

Beau touched the bottle of water in his left hand and his 1911 Colt .45 in the other. The second he realized that it was all he needed, Beau got to his feet and faced the open air.

"Where do you think you're going?"

Beau closed his eyes and cursed before he turned and met Justin's suspicion. "It's been seven days, and I'll be damned if I'm going to let another one pass before I get to Ghazni. Don't try and stop me."

"Actually, that's exactly what I came to do." Justin frowned. "Are you seriously ready for this, Beau?"

"I've been ready since the day she was taken from me."

"That's not what I meant," Justin said quietly. "Do you honestly believe you're ready to face him, after all this time?"

Beau averted his eyes. Finally, he said, "Michael's using Leah as bait, Justin. And he'll kill her, if that's what it takes to get a rise out of me. You know that."

Justin didn't respond.

"So it really doesn't make a difference whether I'm ready or not. I won't sit still and let anyone else die on my behalf. I won't. *I can't.*" Pocketing his gun, Beau stepped past Justin and continued on his way until a firm grip on his shoulder stopped him.

"It's too risky, Beau."

"Risky's my middle name, remember?" Beau retorted, his tone thick with bitterness. Justin caught the edge in his younger cousin's voice and his expression stiffened.

"They'll kill you."

"Good. Then maybe someone will finally win this war."

"And then what, Beau? We die without you? America crashes and burns because we couldn't get the truth out? What if they torture you for information? What if they pit you against the four of us? What then? Shall I, shall Wes, or Luke or Matt have to watch you die on a stake with your blood on our hands because I refrained from doing what you couldn't?"

"Quit being melodramatic."

"Quit running away!" Justin snapped.

"I told you never to stand between me and my path again, Justin." Beau's voice was deadly. "You know what happened the last time."

"Damn it, Beau! My father's death was not your fault!"

"Yes it was!" Beau shouted, his teeth bared. "You know it was! All of this is my fault—*because of him!*" Beau's chest rose and fell harshly.

Justin shook his head. "You're not ready for this, Beau. Michael will tear you apart."

"Let him fucking try."

Justin caught Beau's other arm and twisted it behind his back before his younger cousin could make the move that he knew would come. Beau's gun slid out of his grip and his water spilled to the sand. Justin wrenched at Beau's arms and pulled them tighter together, farther out of place. He was immobilized, but that didn't stop him from trying to thrash his way out. Beau dug his elbows into Justin's chest to try and push him away as he kicked at Justin's knees to try and buckle them so he could make a break for it, but it was all to no avail. Justin twisted his arms behind his back and lined his wrists together. Beau didn't know what was happening until he felt the rope against his skin. He immediately stopped struggling.

His expression was taut with rage, but inside he felt only a strong wave of betrayal. "Always a team, huh? Always on my side, no matter what."

"Shut up," Justin said as he tightened the knot around Beau's wrists to a degree that burned his skin and left no room for defiance. "You know I hate this just as much as you do."

"I doubt that."

Justin sighed and said, "You want inside the shack or out?"

"Out." Beau spit the word venomously.

He didn't fight back because it was pointless. Instead, he followed to where Justin drove a metal sliver deep into the clay with all of his weight and tied the ends of the rope to it. He gave Beau enough slack to move a foot or two, but no more. He could stand, he could sit, he could lie down, but he could not run before the rope jerked him back, and it was tied so tight he knew it would take him days to work his fingers through, days he couldn't afford. Beau felt powerless against everything, chained up as if he were a dog on a leash with every last bit of energy drained from his system. Beau was suddenly very tired, and Justin could tell.

"This wasn't my idea," he said quietly.

Justin waited for a response, but Beau stared

across the deserted landscape stretching out miles and miles before him and said nothing. Justin sighed again, and turned back towards the shack. As he passed, he placed one hand on Beau's shoulder as an act of amends. Beau did not acknowledge the gesture.

As Justin walked away, Beau sensed another's presence. He didn't turn, didn't face him. He did, however, deliver a sharp threat that would remain strong until the second he was released. It was the last bit of strength he could muster. For now.

"You just crossed the line."

"You've left me no choice," Wesley Marshall replied before turning away.

CAUTION

I STRAINED MY EARS to catch the sound of footsteps outside the door to my captivity, but they came and passed a second later. I breathed a sigh of relief and leaned back against the headboard.

Just as I did everyday, I tested the ropes chaining me to the bed. My skin burned at the barest pull, and my eyes immediately began to water. Pretty soon, the rope would be pulled so tight I would feel it non-stop, cutting deeper and deeper into my wrists.

I have to get out of here.

As slowly and with as little movement of my hands as possible, I tilted my head back and patted the top of my head, searching. After almost a minute, my cheeks were stained with tears from the pain, my wrists were dripping blood and in my palm was a black bobby pin.

I really hope this works.

Digging the pin into the center of the knot, I slid it through and began to push on it from both sides using every one of my fingers. My heart soared as the center of the knot loosened the slightest bit. If I could just slide the one end through—

I heard a sharp *ping* as the bobby pin slipped out of my fingers and hit the frame of the bed. I cursed. Scooting myself as far back against the headboard as I could, I dipped my bound hands through the crack and reached down for it, the skin of my wrists protesting greatly. I gritted my teeth as I scoured across every—

There! I cautiously touched the pin so as not to drop it further and secured it between two fingers. Lifting myself up off the bed, I slid it onto the sheet in front of me, then replaced it back into my hands. Finally, I stuck it back into the knot, more careful this time to keep at least two fingers on it at all times.

I worked precariously behind my back for over an hour, struggling to loosen the ropes without losing the pin while also trying to fight the headache that was growing from the pain in my wrists and the lack of energy in my body.

The ropes slacked. *Finally.*

I slid my hands out of the bind, rejoicing with the freedom I'd never thought was so wonderful before now.

I slid off the bed—making sure to be as stealthy and silent as possible—and tip-toed towards the window. Before I even bothered with the latch, I glanced out the smudged glass and tried to discern how high up it was.

Shit. The ground was at least twenty feet away. I deduced that I would probably break at least one of my legs from a fall like that, especially because I had no experience with how to land. If I tried it—which I strongly considered—I probably would have ended up on my face with each of my limbs bent the wrong way.

As tempting as that was, I ran to the door and placed my ear up against it, listening for at least a minute. I was growing antsy, but the last thing I wanted was to kick down the door only to walk straight into Michael's knife. I still felt the blade against my chest from where he'd struck me last time, leaving a deep cut that hadn't really healed.

I waited at least twice as long. Silence.

It was a risk. But what could I do? If I stayed here, waiting longer, the chances of him returning would grow greater. I had no way of knowing where he was, all I had to gamble on was whether or not he was still in the apartment. If he wasn't, I had time—an unknown amount, but time nonetheless. If he was…

I kicked at the door. The wood pulled against the frame, but the locks held it in place. Desperately, I kicked again. It heaved once, and then settled back in place. Defiant. Unyielding.

Two can play that game.

I reached back into my pocket and pulled out the bobby pin I'd taken from my hair. Pursing my lips, I stuck it into the key hole and twisted it. The pin met with resistance, but I turned it further, hoping it would catch and work.

It didn't. I flicked the bobby pin through the air, frustrated. It spun and fell near the corner of the room. Quickly realizing that it was the only valuable tool I had at this point and that discarding it was foolish, I took a deep breath and walked back over to where it fell, my legs weak and tight from being constricted for so long.

As I reached down for the pin, something else caught my eye. In the corner of the room, wedged against the wall was a small, thin piece of metal. Curious, I picked it and the bobby pin back up and returned to the door.

Once, when I was younger, I'd seen Sean do something like this. He'd been playing some video game—*Fallout* or *Assassin's Creed*—and had picked a lock with two small, thin pieces of metal. I eyed the metal, the pin and the lock, and then tried to mimic what my cousin had done. Using one as an anchor, I twisted the other against the bottom, then twisted the one on top. After fumbling around with the idea for over fifteen minutes, I sighed and was ready to give up.

The lock clicked. Open.

I closed my eyes, my heart shouting a joyous *Yes!*

I turned the knob and, to my relief, the door opened. As I stepped out of the room, I held the small piece of metal in my right hand, wielding it as the only weapon I had.

Though it was unnecessary. The place, as I'd hoped, was empty.

I had never been in any other room of Michael's apartment. He must have drug me through the outer rooms initially, but I had been unconscious then, so the scene in front of me was new.

Well, in theory. The place was old. It was all one big room, split off into three subsections: a kitchen, living room and small foyer that led to the front entranceway. There was little furniture in the living room—a couch, which he must have been sleeping on for the past week, a small coffee table and some worn-out exercise equipment in one corner. The kitchen held only a few cabinets, a small box refrigerator and a poor excuse for a dining table—two of the legs were broken. Every surface was covered in a thick layer of dust.

Wrinkling my nose, I headed straight towards the door. I noticed my black boots sitting in the corner of the kitchen and I quickly picked them up and slid my feet into them.

I saw it out of the corner of my eye as I grabbed the doorknob. Sitting on the coffee table in the living room, closed but humming with power, was a laptop fastened to the table like a desktop.

I hesitated, biting my lip. Michael was an important soldier in the organization. He probably had loads of secret information stored on that thing. If I could just get a glimpse—

No. I couldn't risk it. Time was a luxury I did not have right now. Turning back around, I reached for the knob again, even twisted it in my hand.

Just one quick look, I decided. A few minutes couldn't hurt. Beau would have done it, wouldn't have given it a second thought. *Granted, he probably would've waited with a gun until Michael came back...*

Quickly, I ran and sat, uneasily, on the couch. Surprisingly, despite the dust, it was comfortable. I pulled the laptop within reach and flipped it open. It was on and already signed into Michael's account.

Lucky, I wondered, *or a false coincidence?*

Either way, I was too curious to turn back now.

"CAPTAIN!" A VOICE CALLED.

Michael Moiré spun and frowned at the old man approaching, his hands clasped behind his back to conceal his weapon. "Mr. Hassan."

Aziz Hassan glanced at Michael's hidden arm, suspicious. He caught sight of the blood that covered Michael's white T-shirt and his eyes widened.

"You *summoned* me, Aziz?" Michael said, enunciating slowly.

The man frowned and recovered quickly, eyes narrowing again. "Yes. The General requests a word with you."

"How soon?"

"When it is…convenient for you."

Michael slapped the pistol behind his back against Aziz's chest as he passed. "Take care of that, will you?"

Murmuring to himself, Aziz walked off in the opposite direction as Michael headed towards The General's quarters, which just so happened to be on the same level he was currently walking. He arrived at the door moments later.

"Come in," The General said, after a knock.

Striding forward, Michael stepped into the room, bowing his head as per protocol.

"Have a seat, Michael."

Michael had already taken notice of the two other occupants in the room: one a corporal, from U6 of Jackson's crew, the other an older man in his fifties, dressed in a dark suit and tie, whom he had never seen before. Michael sat in the only chair in front of the General's desk, his hands resting at his sides above the weapons he carried at almost all times though few were actually aware of it.

"Would you please give us a moment, Mr. Withe?"

The man nodded respectively, then crossed the room and exited without a glance at him. The other man, the familiar corporal, sat up a little straighter, his hawk eyes fixed solely on Michael. He didn't appear surprised at the blood spattered on Michael's clothing.

"Is this the soldier you claim interfered with your mission, Kye?" The General asked, his tone neutral.

The corporal nodded. "That's him, without a doubt. Though I wouldn't consider him much of a soldier."

"Would you please explain, one more time, the events that took place this morning?"

"Absolutely," the man sneered, leaning forward as if his presence was even remotely intimidating. "I was on recon with a squad from Quadrant 79-03, on the outskirts of Ghazni, when this, this...snake attacked the targets we were assigned to watch. No, a more accurate term would be *slaughter.* He slaughtered them, General!"

"Snake?" Michael maintained a straight face as

he drew his knife out of his pocket with lightning speed and studied it with mock curiosity. "Tell me, corporal. Do you know the time in which it takes a…snake to strike a target less than three feet away?"

The corporal eyed up the distance between them, eyes burning with discomfort. "You see, General? Threatening. Uncontrollable. Just like I said. Why do you think they call him the raz—"

"Thank you, Mr. Hauk," the General said, his tone exhausted. "Rest assured, I will deal with the situation."

The corporal looked exasperated. Nonetheless, he stood up and strode to the door, his eyes shooting daggers at Michael the entire way out.

The door closed and The General looked up at Michael through eyes dark with contempt. "Covert?"

"A minor miscalculation."

"Covert?" the General repeated. "I know you heard me when I gave you those orders. Specifically that this was to be a *covert* operation."

Michael fought very hard to keep his eyes from rolling and, instead, inclined his head. "My apologies…sir."

"How do you think my soldiers will feel if they find out that I have an assassin targeting individuals inside the city? What if the media caught wind of this?"

"Now this is a political debate?"

"This is not a debate. This is an adult scolding a child for insubordination—a crime that you would do well to discontinue your repetition of. Remember why you sit here, Michael Moiré."

Michael pursed his lips at the threat but said nothing.

The General studied him. "Fortunately, I will overlook this rather large error and trust that, in the future, you will do *much better* at keeping your missions covert. Am I understood?"

"Yes, General," Michael said, the perfect tone of obedience.

The General waved his hand in dismissal and, bowing once more before he left, Michael exited the room. The second he did, he pulled out the blinking walkie talkie clipped to his belt and lifted it to his lips after he'd discerned the current corridor to be empty.

"What the fuck did I say about a low profile?"

The device beeped once and then buzzed with static. Finally, an irritated voice came on the line.

"What did you expect, Moiré? You asked me to take them out, I took them out. What difference does it make how I do it?"

"Because," Michael said, rubbing his temples, "that damned rat Kye Hauk saw me and reported it."

The man cursed in Arabic. "Did he see my guy?"

"No, asshole. He saw me."

"Weren't you on a mission for...uh...you know?"

Michael glanced down at his blood-covered shirt and replied, "Yes. It went well, though. I was headed back to my apartment when I stopped in the recon vicinity to see how your man did."

"And?"

"And nothing. He bailed. Got cold-feet. I had to finish it myself and that's why Hauk caught *me*."

"Ah, shit…All right. I'll take care of him."

"Do that." Glancing to the sides, Michael lowered his voice and said, "I need to speak with you in person, Dez. He gave me word that he'd be arriving soon to meet with each of us individually."

"Ah, shit…"

"Relax. I covered your tracks—God knows you can't handle that yourself."

"You're an angel, Michael. Truly."

"Next time, Dezuriel, get the timing right," Michael said sharply. "You're lucky I was there to take the fall for you, like I always do, or they would have executed your ass months ago. Hell, you're lucky The General hasn't come down on you yet."

"You think he knows about my team?"

"Yes," Michael snorted. "He just knows how little of a threat you are to his plans."

"He needs me more than he needs you."

"That's why you're still alive. For now." Michael clicked his walkie off and replaced it on his belt.

Shaking his head, he took off towards the elevator. Seven levels later, he was walking out the door, through the disinteresting city of Ghazni, towards his apartment on the south side.

MY EYES WERE WIDE. There was so much information, all of it only a click away.

Each individual file was marked by an icon—and there were hundreds of them on the desktop. The only problem was that I didn't know what half of the titles meant.

The first one I clicked on brought up a map. There were markings on it, symbols and etchings written in a language I guessed was Arabic. The words, however, were in English.

A map of Beau's whereabouts, titled *Yankee Two*, told me he was in the outskirts of a city called Zaranj. I don't know how they managed to track him or how Michael had gotten a hold of this, but I made a mental note of the map itself, then exited out of the icon, highlighted it and pressed DELETE.

Maybe it wouldn't delete their tracker, wouldn't change anything. Maybe it would. Either way, it was an act against D79, a blow—no matter how small.

The second file I discovered was different.

The title *Yankee* caught my eye, and, curious, I clicked on it. Instead of a map like the one on the other link, this one led me to an article from USA Today.

"September 23rd, 1996," I read quietly to myself. "A jet departing from Ghazni, Afghanistan at approximately 2:43pm eastern time, expected to arrive in the U.S. the same evening, crashed down six miles off the coast of New Jersey. The coast guard reported the cause of the crash due to uncharted, violent wind currents. No bodies were recovered, but the full passenger list was taken from the airport in Afghanistan. The death toll included thirteen passengers; no survivors, nor conclusive wreckage.

"The jet was evidently carrying U.S. Army soldiers on leave, and we regret this loss as a devastating one. The tragedy, as it stands, was deemed an accident. No further investigation was explored…"
I scrolled down the page, skimming over the names. The tenth line down made my eyes widen.

Mr. and Mrs. Alexander Moiré, ages twenty-two and twenty-three.

That couldn't be right. Beau had told me that his parents were murdered when he was five years old, not killed in a plane crash. And if they had died when he was five, it would have been in 2005—unless Beau was actually older than twenty, which, given his track record on secrets, wasn't entirely out of the question. So, was he lying again? Or was this some sort of trick? A cover-up? Or just a simple mistake? Somehow, it all didn't add up.

I scrolled further.

Wyatt Vendelle, age twenty-two. Scottran "Scott" Dellis, age twenty-six. Raymond Roland, age twenty-three.

My mind was spinning. So, the report had to be wrong, or at least falsified. Raymond hadn't died in a plane crash; he was alive until a few days ago. Unless the man who Beau and the others called Raymond was someone else entirely, disguising himself as Beau's uncle and Justin and Matt's father…

I slipped my head into my hands, trying to dull the ache that was forming as I felt like I had become someone else. Someone who didn't know right from wrong, truth from lie. Someone who questioned everything. Suspicious, untrusting. Was there anything solid about my life anymore?

Keeping a steady hand to my left temple, I directed the mouse across the screen, searching for anything else notable before I left this place for good.

The next icon I selected was titled "Logbook."

Instead of a map or an article, this one was a simple notepad, almost like a journal. It contained entries, but no dates.

"'I wrote down everything,'" I read. "'My thoughts, my ideas, my suspicions. Every map, every piece of sacred information, every guarded scrap of Intel. Perhaps it will be useful to future generations. Perhaps not. Either way, from my experience, I have learned that it is always better to be prepared...' 'Life and death, right and wrong. Sometimes I question whether they are truly opposites, or rather compliments of one another...' 'There's always another secret, another trick. Another betrayal. In a way, deception is predictable...'"

I frowned, squinting at the screen, confused further—as if that were even possible. First the alleged plane crash, now this? I searched the link for the author's name. It didn't list any.

Unnerved, I moved onto the next, titled *Sgt. Class. Indx.* I perked up. Sergeant Classification Index?

What caught my attention was the insignia on it—one I recognized from the day Wes and Beau had informed me that Sean had been recruited to the terrorist organization D79. He'd worn the classification patch of a sergeant.

I scanned the list of names; each one included an attachment that detailed the individual's life and service. I scrolled down to "C" and there, halfway down, I found the name I was searching for.

Collins, Sgt. Sean Austin.

It had been a while since I'd heard Sean's middle name. He didn't use it often.

Clicking on the attachment, I read everything it displayed. His childhood details, his service, the Army Reserves, his college degree and previous job experience and then, finally, his stationing.

My jaw dropped. *Impossible.* According to the index, Sean was stationed in—

A hand shot forward and slammed the top of the computer down. I gasped, standing up and backing away quickly, guiltily.

Fearfully.

"Well, well, *well.*"

CAREFUL CALCULATION

BEAU GRIMACED AS THE rope dug into his wrists, but he knew better than to fight back. They weren't trying to hurt him. They were, again, trying to reason with him—something he had no interest in.

"We're all we have left," Wes said. "And we have far too strong of an enemy to be fighting amongst ourselves. I want to release you, Beau. I don't want you to feel as if you're a captive."

"Then don't treat me like one," he replied coldly.

Justin yanked against the rope, and Beau closed his eyes as he tried to suppress the sharp, burning pain.

"Will you cooperate?" Wes asked coolly. "And by cooperate, I mean not attempt to run off on your fucking family every second."

"Yeah, every *other* second we could handle."

"Shut up, Justin."

"Beau," Justin pleaded further, anticipating his response. "Just say it. Even if you don't mean it! Stop fighting this."

Beau gritted his teeth and replied, again, "No."

Wes pursed his lips and shifted his eyes. Shaking his head ever so slightly, he flicked his wrist through the air. Justin gripped the rope with two hands and twisted it at a sharp angle so that it cut into Beau's raw skin further. Beau jerked his wrists away, cursing loudly, which only intensified the effect.

"Stop." Matt strode out of the shack, his ever-patient face grim with anger. "Let him go."

Justin loosened the rope and, momentarily relieved, Beau slid down onto his hands and knees.

"Look at him," Matt snapped. "He's not going to submit and the both of you already know that. He'll die before he gives in. Is that what you want?"

"Of course not," Justin said defensively, appalled at the thought.

Wes was a little less contrite. "I think he's a bit tougher than a piece of rope, Matthew. You know the circumstances at hand."

"I do," Matt agreed. "I do not, however, support the way you're handling them, Wesley."

"Don't pretend we have a choice," Wes said sharply. "You know as well as I that if we let him go he'll run straight to Ghazni and get himself killed. I would like to see him live a little while longer than that, wouldn't you?"

"Torturing him is not the answer."

"Then why don't you tell me what is."

"Guys," Justin said, "cut it out. We're all on the same side here."

"Are we?" Matt replied, as he folded his arms across his chest and raised a mocking eyebrow at Beau. "You could have fooled me."

Wes narrowed his eyes. "I asked him to cooperate. I begged him to reconsider. As you can see, he won't and we can't just let him go. If you've any better suggestions, now would be an excellent time to share them."

Matt glanced back and forth from Justin to Wes and then walked over to Beau. He folded his feet underneath him and sat down in the dirt beside his younger cousin.

"We will rescue Leah," Matt said reasonably. "I promise you that. Do you believe me?"

Beau's chest rose and fell. He closed his eyes and, after a moment, he nodded.

"You know what we're up against," Matt continued. "We can't gamble on this, Beau. Not now."

"If it were anyone else," Beau said quietly, "you'd have planned the rescue by now."

"That's not true."

"You know it is."

Matt sighed. Beau stood up, pushing aside the stinging pain in his wrists and turning to glare at them, one by one. "If it were me—if Michael had taken *me* prisoner instead of Leah—say you wouldn't have dropped *everything* to find me. Say you would've done nothing. *Lie to me.*"

Justin, Wes and Matt shared a look.

"All right," Justin said. "We get it."

"How is this any different? How is this fair?"

"It's not!" Matt snapped, his calm exterior wavering unexpectedly. "It's *not* fair, Beau. Don't pretend you're the only one who cares for Leah! We

53

regret her capture just as you do, but we're not blinded by love. We have what you never will and that is perspective. If Leah knew the situation, she would want us to do our job, our mission, *first.* Even she understands what's at stake here. You, Beau, seem to be the only one who truly does not."

Beau shifted his aim to Wes. "What if it were Laci?" he snapped. "How would you feel if she were the one taken while you stood by and let it happen?"

"Laci is dead," Wes replied coldly. "My fiancée died because of D79, and I'll be damned if I'm going to let her death be in vain. She, too, would want me to focus on our mission—now more than ever. That, Beau, is something you have yet to learn."

"Sacrifice?" he snorted.

"Responsibility."

"Just let me go," Beau reasoned. "I swear to you, I'll come back alive. I'll find Leah and bring her back. Give me twenty-four hours."

Matt shook his head. "You'll confront Michael, and he won't hesitate like you will. He doesn't have the heart that you do, Beau. You feel remorse for the people you kill. He never has."

That's not true, Beau thought. *He used to.*

"Just one day."

Matt sat back on his heels and sighed. It wasn't a frustrated sigh, or a defeated sigh.

It was a tired one.

"You can't ask us to forfeit you, just as we can't ask you to forfeit her." Matt lowered his head. "So we're stuck here until we come to some sort of compromise."

"Justin?" Beau said, appealing to his older cousin, his role model, his comrade; the one Beau could always count on to be on his side.

Justin, too, lowered his head.

"Wes?" Beau's hands were trembling.

Wes shook his head. "I sympathize with you, my friend. You know I do. But I'm afraid there are a lot more people who will suffer because of your death than hers. That's the hard truth here, Beau."

Beau stared at the earth. He knew they were right, that he couldn't drop everything and risk going into Ghazni where Michael, The General and probably three-quarters of Division-7-9 were waiting for him. At the same time, however, he wasn't sure his heart could take another second of guilt at the thought of *not* going.

He barely felt it when Justin rested his hand on his forearm. No one needed to tie his wrists behind his back this time. He jerked his arms away from Justin, away from Wes, from Matt, and walked back into the confined shack that had become his cell.

I FOUGHT THE URGE to gasp at how similar he looked to Beau—the tall physique, muscular build, dark eyes. His hair was less curly, however, and very blond. He wore the same outfit I'd last seen him in, though there were two key differences: his pants were gray camouflage instead of brown, and the white t-shirt that accentuated the hard muscles of his chest was splattered with blood.

His eyes, I noticed, were cold as ice.

"Beautiful and deceptive. An interesting combination," Michael Moiré said darkly. "Very *promising.*"

My hands were trembling fully now, my lips quivering, my eyes darting around the room trying to find an escape route. Several times I considered the open door. I glanced back at Michael, sizing him up. It would be a contest of speed; something I'd always had an advantage of...

He caught my eye and smiled, daringly.

I bolted towards the door, digging my heels into the thin carpet and using every muscle in my legs to push me as fast as my body would go. I reached the entranceway at the same time Michael slammed me back against the side wall as he kicked the door shut.

"I come home from a long day of work—as you can see," Michael said, his tone mockingly dramatic as he gestured to his bloody shirt, "expecting to get some rest on my couch considering there's been a very unfriendly woman in my bed when, *lo and behold*, I find my one and only captive...*out* of captivity."

My mouth was sealed shut. Michael moved slowly towards me, his expression impressively controlled and leaned his elbow onto the wall behind me. I smashed myself back against the wall, my pulse racing, but there was no escape this time.

"What am I supposed to do with you?"

My hands shook. "You can let me go."

"Tell me why," he said derisively, "I would ever

do that."

"Because you don't need me," I said. "You've already pissed him off. Beau will come and he'll fight now. Keeping me locked in here is pointless—"

"Bitch bitch *bitch*. Is that all you ever do? Honestly. I surrender my room and my bed to you and this is how you show your gratitude?"

"My *gratitude*?" Exasperated, I momentarily forgot my fear and pushed back. "First you stab Luke and then drag me to who the hell knows where, then you lock me in a room for a week with barely a drop of water or food, and then you expect me to *thank* you?"

Michael's eyebrows shot up. "Beautiful, deceptive and bold. Now that," he said, smiling, "is a dangerous combination."

I didn't see him pull the knife until it was against my skin.

I inhaled deeply, pressing myself further back but unable to move. Trapped.

"Let's see what else you're made of."

I shook my head rapidly.

"Come now." Michael slid the tip of the blade down my arm, the cold metal cutting into my skin just enough to sting. He smiled. "Surely my brother must have taught you something. Fight back."

I continued shaking my head. Michael brushed the knife across my palm and then twisted it at the base of my wrist. I tilted my head back against the wall and closed my eyes, my fists clenched. It took everything in me not to flinch or fight back. A thin line of blood ran down the length of my arm.

"Can I tell you a secret?"

He twisted it further, harder. I bit my tongue.

"I trained Sean how to fight."

I gasped—though, this time, not from the pain. "You're lying."

"Am I?"

I reached out and slapped him across the face because he had just crossed the line. His expression was surprised for one split-second before he controlled it again. *What have I done?*

Now, however, his eyes were blazing.

Michael took the knife into his fist and slammed it against the wall beside my head, digging the blade into the wall where it stuck out a mere three inches. And then he backed away, his derisive smile a ploy to riot me as much as possible.

"Sean was so weak," he remarked. "Luckily for him, he had an excellent mentor. Honestly, Leah, you should see the progress he's made." His eyes glittered. "He's just like me."

"Stop it!" Eyes narrowed, I yanked the knife out of the wall and stepped up to his challenge. "Why do you want to fight me?"

He smiled. "Curiosity."

"Are you sure it isn't cold-hearted *arrogance?*" I snapped.

"Passionate," he said. "It's a shame you're just his pet. You could make a fine hit man...woman...All you need is some practice. And muscles."

Angrily, I threw the knife at his mocking face. He twisted to the left, dodging it easily. I didn't give up. I spun to where he'd moved and swung my right arm out to clip him in the stomach while simultaneously aiming a kick to his groin. Again, he moved out of the way a fraction of a second before I could make any contact.

"Persistence," he said calmly, nodding.

I bared my teeth, his indifferent attitude grating against my nerves. I glanced around the room, trying to find something I could utilize quickly and easily that would wipe away that arrogant smirk.

"Resourceful."

Behind me, I saw a pair of scissors. Gripping them like a dart, I snapped my wrist and sent them flying straight at his neck. He didn't even have to dodge this time. My throw went so far left it smashed against a window and rebounded. Bulletproof glass? I cursed.

"Dreadful aim."

"Shut up!" I growled, my eyes searching for another tool.

"Poor attitude."

Finally, I gave up on weapons and used the heel of my boot, high-kicking him square in the face. It happened before I even had a chance to calculate it so this time, it worked. His head jerked back and I heard the harsh sound of his nose *crack*.

There was blood on his face, but he came up laughing.

While I had him, I sent a punch at his chest with all of my strength, only to feel like my fist collided with concrete. I recoiled instantly and fought the urge to rub my knuckles.

"Weak arm muscles," he commented.

My chest was rising and falling rapidly now. I circled him for a moment, trying to find any weaknesses. His entire body appeared strong, unbreakable, which was little to my surprise; particularly his arms, corded thick with muscle.

His hands, however, drew my attention.

"You're right-handed." On his right hand was a long, deep rift that had scarred over. Both times I had seen Michael wield a gun, he had used his left hand—which, don't get me wrong, was accurate enough to shoot through a one-inch thick rope from several yards away—but I had a feeling that it wasn't his dominant hand. Several times, despite the scarred injury, I remembered him using his right hand with slightly more coordination than one should have had, such as when he jammed the knife into the wall and when he was tying the rope around my wrists. The real tell, however, was the way he curled in the fingers on his right hand every time he used his left, as if forcing himself to keep his dominant hand stationary.

He smiled calmly—beneath his careful reserve, however, I could see a faint glimpse of shock. "Perceptive," he said. I noticed how he, again, curled the fingers on his right hand, almost self-consciously now.

And while my attention was preoccupied with it, he chose that moment to strike. Michael lunged at me, his movements so quick I had no time to anticipate the attack or defend myself from it. He caught me by the wrist—my weakest point, thanks to the rope binds—and jerked his arm back, pulling my arm and twisting me so hard I spun forward, then backwards as I tried to recover. My knee caught against the edge of the small coffee table and I crashed to the floor, sliding at least two feet and rolling several more.

There was a four-inch gash on my knee, as well as a brush burn that spanned the entire length of my leg. I exhaled, trying to block out the sharp pain I felt in my back.

"You need to be aware of everything going on around you at all times. Never commit yourself to one direction. Perception doesn't have to be limited. Open your senses, stay focused, but even more importantly, stay alert and you will never be caught off-guard."

I exhaled roughly and coughed, my throat burning from the dust.

"Get up now or stay down."

Honestly, staying down had so much appeal at the moment. Michael stood in front of me, his left hand extended.

Pushing myself up off of my stomach, I hesitantly took Michael's hand because I was afraid he would stab me with it if I didn't, and he pulled me to my feet. Without missing a beat, he kicked my feet out from under me and slammed me back down against the floor so hard I began to see stars.

When I was able, I sent him a glare. "Why are you doing this?"

"Never accept help from your enemy. It's just an easy way for them to control you," he said shortly, as if this should have been obvious. "Get up and stay up before I kick you the way I used to kick your worthless cousin. He bitched a lot like you do, by the way."

My blood boiled as I realized, again, that he was toying with me. Brushing the dust from my elbows, I forced myself up despite the pain that shot through my limbs and moved away from him. We circled each other for a time, his eyes never leaving mine. I struggled to do the same, for he kept shifting so much it was distracting. I tried to control my emotions, my fear. To breathe, center myself and block all else out.

"Good stance," he said, and sent a half-powered kick to my shins. I stumbled for a moment, but bent my knees a little and steadied. "Always maintain stability, but never rest on the balls of your heels—it'll slow you down if you need to strike or, in your case, quickly run away."

I rolled my eyes. Michael dropped his steady posture and walked towards me. I tensed immediately and started to back away, but he held his hand up and said, "Relax," which did not relax me in the slightest. As he came within hitting distance, I aimed my fist at his face and, with the full force of his right arm— proving that it was just as strong as his left—he twisted my arm behind my back and spun me around so that he was directly behind me and had my arms in a pretzel. I gasped as the pain bolted through me like an electric shock. His lips touched my ear.

"I said *relax.*"

He released me roughly. I stood rigid this time, my hands balled into fists as he came close and circled me twice, studying me up and down. His scrutiny was unnerving and I felt vulnerable to the point that it became difficult to remain still while an enemy was so close.

"Strong legs," he noted. "Probably a treadmill junkie."

Through my teeth I said, "I was a lifeguard," though I wasn't sure why I even felt the need to explain myself to him.

"Not a very good one, I imagine," he replied offhandedly.

It took everything in me to stay still. Michael continued to study me impassively, crossing behind me and moving around my back. I clenched my fists, bracing myself for a blow, an insult or both.

"Nice ass."

I spun and gaped at him, my eyes narrowed menacingly. Ignoring his orders to relax, I sent a fist at his face that clipped him in the ear as he turned away, shifting just a step but somehow ending up right in front of me, completely unharmed but for a light tap on the ear.

He reached around and touched the back of my arms like I had never moved, his fingers cold against my skin. I tensed like a rock. His rough hands felt my biceps—or lack of them—and then he released me and backed up.

And then came at me again.

This time, I was ready for it. Michael actually aimed a blow at my face, but I stuck my hand up to block it as I ducked my head out of the way. Just as he claimed, my arm muscles didn't hold up against the attack, and he knocked me backwards and off my feet just as easily as before.

But I didn't quit, and neither did he. I jumped to my feet and dashed left as he swung at me from the right. I missed the coffee table this time by centimeters and pressed my back against the wall to steady myself but quickly moved away as to not trap myself. As his eyes never left my face, mine never left his body, particularly his core. I rocked on my heels, ready for another attack. My pulse raced. Blood pumped fast in my veins from the adrenaline. My mind, I noticed, was more clear, sharp and perceptive than ever before as I tried to anticipate his next move.

I felt so alive.

When Michael changed direction and I spun to keep him in my sight, I was smiling through the pain, through the anger that kept building within me. It was a cold, hateful smile that I had never worn before—before I realized that I was stronger than I could have ever imagined. Heat coursed through my veins, adrenaline like I had never felt before giving me a renewed sense of power.

Michael raised an eyebrow at the sudden shift in my demeanor. Then he faked right and raced at me from the left. I fell for the move but recovered in just enough time to spin my body sideways, feeling the wind rush my body where Michael's fist had aimed. I sent a punch at his face but he twisted to the side while simultaneously kicking his foot out to trip me as I tried to shift my position again. My fingers gripped the edge of Michael's knee and, as I fell, he fell with me. We crash landed on the floor on the opposite side of the room where we'd begun the fight. The coffee table was turned over and his computer with it. Broken dishes, dirt and dust particles were kicked up and strewn everywhere and I hadn't realized just how much of the room we'd traversed in such a short time. It was as if I had blacked out and was now coming-to.

I coughed from the dust, sitting up despite the pain it caused me in several areas, muscles strained in places I had never thought I had them. I crawled on my elbows over to Michael, who was on his back a few feet from me.

"Does this mean it's a draw?"

He snorted and, before I could even tense up, grabbed both of my arms and used them to lift himself up while slamming me down at the same time. I gasped, the breath knocked out of me. Directly over my heart, Michael held the knife he'd started with.

"Hardly."

I closed my eyes as I tried to steady my breathing to keep my chest from the knife, my fists clenched and unclenched as I struggled. "How are you always one step ahead of me?"

"You're predictable. And that," he said, hoisting himself up by the strength of his legs and sheathing his knife, "is the most important of every attribute I pointed out to you."

"You were testing me?" I challenged, lifting myself up with a great effort, my body aching.

"You didn't think I was actually trying, did you?"

I frowned, heated, angry and embarrassed. There were times when I believed he might have been trying, times when my confidence had soared as I thought I had outmaneuvered, or at least outsmarted him. "So?"

"All in all," he smiled, his eyes burning bright with icy amusement, "you're pathetic and I could've killed you in the time it takes you to blink. But you have potential."

I studied him, trying to decide how to process all of this. If I should be scared, angry or excited.

"If only you knew how to pick and choose your battles." With his speed, Michael smacked me across the face and kicked at the back of my legs, dropping me to my knees, dazed, in an instant. He jerked my hands behind my back and I pulled against him, trying to fight it, but my energy was spent and he was endlessly unyielding. Wrapping my arm with a thin white cloth, he tied my hands together with a rope I hadn't seen him grab or conceal and cinched it too tight into the same rifts it had dug before, drawing a cry from my lips that he ignored.

I couldn't fight back as he pushed me, surprisingly, away from his room instead of towards it. Seconds later, we came to a room I recognized, with a sinking feeling, as an old laundry/bath room.

"Since you wanted out of my room so desperately," he remarked, his tone no longer playful. He pushed me inside, hard, and flicked the light switch beside the door. It flickered and died. He shrugged and turned to go, leaving me in complete darkness with little space to even sit. At least there was a toilet in the corner, but it had no handle. I felt my despair returning.

"Wait."

Michael turned and raised an irritated eyebrow.

"My cousin," I said. "Sean. Is it true? Is he...here?"

"For now," Michael said shortly, confirming the fact that Sean was stationed in Ghazni like the information on his laptop had told me only several minutes before.

He studied my face quietly. His dark eyes were penetrating. "What else did you see?"

I pressed my mouth shut.

Michael shook his head, his lip curled up the tiniest bit. "Hold onto that," he said.

"To what?"

"Defiance. It just might keep you alive." Michael spun to leave again, but just before he did, he turned his head and met my eyes over his shoulder, his expression stone cold again. "I suggest you keep your nosiness at bay," he warned. "Some things should *stay* secret. Understand?"

"I understand."

Crossing his arms at the base of his torso, Michael pulled his bloody white t-shirt over his head and tossed it into a basket of old clothes in the corner of the room. His back, I couldn't help but notice, was just as scarred as his front—but covered by a giant black-inked bird, its wings outstretched over his shoulder muscles, its head just below his neck and its body following the curve of his figure into a strong, defined "V." The tattooed bird's claws were detailed sharply, its eyes nearly as black and piercing as his own.

It was an eagle. The symbol of freedom.

Michael closed the door behind him and locked it, the metal clicking harshly against the rusted frame. I closed my eyes—there were no lights or windows, so I couldn't see anyway—and sat down right where I'd been standing, in the very center of the small room, my knees squished against the cluttered porcelain.

My mind raced. Not from adrenaline, pain, the new knowledge I'd gained or even from Michael's dark pull. It was from the way he'd stated those last words. The look in his eyes, the threat in his tone.

Some things should stay secret.

It wasn't just a warning to keep me from digging to discover what I could find. It was a challenge to see just what he was hiding.

✦   ✦   ✦

NOSY LITTLE BITCH, HE thought as he stretched his right hand, his eyes studying the scarred tissue that was just barely visible yet rendered his dominant hand all but useless. Shaking his head, Michael walked over to the coffee table and straightened it right-side up.

He killed the power on his computer and closed the top as he stood up and reached for his army boots. Not long after he sat down on the couch and began lacing up the front of his boots, a subtle yet commanding buzz shook the left pocket of his pants.

Michael pulled out Luke Marshall's communicator, accepted the contact and hit the speaker button so he could talk freely without requiring his hands.

"What *the hell* are you playing at, Michael Moiré?"

The voice that shot through the speakers was sharp, angry and so familiar that he'd have known it anywhere.

"You'll have to be a little more specific than that, Wes."

"*Shooting* at me in California? Stabbing *my brother* in Kandahar? Selling me out to Leah when you knew *damn* well that Beau was listening!"

"I didn't shoot you."

"You meant to. And you missed, by the way."

"A careful calculation. Also, I never liked that obnoxious little brother of yours," Michael said flatly as he continued to lace up his boots. "He reminds me too much of…me."

"Control yourself, Michael. I will not continue to clean up after your messes and have my loyalty rewarded with outright disrespect."

"Have some faith, Wesley. Everything I do, I do with reason. You know that. Do not patronize me."

There was a pause, then a sigh. "Very well. I trust your judgment. There's something we need to discuss."

"And that is…"

"Leah."

Michael paused. He glanced over his shoulder once, then reached for the communicator and took it off speaker.

"I know you have her; don't deny it," Wesley Marshall continued. "I only mention it because I feel the need to warn you."

"About *my* obnoxious little brother, I assume."

"I can only stall him for so long. You know

Beau, he is anxious and rash and quick to fight for what he wants. Leah is no exception. Scratch that— she's *the only* exception."

"I need more time."

"I still don't see what you have to gain from this."

Michael smirked. Dodging the question, he replied, "Faith, Wes."

"Yes, well. You make it very difficult for others to have faith in you and your preposterously aloof schemes."

Because information is power, and power is control, Michael thought. He didn't say that. Instead, he simply replied, "Are you with me, or are you against me?"

Another pause.

"I'm with you."

"Good." After a brief glance at his watch, Michael finished with the lacing and stood. "Keep Beau busy. And whatever you do, keep him away from Ghazni. The last thing I need is that pathetic pain in the ass causing problems for me again."

"I'm trying," Wesley replied. "He is persistent, and the others are getting restless too. I do not know how much longer I have, Michael. I'll contact you if anything changes, as always."

"Wesley," Michael said quietly, before ending the conversation. "Beau and the others aren't to know any of this, or I'll kill every last one of you. Understood?"

"Of course," Wesley said, equally as quiet, a dark note to his voice. "I've told them nothing."

"As always," Michael replied, with a satisfied smile.

"As always."

✦   ✦   ✦

PART TWO

LOST

At eight, I hated myself—and maybe that's what pushed me
over the edge at eighteen.
Maybe that's why, when I was forced with the decision
between living out my dream as a soldier or accepting my
skill as an assassin, I chose the latter.
When Division-7-9 first recruited me, I caught a glimpse of
the old contentment I had once known before my parents'
deaths. I trained again, harder, better. I soared through the
ranks, reaching an officer position—one I should've had to
wait years for—in just a few short months. Like the first day
my father had let me hold his gun. Again, I was arrogant.
Because again, I was unstoppable.
The death toll surrounding me rose, and I thrived from it. In
enemy territory, I shot Arab after Arab.
Something from the exhilaration took hold of me. So much
so, that I didn't even realize when my targets had changed.
Instead of Arabs, I was killing American after American.
Mercilessly.

October 10, 2019
Five months after The Breach
Location: Ghazni
Entry: Ten

NEEDLE IN A HAYSTACK

FBI Headquarters
Washington, D.C.
August 2, 2020

THOMAS LAWTON STARED AT the file, his eyes unblinking, yet his mind registering nothing—at least, nothing that existed on the quarter-length page that lay on the desk before him.

Something's going on here. Something that you, me, Eric Renton and the CIA aren't supposed to be talking about.

Those words, the words spoken by his—for all intents and purposes—boss, hadn't left his mind since the day three months ago when Derek Vince had spoken them. Right here, in this very office in the nation's capital as angry citizens had stormed the white house gates like they were the beaches of Normandy and America never seemed closer to the brink.

The brink of what, however, Lawton still had absolutely no idea.

The Justice Department, the Department of Defense, the Joint Chiefs of Staff, the White House—you name it. They've charged every agency in the country to limit media interaction involving war-related issues.

Lawton tapped his fingers against the curved edge of his ancient oak desk, his fingers pressing against the rivets that had formed, its surface smooth yet jagged-shaped and worn from how many times over the past fifteen years he'd racked his brain. The box television in the corner of the room was just barely audible, the presumptive Democratic presidential nominee, one Tyler Millerton of Nebraska, speaking at a rally in New York City.

"This 'war' the GOP call it has been going on for far too long," the man preached, his voice tinged with a deep Western accent as he spoke to the crowd without the use of a microphone. "How many of our troops have been shipped off to countries that want nothing more than to see our men dead? Our women dead? Our children dead? And yet we hear nothing about it from the current cabinet, the Senate, the House of Representatives—all Republican. All silent."

The crowd gave a resounding cheer, responses like "fuck war," "damn the GOP" and "we have a right to know" were particularly clear to Lawton's ear as he tried to ignore the voices entirely.

Besides, the case in question that Derek Vince, head of the FBI Counterterrorism Division (CTD), had saddled Lawton with regarded a headline that had disappeared from the media's attention a long time ago—yet somehow, both streams of thought began to merge as he fought to sort it all out.

Case of the missing fugitives that don't exist, he mused cynically. *Domestic Terrorism G894. Two years ago, a United States Army soldier named Joseph Locke went Absent*

Without Leave (AWOL).

Locke was later reported as, and charged with, conspiring against America. His file included sedition, levying war, and of course, deserting his contracted place in the Army. Some believed there was Al Qaeda affiliation, though Lawton had his doubts—Al Qaeda and the Taliban had lost a lot of steam at the turn of the war, and this didn't seem like theirs. In fact, it had ISIS's name written all over it, yet, somehow, Lawton doubted that the Islamic State were behind it, either.

"No more terrorists, both in *and* out of our country," Millerton shouted from the television, breaking Lawton's train of thought. He moved to grab the remote to silence the box, but for some reason, his fingers stopped short of the power button.

Millerton continued, "I don't know about you fine folks, but I'm tired of turning on the news or walking down the street and hearing police sirens and ambulances because someone in America decided that today would be the day they'd pick up a gun and join the Islamic State or the FBI's Most Wanted list. I'm tired of it being too damn easy for anyone to be a criminal."

Lawton perked up as he recalled what Vince had said after digging up research from the National Archives on Joseph Locke.

He's listed in the FBI's Most Wanted as a judicial fugitive, not a terrorist.

A criminal, under the jurisdiction of the Justice system.

Lawton realized that perhaps he'd been looking in the wrong place for information that would never exist there—not necessarily because it didn't exist at all.

Anything on Joseph Locke's alleged accomplices?

Two. One a fellow soldier, the other linked to the Army through a selective intelligence agency, and both charged with the same crimes, Vince had said. *Wesley Marshall and Justin Roland, accomplices to Joseph Locke, aka Beau Moiré, whose alias matched up. All of which had no recorded existence after August 18, 2016, but would eventually be found deserting their contracted roles in the United States Army in 2018.*

2016. 2018. It was as if they had dropped off the face of the earth for two full years before they fell under the radar again.

Wesley Marshall the academic braniac, Justin Roland the military academy star and Beau Moiré the troubled orphan all existed in the National Archives. What had been erased was Marshall the Army intelligence agent, Roland the soldier and Locke the terrorist—those pieces had to be uncovered from avenues that anyone without the highest degree of security clearance would never have been able to find, from hidden files that had to be retrieved from camera glimpses and recorded sightings that not even Thomas Lawton had access to.

When this case had been placed on his desk many months back from higher-ups, Lawton had researched as much as he could about the Army Controversy of 2018 and the fugitives' desertion; how they had been tracked all across the Middle East for months and months until the trail went cold and he was forced to reassess the details of the case and who these men were, try to fit the puzzle together without half of the pieces. And every time, with every extraneous search, he came up with nothing more than what he'd started with.

From 2016 to 2018, there was just nothing.

2016, Lawton mused suddenly. To Lawton, the magic number had always been 2018—the year they were caught and wanted for treason. His task was to find the fugitives and bring them to justice, and to do so, he believed he needed to start where they'd left off, at the end of the trail. But, now that he thought of it, the beginning seemed far more important.

All of which had no recorded existence after August 18, 2016. Two years before the Army desertion of 2018, which was two years before Thomas Lawton now took the case in 2020.

Four years ago, they all blacked out at the same time.

"The year of the draft," Lawton said suddenly aloud.

Lawton sat back in his swivel chair, his eyes on the ceiling as he touched the stubble on his face that was well beyond five-o'clock shadow. When was the last time he'd been home long enough to have a good shave? Lawton couldn't remember. He thought only of the fact that perhaps he'd been speculating in the exact wrong place and focusing on the wrong timeframe.

Now, perhaps, he was onto something.

They all blacked out at the same time—2016. The year of the first draft call since 1972. Five months after the United States declared war on the Middle Eastern Council, Wesley Marshall, Justin Roland and Beau Moiré vanished.

Why?

"The Republicans want you to be afraid," Tyler Millerton said, his voice rising over Lawton's thoughts. He'd almost forgotten the man had been speaking, though no one else in the televised crowd seemed to have that problem. "They want to instill a fear in the American people that rallies us all to do unspeakable things. Fear is the key and guess what—it's working. We're afraid to walk down the street at night, to leave our doors unlocked in broad daylight. When we enter a nightclub, or a school, or a shopping mall, we take note of everyone around us and watch our backs because we're afraid someone will have a weapon and do us harm. Let me ask you this—do you trust the American people?" The crowd was silent. "Do you trust the NRA? Law enforcement? Do you trust your government?" Again, silence pervaded the stands.

"Do you trust me?"

All of a sudden, the crowd burst alive as if out of a dead sleep and cheered in an affirmation that knocked Lawton out of his seat in alarm. From where his swivel chair had given way, Lawton looked up at the screen as the presidential nominee stared out into the crowd, his eyes wielding a particularly satisfied expression.

At the same time, a knock sounded against the door, unnerving Lawton further. He glanced at the clock on the wall as he got to his feet.

11:42 p.m.

Mostly everyone in the building had gone home hours ago.

Lawton hesitated before he said, "Come in."

The door opened to reveal a woman he had never met before; Lawton was sure of it—particularly so because she was a red-haired bombshell that couldn't have been any older than twenty-six. Her fire-colored hair was pinned straight back into a neat ponytail and her thin frame was clothed in a chestnut pantsuit that looked more expensive than anything Thomas owned. She held the grace of a woman much older, yet there was a curiosity in her eyes that proved she was on a mission that called for her youth.

Suddenly, Lawton recalled where he'd seen her in the building before, almost five floors below his.

"I'm sorry, I don't believe we have met," Lawton said abruptly, realizing he was the professional and that it was his duty to hold out his hand. He cleared his throat, sounding like an ancient record-player coming to life, or perhaps a frog coming out of it. "You work in the secretaries' offices?"

The woman smiled but did not address the assumption. "Special Agent Thomas Lawton." She paused only a moment to survey the room and Lawton himself. "Your friend Logan speaks very highly of you. Forgive me, I must admit I was curious to see for myself."

Lawton eyed her again. "Ah, yes. Mr. Williams may have mentioned you at one point or another," he said, though it was an obvious lie. If Logan Williams, perhaps the most inappropriate and horny fifty-year-old on the planet hadn't mentioned this woman, it was mostly certainly because he had never met her before.

"What can I do for you?" Lawton asked, playing

into her bluff regardless.

Her eyes were a clouded gray color that revealed nothing. Again, dodging the question, she glanced at the television in the corner of the room, recognizing the speaker immediately and said instead, "Do you like him?"

"Do I like him?" Lawton hesitated for a second. Politics was the last thing he had been expecting to come from this woman's lips. "Sure," he said with an easy smile. "I'm a Democrat. He's my party's candidate."

"But do you like him?" she asked again.

Thomas Lawton glanced back at the television, at Tyler Millerton as he waved at the crowd with one steady stroke of his hand moving through the air, a wide grin on his face. His eyes were what caught Lawton's attention, however, and what he had never been able to get past. Steely gray and lacking any sort of sincerity or life behind them. Gray like a robot.

Gray like the woman's standing before him.

"I like him," Lawton lied. "My apologies, I'm afraid I never caught your name, Miss...?"

"Savanna," she said softly. And that was all that she said. There was a quiet mystery about her, an allusive radiation that set Lawton's mind at work all over again. But every time a train of thought began, her lips broke out into an innocent smile that shut everything back down. "You're very handsome, Mr. Lawton."

"Thomas," he replied suddenly, then wondered why he'd said it.

"Thomas," she said with a wider smile. "It was

nice to finally meet you. Forgive me for intruding, you seem like a very busy man. I'll leave you to your work. Good night."

Lawton inclined his head as she turned for the door, twisting her long legs at the base as she spun on her long high-heels and departed in one abrupt motion. She was gone before Lawton could realize that she'd said goodbye.

Or, rather, *good night.*

Lawton brushed his hand through his dark hair, feeling like he'd just stepped in and out of a dream. Suddenly he couldn't remember why his television was on and a file was open on his desk, plainly displaying its title *Domestic Terrorism G894.*

He didn't understand why the clock flashed midnight when it had just been a quarter-till, or why he'd fallen on the floor and was still holding the remote control for the television.

In fact, the only thing Thomas Lawton knew for certain was that the woman who'd come and gone in the blink of an eye had most certainly never worked a day in her life as a secretary for the Federal Bureau of Investigation.

THIRTY-TWO-YEAR-OLD Savanna Vienne stepped out into the night and waited at the curb of the corner of 10th Street and Pennsylvania Avenue Northwest for only a second before a black Buick pulled up. Slipping off the obnoxiously high heels she'd dawned for the occasion, she opened the door to the backseat and stepped in. Without hesitation, the driver, an African American man with a chrome watch and matching sunglasses, put his foot to the pedal and drove off into the night. When they were a few blocks away, he pulled over on the side of the road and removed his glasses.

"Well?"

"You were right. They're oblivious, save for one," Savanna said as she pulled the elastic out of her hair, ruining the sleek ponytail she'd sported, and pulled her strawberry locks into a messy bun that was much more comfortable. "Criminal Investigative Division, Special Agent Thomas—"

"Lawton." The man smirked into the rear-view mirror. "Ole Tommy. Why does that not surprise me."

"You know him," the woman replied, pulling her pocket mirror from her purse to remove the eye liner she'd applied a few hours before. "Why does *that* not surprise me."

"Tommy's not a threat to our cause," the man said shortly. "But time will tell whether he is an ally."

"You think he knows about our department?" Savanna Vienne asked, a touch of curiosity to her voice.

"I think he's got bigger things to worry about with his own."

NO ONE LEAVES

Ghazni, Afghanistan

I TWISTED TO THE right and dove to the floor, cushioning my head as I rolled several feet, just as a glass bottle smashed against the wall where I had just been standing. The force of the throw shattered the glass into a million pieces across the floor, creating a minefield of glistening, glittering shards.

"I thought you weren't trying to kill me!" I snapped, my breath coming in quick and hard after nearly an hour of this.

Michael cracked the top off another bottle of beer and flicked the cap onto the floor as he took a long drink.

"I never said I wasn't trying to kill you," he said, voice slurring as he raised the bottle and poured the rest of the beer right onto the floor. "I said give me your best...*shot.*"

My pulse raced as I ran back to the left, dodging the broken glass and tripping over the couch just in time to slide to the floor as the bottle flew through the air. This time, I wasn't quick enough and the edge of the bottle clipped me in the back, cracking against my left shoulder blade and spilling what little beer was left in the bottle all over my white shirt, which was already ripped down the side and covered in dust, dirt and beer.

I let out a long, agonized cry as I knelt to the floor. I pressed my fingers to my shoulder. They came back dripping with blood.

A shadow formed over me and I knew it was him, but I couldn't bring myself to move.

"Get up."

I gritted my teeth. "No."

I screamed as he grabbed a fist-full of my hair and yanked me to my feet. I whipped my fist through the air, smacking into his forearm just strong enough for him to release me.

I backed up and raked a hand through my hair, my scalp on fire, back in flames. I sent him a dark look. "Stop this. I don't want to play anymore."

Michael smirked and took one step towards me. A flash of silver gleamed at his waistline. "Who says we're playing?"

I backed up again. "You're drunk."

"I don't get drunk."

"You look drunk," I said, reaching the wall as he took the final step towards me and leaned his hand beside my shoulder on the wall behind me. "And the floor says otherwise."

Michael laughed, his eyes reveling in every moment. I glanced down at the shards covering nearly every inch of Michael's dingy little apartment and tried to think of a way out of this.

The gem of his necklace caught my eye from where it lay just beneath the neckline of his shirt, a perfect replica of Beau's, minus the initials. And suddenly, I remembered who I was up against—not just an enemy with Beau's physique, but, perhaps, one with his temper, too.

Without further thought, I spit at him. A spray of saliva splattered his face, and I readied myself for the backlash but even with alcohol on my side, Michael didn't burst out in anger and get reckless the way I anticipated; the way Beau would've.

Instead, he took a step even closer to me, his eyes locked onto mine, and grabbed a fist full of my shirt, pulling me against him suddenly. Putting both of his hands underneath, brushing against the tips of my skin, Michael pulled my shirt up farther than necessary and wiped my spit off of his face with it.

After several long seconds of toying with me, he finally let go and, rather than backing up, I used the proximity to aim a kick with my knee at his groin area. Because I hadn't planned it, I didn't expect him to see it coming, but somehow Michael had his left hand around the place where your knee meets your thigh just before it could strike him. Again, the force of the pull brought me in closer, my lower body basically straddling his until he finally released me and I backed away abruptly this time.

For some reason, I was the only one getting heated.

"You have no control over yourself," Michael said, as if reading my mind and picking out the very source of my frustration with ease. His tone was calm.

"If I wanted to kill you, right now," as he spoke, he circled his right hand around my throat and pressed me back against the wall, "it would be all too easy."

I tried to steady my breath and defy his words, but I knew he was right just by the way his hold on my neck was soft, loose and didn't block me from breathing the way it could have if he only pressed just an inch further, a muscle tighter. I curled my fingers into my palm and breathed out, feeling suffocated in more ways than one.

He capitalized on it instantly.

"If I wanted to take advantage of you," Michael lowered his fingers from my neck and let them trail down the contours of my chest, in-sync with my rising heartbeat, though he stopped abruptly there. "I could do that, too."

I levelled my stare at his neckline and searched for the words or the strength to fight back, but again, there was nothing. And the way he regarded me now, his fingers soft and gentle yet invasive, only confirmed how powerless I truly was, and had been, this entire time. He stopped. But he didn't have to.

That lit something inside of me on fire. I curled my fingers in, ready to defend myself this time.

At that moment, a crackling static echoed throughout the room, startling me out of my head. Michael's expression did not change as he backed away from me, finally giving me room to breathe and to think for the first time, and searched for the source of the sound.

"Moiré," a loud, hissing voice sounded over the intercom. It came from under the couch, reverberating from what sounded like a walkie talkie. "Moiré, answer. I need you to tell me what Vendelle—"

The voice was Middle Eastern. I momentarily froze, all thoughts of our intimate encounter subdued. *Vendelle.* Why did that name sound familiar?

And then it hit me.

September 23rd, 1996. A jet departing from Ghazni, Afghanistan at approximately 2:43pm Eastern Time, expected to arrive in the U.S. the same evening, crashed down six miles off the coast of New Jersey. The local coast guard reported the cause of the crash due to uncharted, violent wind currents. No bodies were recovered, but the full passenger list was taken from the airport in Afghanistan. The death toll was complete with thirteen passengers; no survivors, nor conclusive wreckage. The jet was evidently carrying U.S. Army soldiers on leave... Alexander and Diane Moiré, age twenty-two and twenty-three. Raymond Roland, age twenty-two. Scottran "Scott" Dellis, twenty-six. Wyatt Vendelle, age twenty-three.

"Wyatt Vendelle," I said aloud.

Michael flipped the switch on the device, silencing it. He turned back around slowly, fully analyzing my face. His was a mask of concealment, tinged with a little something else now.

"How do you know that name?"

I hesitated, my expression betraying my thoughts entirely too much. Before I could formulate a cohesive response, Michael placed himself directly in front of me, closer this time, so close I could feel the heat of his breath against my forehead, smell the thick scent of beer on it. His stance, however, was entirely sober—as if the drunk state had all just been an act.

Curious. I leveled my stare at his chest, refusing to meet his eyes. As a result, he tipped my chin up forcefully with his left hand.

And while his side was exposed, I snatched the silver that had been gleaming under his belt—that I'd been eyeing up, waiting for an opportunity—since the beginning of the encounter and held it up to *his* chin, in return.

Michael didn't glance at the silver knife that was now inches from his throat. If the move surprised him, he didn't show it. With steady serenity, he dipped his fingers into the front pocket on his other side and flipped out a knife slightly smaller than the one I'd taken, yet more jagged, with a hilt as black as death and a blade sharper than the point of a needle.

My heart skipped a beat because I knew what I had just done.

I dropped quickly to the floor with a gasp as Michael whipped his pocket knife out at me and slashed it through the air where I had just been. Twisting around vigorously, I kicked at the backs of his knees and rolled across the floor a few feet to clear myself from his anticipated fall. He staggered but regained his footing just as easily and spun to face me as I rose to my feet also, the knife gripped tightly in my fisted right hand that shook tremendously now.

Michael noticed, his leering smile returning as he took his knife by the blade and tossed it up into the air and then into his other hand, catching it just as smoothly. His eyes never left mine.

All of a sudden, I felt a sharp, rioting pain in my right forearm, a burning sting so hot the knife slid out of my fingers as my body panicked. Memories of the burning jolt of a bullet in my arm, my side, my leg were an inferno in my head, dispersing itself into each of my limbs as my body burned.

Michael's pocket knife clattered to the floor along with the one I'd been wielding as blood ran in streams down my arm from where the knife he threw—the one he'd just tossed up into the air and caught—had hit and cut me in the time it took me to blink.

I pressed my fingers to my forearm trying to put pressure on the wound, but blood came through my hand and dripped down my fingers, pooling discreetly on the musty floor.

I looked up incredulously.

"You'll have to do better than that, love."

Teeth clenched, I dropped my hand and lunged at him, foregoing the knives in favor of sinking all the fury of my own flesh into his however I could.

Even intoxicated as he must've been, even slightly impaired by a weak right wrist and tired from kicking my ass for hours every day, Michael was better, faster and stronger than ever. His persistence was relentless, yet his composure never wavered. His body language told me he was enjoying this, relishing in my constant defeat, but his eyes remained indifferent. A cool, passive force that somehow penetrated every last nerve I had as he sent me spinning to the ground with moves that seemed simultaneously half-assed and perfect all at once.

"Do better," he said offhandedly.

I pushed harder, centered the tips of my control

to a resolute *T* and fought back relentlessly. But it got me nowhere as he put me on the ground just as easily as before.

"Do better."

I landed on my butt for the third time and cursed. This time I didn't even want to get up, my body was so bruised and battered, but I somehow found the will to. I couldn't let this be my final stand, couldn't give him the satisfaction of breaking me into submission. I stood in front of him again, my exterior aching, and tried again.

"Do better," he repeated, as I went sailing to the concrete floor. He knocked me off my feet without even the slightest exertion.

I pressed my forearms to the ground and screamed, teeth gritted as I bit my tongue. His arrogance was unending, so much so that I instantaneously snapped. I jumped up and ran at him, every muscle in my body aching from hitting the floor so many times, so many ways. My teeth were bared like an animal's. I couldn't take this anymore. I pushed against him, using the full force of my right shoulder and my back instead of just the force of my legs, delivering everything I had in me, uncaring of the consequences or the subsequent pain that would undoubtedly befall me.

Michael's back hit the wall, even if it was just barely. Victory.

When I lifted my fiery gaze up to his from where the force of the blow had put me on the floor hard, he nodded his head the tiniest bit. "Good." I smiled; he smirked. "Now *do better.*"

I blew out a frustrated breath and smacked my hands against the concrete. "This is pointless."

"Is it?" Michael's eyes were hard, his voice cold. "You have passion, but no drive. You have ferocity, yet you lack the focus to channel it into anything positive."

"I'm not as good as you," I said irritably. "You expect me to be able to beat you when I have no training, no experience."

"Experience means nothing when you have drive."

"Experience means everything!" I snapped. "Look at you!" I gestured up at his figure, his muscles tight against his white shirt, his stance that was both nonchalant and full of strength, the scars that proved he'd endured. "Look at what you are, what you've done!"

Michael shook his head. The fingers of his right hand twitched uncomfortably. "I didn't do this," he replied. "This is what happens when you are a product of your environment."

Our eyes met for a long moment as his words registered fully beyond his intention. *This is what Division did to me, Leah.* That's what Beau had said back at the hotel in Kandahar, when I had seen, for the first time, the real scars his past had left him with. Scars that didn't show up on his body the way Michael's did. *I'm a monster, a machine. This is what I have to be if I'm to fix my mistakes.*

"This is pointless," I said again, feeling even more distant now.

"Defending your life is pointless?"

"You're not giving me a chance to defend myself!"

"No one will ever give you that chance," he said as he reached down and yanked me up by my non-bloody forearm. "Your life is your own, and you should automatically defend yourself at all costs, especially when someone is threatening you because they *won't* give you that chance. They won't go easy on you."

"Like you are?" I challenged.

"Yes," he said through his teeth. Shockingly, his tone had a touch of emotion in it. Anger. Frustration. The first I'd seen since all of this began.

"Why?" I snapped back, pushing him emotionally the way he'd pushed me physically. "I'm supposed to be your enemy. Why go easy on me?"

Michael clenched his fists the way Beau did when he was holding back, and I pushed further, "Why tell me all of this? You say you can kill me, so why don't you?" I took a step towards him. "You say you can take advantage of me, yet you haven't done that either."

He didn't respond, but he radiated rage.

"Why? Why keep me alive only to make me suffer? *Why?*"

He met my eyes again and held them, his a solid black color devoid of any emerald light.

When he still didn't respond, I jerked my hand out of his grip and shouted, *"Why, you fucking coward?"*

So fast I didn't see it coming, Michael whipped the full length of his arm out and backhanded me across the face with every ounce of power he had.

I staggered to the left and then sank straight to my knees, my vision blurring for over a minute as my face stung like a hornet on fire. The force of the blow was like nothing I had ever felt before, not even the bullets he'd fired at me, all those weeks ago, nor the cuts and bruises that were beginning to add up on my body.

As tears welled unwillingly, I realized I had fallen on the flat end of the knives we'd dropped. Without looking down, I pressed my knees firmly against them, crushing the blades out of view. Michael's fists were tight, his eyes too distracted to notice. I narrowed mine in response and fought the urge to touch my reddened skin, to show any weakness in the face of his strength. Rather, I leveled my stare at him from where he stood powerfully above me.

He'd pushed me close to the edge, and I knew that he could feel it. At the same time, I had pushed him, too, and I could feel that too.

Quietly, discreetly, I smiled through the pain.

MICHAEL STARED OUT AT the endless ramparts of Ghazni, his lips pressed tightly together and his fingers tapping against the rusted metal railing in a quick *pat pat* that distracted him from the fire that was growing inside of his head, his body, his soul.

It was well past midnight, but despite the fact that he had to be up in less than four hours for a Council meeting with the General, Michael couldn't sleep. He studied the dark sky restlessly; full of an adrenaline he couldn't quite understand, anxiously awaiting the call.

When it came, his mind shut off, like it always did.

Michael reached into the pocket of his faded-brown combat slacks and pulled out his blinking cell phone. With a flat stare at the half-crescent moon above, Michael pressed *accept*.

A cold, careful voice said, "Well?"

"All the cards are in our hands," Michael said emotionlessly.

"Is it done?"

"It is," he replied, fingering the military tags in his pocket.

"I have heard rumors," the voice growled, "that you have been keeping a low profile…recently. That you have been distracted."

"Clearly, you have an unreliable source," Michael replied flatly.

"Dezuriel is more loyal to me than you have ever been."

"Loyalty is twisted. You of anyone should know that."

"I know you have the girl, Moiré. Do not deny it. So perhaps the only one with a truly twisted sense of loyalty is you."

Glancing over his shoulder, past the screened door that led to the pint-sized porch attached to the back of his apartment, he thought of Leah in the old laundry room, probably crunched up in a ball, asleep with a baseball-sized bruise on her face. Michael leaned out over the railing, resting both hands against the steel surface and said, "What do you want?"

"Contact your friend in Quad 79-07. Stubler. I want you to gain me his trust."

Michael frowned. "Stubler, why? He's the lowest in his branch; the rest of the technicians mock him in their spare time."

"The best moles are always the ones no one suspects."

Michael stared straight ahead, wordlessly.

"Do I sense a certain reluctance in you, Moiré?"

Again, he did not respond.

"Careful, Michael," the man said stiffly. "These are shallow waters you tread."

"I'm not at sea."

"You've been at sea your entire life, Michael Moiré," the man said. "And you've been drowning a lot longer than you care to realize."

"What do you want from me?" Michael repeated, his knuckles grinding against the cold steel rail, though he felt none of the pain.

"I want you to tell me why."

"Why what?"

"Why not just kill her and be done with it? Why toy with the girl?"

Michael glanced at the device, his eyes narrowing the slightest bit as the same questions echoed in his head from hours before. "Have you nothing better to do than muddle in my private life?"

The voice on the line did not reply. Even from his side, from half a world away, Michael could feel the tension.

Regardless, he touched the tips of his fingers against the railing the slightest bit, his thoughts drifting far from where they should be. His expression was inanimate. Yet his eyes burned as bright as the stars would have if they were visible. He thought of the sea, the waves on the Atlantic Coast, the birds and the shore. He thought of his mother's wild brown curls and the strength she'd carried until her last breath.

"I didn't think anyone knew how to get under my skin the way Beau does," Michael said, his nails chipping away at the rust on the railing. A sliver slid under his fingernail, cutting its way in. "I was wrong."

"Then kill her."

"I will," Michael replied, nodding his head the slightest bit. "But I'll kill her when I no longer have use for her."

"What use is a fragile little girl?"

Michael's lips curved up the tiniest bit. "What indeed."

The man on the line sounded irritable. "When all of this comes to a close, I suggest you arrange your priorities," he said and finished his sentence with a resounding *click* that brought Michael more relief than he cared to acknowledge. Relief that was short-lived.

"*¿Cual es su nombre, Miguel?*"

Just like that, Michael's tension returned. He didn't stir, but he sensed her presence from the side of the porch to the left where she'd hopped over the railing, her lithe step ever soundless and fused with grace.

"*Miguel.*" Reluctantly, Michael glanced aside and studied the thin silhouette of the unexpected arrival, her caramel-colored skin shining against the tight black clothes she wore under her costumed *abaya.* The traditional female dress. She licked her Latina lips and repeated, "Her name?"

Michael studied her carefully. "You shouldn't be here, Rya."

"Neither should she," Rya said, slinking her way closer to him, her dark brows furrowed, teasing. "Is she your new lover?"

"You know I've only ever had eyes for you."

Rya smiled and dipped her head. "I wish I knew whether you were lying or not," she said cautiously. "I was never able to tell."

"Or care, really." Michael smirked and turned away. He rested his elbows against the railing again, this time keeping his body forward, closed off and concealed from her.

But she broke through anyway. Rya lifted her hand onto his back, the soft feel of her touch making him want to shiver. She slid her slender fingers up his back, the tips of her nails biting in as if they were claws of a lioness.

Her movements were deliberate, sharp. When she spoke, it sounded more like a purr.

"*¿Qué deseas?*"

"You know I don't speak Spanish."

Rya smiled and said, "*No verdad.* You had a good teacher."

"Déjame solo," Michael said at last, his tongue finding the words strange as opposed to the Arabic he was immersed in. *Leave me alone.*

Rya ignored that. Instead, she took a step, the move bringing her closer, and slid her hands up onto his chest and positioned her body against his. Michael's muscles tightened against her touch, bringing a smile to her face. The slinky black outfit she wore under traditionally Arabic garb blew back from the wind to reveal long, slender limbs.

Michael closed his eyes as she hovered her lips over his. For the last time, her seductive voice was a fragile whisper that whisked the stubble on his chin as she said, *"Qué deseas,* Mi—"

Michael had his hands around her back and his lips against hers before she could end her question: *What do you want?*

It was obvious what he wanted, and Michael knew that she knew that, too.

Rya leaned against him for support, hands coiled around his hips as he kissed her long, hard and deeply until her back was against the apartment siding and his heart was pounding beneath his chest.

She bit his lip and pulled away. Her almond eyes were bright and gleaming through the night; yet, like always, there was no emotion behind them. No remorse for the fact that she had come to steal only a kiss. Michael had grown to expect that, however reluctantly.

He brushed his fingers over the smooth, silver jewel on the fourth finger of her left hand. She wiggled it out of his grasp and stepped away, turning to go, her hand balled into a fist to hide the diamond wedding ring that was the newest addition to her new life.

"Why did you come back?" Michael said, his voice as thick as steel and his chest feeling remarkably similar. "You left the organization. Married a diplomat. *Dígame.*" *Tell me.*

Rya's face was expressionless. Twisting her pixie hair into a knot with two fingers, she met his eyes, blew him a kiss and hopped back over the rail. Her smile, through the dark, was eerie.

"Nadie se va," she said.

No one leaves.

✦ ✦ ✦

ALTERATIONS

"JUST LIKE OLD TIMES."

Wesley Marshall smirked at his comrade, Justin, who was surveying the landscape of outer-city Zaranj in the distance, his eyes completely covered by high-powered binoculars.

"Remarkably, old times seem like ages ago," Wesley said.

"Not long enough," Justin replied as he lowered the binoculars and glanced with his own amber eyes at the immediate surroundings. He lowered his voice and spoke into the black earpiece encircled around his left ear. "Matt, all clear?"

The communicator's line crackled with static as Mathew Roland repeated, his voice soft, "Clear."

"Luke?"

It crackled again, this time more distinctly as a result of the distance between their position and the shack where Luke had stayed behind. "I'm fine," Luke Marshall said irritably. "Aside from the fact that I'm lying in bed like a seven-year-old while you're all out playing G. I. Jane without me."

"It's Joe," Justin retorted. "G. I. Joe. Maybe someday you'll get to hang with the big kids, Luke, but for now—"

"Piss-off, Jane."

"Luke," Wesley interjected as he began moving forward out of the ditch they'd been crouched in. "How's Beau?"

"Stationary as ever. But I can go poke him with a stick, if you really want me to tell you something different."

Wesley exhaled. "Keep us updated; communicate to us your status and we'll quit checking in."

"Yes, mom."

The static died out. Wesley shook his head and then glanced at Justin. "Ready?"

"Ready," Justin and Matt replied simultaneously, one in person and one over their frequency. "Let's take this one slower," Matt added, his voice skewed by the static that seemed to be growing stronger the closer they got to their target.

Even though it had only been a little over three years since he'd stepped foot in the place, the military compound in Zaranj held little resemblance to the lean-to Wesley had grown accustomed to in his time with the organization. Much like the Nimruz province to the south, the compound had become built-up defensively, enclosed with a fifteen-foot tall fence that was electrically charged by the overarching solar panels that rose every thirty-feet or so around the perimeter—which used to stretch one to two acres, but was now upwards of five, spanning over two-hundred thousand square feet.

Parallel to the electric fence, there had been dug five-foot deep ditches, rivets wide enough to prevent one from easily jumping up and across, and long enough to circle around the entire base of the compound in a calculated, intricate spiral.

Justin's eyes were wide, his lips parted the barest width. "Is it just me, or did breaking into Zaranj to hijack weapons suddenly become impossible?"

"I assume this is new," Matt said over the radio com. His voice sounded far though he was only an acre away, adjacent to the base, in a similar position as they were. He had offered to go it alone, despite the others' protests that Wesley should be the one to do it since he was the most familiar with Zaranj. "Wes? Thoughts?"

Wesley scanned the horizon and brushed a hand over his blond hair, which was short but growing longer with each day it hadn't been routinely trimmed. Justin was equally rugged, his dark brown hair unkempt and his chin thick with stubble. It had only been a couple of weeks since they'd departed California and touched down in Kandahar, but, to each of them, it had begun to feel like an eternity.

"Let's go back."

Wesley kept his thoughts to himself as he traipsed through the hilly landscape, hazel eyes downcast as he walked beside Justin, and Matt who'd joined them along the way.

"How much farther out?" Justin asked, brushing a brim of sweat off of his forehead that had been gathering for over twenty minutes.

Wesley glanced around, calculating the distance of the base behind them and the tops of buildings that were beginning to come into view. "Approximately six miles."

"Six point two," Matt confirmed, glancing up from his digital map briefly to give Wesley an incredulous stare.

Wesley didn't shift his focus, but he could feel two sets of eyes on him. "We should veer right," he said. "This path becomes exposed."

As they neared the outskirts of what appeared to be a small village, Wesley raised his black hood to cover all of his head and most his face, as did the other two. Two children came scurrying towards them, kicking a ball that was about as round as a brick and, to the newcomers' relief, didn't spare them a glance.

They walked through the village this way, doing their best not to act suspicious or let their eyes do too much scanning. Every now and again, they would catch a glimpse of a man in uniform wielding an Ak-47, either adorned with the insignia of the Afghan militia or the symbol of Division-7-9. The ratio was about fifty-fifty.

No one commented about this, careful not to let their American accents be heard, but it troubled them nonetheless. Zaranj had been a warzone in the fall of 2017, when the American military had targeted it with drone strikes in an effort to kill an alleged leader of the Islamic State. As it turned out, the man wasn't within a fifty-mile radius, off gambling in a ritzy hotel in the middle of Kabul, the nation's capital. The locals of Zaranj knew this. The Americans did not. Ever since, Americans were only welcome if they left their heads at the city gate.

What the others didn't know was that it hadn't always been like that; that they were passing one particular residence that was once the home of Wesley Marshall and his newly engaged fiancée, Laci Green, who, by a small miracle, had been relocated to Ghazni, Afghanistan just weeks before the attacks. The building they'd spent months in, shared their fears of the present and hopes for the future, made love on every surface and dreamed about the day they could go home in, had been leveled.

As had ninety percent of Zaranj. The village they now walked through represented the ten-percent that withstood the bombing.

Hours later, as they brimmed the top of a particularly high mound, Justin caught sight of the shack they'd commandeered and cheered with every last bit of strength he'd had in him. Matt's expression was similar, devoid of his typical reserve. The long-sleeves they wore were dripping with sweat in the hundred-degree sun that had proven relentless since the moment they'd set out that morning. They now returned as the sun was beginning to set.

Just then, the radio at Wes's ear crackled, the sound deafening.

"Wes! Justin! Matt! You nag me over stupid shit all day and then ignore me when it matters! Hey fuckers, answer me!"

Wesley, Justin and Matt shared a look. Wesley clicked his earpiece and said, "Luke? What's wrong?"

"You haven't heard a damn word I've said?" Luke's voice rasped through the device, static looming over the frequency despite the fact that they were less than thirty yards away. With such a proximity, the line should've been clear. "I said you need to come back ASAP."

Wesley had a feeling he knew where this was headed. "Why?" he asked cautiously, his fingers touching another device in his front right pocket. "What's happened?"

"Beau's gone," Luke said.

Justin and Matt's eyes were wide. As if they hadn't been walking through the desert all day, the pair of them sprinted towards the shack while, over the radio, Luke continued speaking breathlessly.

"I tried to stop him! I tried. I'm so sorry guys, I did everything I could and I've been trying to reach you. He left over an hour ago..."

Wesley reached up to his ear and yanked the device out of it, deactivating his signal. Shoving it in his pocket, he slipped the other one out. Typing in an access code that none of the others were familiar with, Wes lifted the communicator to his ear.

Before the voice on the other end of the line could even speak, Wesley barked into the device, "There's been a change of plans."

OPTIONS

I GRIPPED THE KNIFE tightly between the base of my palm and the tips of my fingers, the metal pressing cold against my skin. It was a horrible idea, but for some reason, I was standing at the edge of the corner that separated Michael's bedroom and the bathroom, my body poised and ready to strike.

When the moment came, I lowered my breathing, steadied my heartrate and focused my vision on the door that was sealed.

It opened faster than I expected it to, and to my complete and utter shock, Michael walked out naked.

Well, not entirely. But the sight of him was enough to bring a rose-colored blush to my cheeks. He wore thick gray boxer briefs, no shirt, and was slipping on a pair of dark blue jeans, his lightly-tanned skin and bright blond hair glisteningly wet. I cursed in my head for not hearing the shower run and tried to refocus on my mission.

As quiet as a mouse, I ducked to the floor and edged with a lithe step so that I was just close enough to see the rugged outline of the tattooed eagle on his back. It was almost dusk—a time I chose intentionally, for the absence of the sun cast shadows everywhere, disallowing one from discerning what was real and what was an illusion. A trick of the light.

So he didn't see me coming when I came up behind him and sank my knife into the back of his shoulder. The blade met with resistance, so the hilt was kept only inches from the surface of his skin. As fast as I could, I snaked the other knife I had possession of from the last fight we'd had and wielded it, ready to be the one with the upper hand. If he wasn't going to give me what I wanted, I would take it by force. Kill him, if I could, if I had to.

He turned around, blood dripping down the slippery surface of his skin. It wasn't Michael.

It was Beau.

His lips were parted the barest width, his fingers, covered thick with red as my eyes filled with tears, reached out and whisked the side of my face before he collapsed onto the floor at my feet.

No no no! I knelt down and took his head into my hands, pressing him against me to shelter him from his pain. Pain because of me.

What have I done?

Frantically, I tilted his chin up and pressed my lips against his, drawing every breath in my body to breathe whatever life into him I had left in me.

He kissed me back, and his hands slid around my waist tighter than I thought he was capable of, pulling me so that my body fit firmly against his, opening my mouth forcefully with an exertion that I didn't even try to fight. My eyelids fluttered shut. I let him move me, let him press me back against the wall, slide his strong hand over my skin, leaving traces of fire in its wake that pushed me further and further from control.

He smiled and bit my lip, hard. I opened my eyes. It was Michael.

I woke up dripping with sweat, my heartbeat pounding right out of my chest and slid my hands up and down my body, frantic, feeling burned from the dream. Tears stained my cheeks. There was a pool of water on the ground across from me where the sink was leaking. Aside from the infrequent sound of *drip, drip, drip,* the air was cool and the little room I'd come to know was silent as the grave.

The door was cracked the slightest bit, letting in a soft wind that whisked my skin, leaving a minefield of goosebumps.

Open.

I furrowed my brows and slowly got to my feet, my body tired, sore and harboring an ache that had only grown denser in the past forty-eight hours. I hardly remembered Michael tossing me into the room this time. I must have been unconscious again.

My feet touched the tile floor and barely felt a thing, they had become so calloused and worn. My wrists were raw and crusted, but had stopped bleeding a long time ago. My lips were hard, having been bitten down on so many times out of frustration and to dim the pain inflicted on the rest of my body. Bruises lined the surface of my legs all the way up, but they didn't bother me anymore.

I stood up to my full five-foot-seven height for the first time in what felt like forever and noticed there was a mirror on the wall, positioned adjacent to the doorway, which remained open. I spared not a glance at the door, unhurried to face Michael again, to step up to his challenge like I had every day for as many days as I could remember, and instead squared myself, prepared for a new challenge.

Slowly, hesitantly, I lifted my head and glanced in the mirror. The person I saw staring back at me was the same one I'd seen for years. Except, somehow, she was different, too. She was older, more experienced. Her curly blonde hair hung past her delicate shoulders in messy waves, falling just above her chest and partially covering the tattered white shirt that fit loosely against her body. She had on dark brown pants and her black boots were sitting out by the front door of Michael's apartment, for she was barefoot the way she'd been her entire life growing up on the American west coast.

There were the slightest traces of make-up on her face—some mascara, worn eye-liner, and dried-up lip gloss that crusted her thin lips. Overall, she looked the same. Normal. Aside from the bruises, she could've almost been that girl on the beach. Almost.

It was the eyes that gave her away. The dark, emerald pools that suddenly weren't so full of innocence anymore. Now they were hard, unwavering instead of liquid soft. Intense, devoid of the sweetness, the uncertainty, the pain that had come to define her very essence. Now, there was only raw determination, strength to survive this war.

I tore my eyes away from my reflection and it finally dawned on me that the door was open and I was free to get the hell out of this claustrophobic space. Gripping the knife I had fallen asleep with in my hand, I touched the door with my fingertips, sliding it open a few more inches to allow room for me to snake my body through.

Like it had been in my dream, the apartment was dimly lit by the moon outside that filtered in through the windows in slanting forms, casting shadows and tricks of the light at every turn. The door to Michael's room was cracked as well, but all other doors were sealed shut. I crept past the bathroom quickly, unwilling to spare it a glance or a thought back to what I'd seen in my head only minutes before. The sights and sense of Michael's body, Beau's wound and the passionate kiss that could have been either of them, I pushed it all out of my head.

Finish this. With a touch as light as a feather, I pressed my fingers against the door to Michael's bedroom and moved forward as it opened. It did not creak, didn't swing forward in announcement of my presence as I half expected it to. I entered his room without so much as a sound, and for a moment, I listened and heard nothing. Empty?

No. After a few seconds of adjusting, I was able to make out the rough edges of Michael's form through the dark. He was lying on his back with his hands resting at his sides, coverless and bare-chested with only loose camouflage pants the color of the desert. Ironically, they did more to illuminate him than anything.

Breathing soundlessly as he was, I cautiously stepped forward, reaching his bedside within five steps. The room looked smaller now than it had when he'd kept me chained up in here before I'd picked the lock and begun a series of battles that led us to this very moment. The knife suddenly felt very hot against my palm, my fingers growing numb as they attempted to steady themselves while simultaneously maintaining their grip on the only weapon that would save my life, if he were to wake.

I lifted my eyes to his figure, only to wish I hadn't.

Lying stretched out to his full length, Michael didn't have the same bitterness, same hardness he had when he was conscious and employing his strength. His legs were strong, but lean. He didn't eat very much, if anything really, and his silhouette reflected it. His torso was scarred at almost every inch. His hair was a tousled mess, like Beau's, but it was blonder than blond, like mine, and made his face seem paler than it was, especially his lips. Softer, less dangerous.

So I was staring at his lips when they moved.

"Go ahead," he said quietly, his voice devoid of the grogginess one has when they awake, and I got the feeling he had never actually been asleep at all. "You don't know how many times I've tried."

I set my eyes on the knife that was poised directly above his heart, slightly angled so as to slide through the ribs, frozen in place with my fingers held tight against its hilt.

"Why?" I said, stalling though unwilling to admit it.

"Because I deserve it." His tone was low and sincere the way I'd never heard it before. There was no malice in his voice, no sarcasm or bravo. He wasn't afraid and if he were, he did a perfect job of disguising it. "Isn't that what've willed yourself to believe?"

I started as I felt the cold touch of his fingers against mine where they were gripping the knife. He positioned his precisely where mine were and pressed down. I jerked my hand back up and, in an instant, everything twisted. Michael released the knife, but I lost control of it too and though I couldn't see it, I heard it fall to the floor with what sounded in the silence like a deafening *ping*.

Michael was off the bed in an instant and reaching for me so fast I stumbled back against what I thought was the wall, but was actually the door. It slammed shut with an even louder sound, mimicking the blood that was pounding through my head. I ducked to the floor and scoured for the knife. My fingers made contact at the same time I caught a glimpse of him coming closer to me, his actions no longer calm or complacent. I grabbed ahold of the knife and rolled under the bed, feeling his fingertips whisk the ends of my shirt and rip a piece of fabric off as I went spinning in the other direction.

I reached the other side of the room from under the bed and stayed low, crouched behind the bed that hid me from view. At that moment, the room went silent. All that was audible was the sound of my heart beating wildly out of my chest at the unexpected retaliation that should've been all too expected.

Somehow, when he spoke, his voice came from behind me.

"Don't underestimate your opponent."

I swung my arm around, feeling the knife make contact with some part of his skin before he caught hold of my wrist and jerked me forward. I fell into him, my legs losing themselves to the fall but my upper body held in place by his arms, the muscles of which were taut and unrelenting.

Miraculously, I managed to steady the tip of the knife against his chest, against the same place over his heart where it began. This time, I held it more firmly—or tried to.

What I didn't realize was the inch-thick barrel of a pistol that was suddenly against my neck, the cold metal pressing into my throat. Michael was always one step ahead of me.

"Don't get into a stalemate," he said quietly. "Unless, of course, you're not bluffing. Which you are."

"How do you know I'm bluffing?" I fired back in an attempt to sound strong, but my voice was anything but.

Through the dark, his teeth gleamed as he smiled for the first time in a long time. It was an unnerving smile. I gasped as I felt his fingers touch the edge of my wrist, but he simply took my hand into his. Mine was shaking.

"Drop it."

I opened my trembling hand and let the knife fall through. It made a quiet *ping* against the floor, the sound drowned out by the drum inside my chest that unnerved me further. Michael released my hand but did not lower the barrel poised directly under my chin, angled straight for my brain, capable of killing me instantly.

"Lastly, do yourself a favor," he said, breath whisking my cheeks, "and don't ever do that again."

"Do what?" I asked breathlessly, expecting him to threaten me for threatening him, for leaving my captivity, for wielding his weapon.

"Hesitate," he said.

I looked up and our eyes met. Prepared for the backlash, I steadied my lips and said daringly, "Is that what you did?"

The barrel of his gun pressed against my windpipe, all but cutting off my breath. The tips of two fingers were rested on the trigger. And I knew that, unlike me, Michael was not bluffing. He pressed the gun deeper into my skin and I gasped, instinctively trying to back away, but he had his other hand behind my back, holding me to him. I looked up into his eyes again which were just barely visible. We stayed like that for a few more seconds before I finally surrendered.

"Fine," I said as I locked my jaw. "Go ahead and do it. You don't know how many times *I've* tried."

"Careful, sweetheart."

I shook my head, tired of the banter, the games and the threats. "This is what you kidnapped me for. What you wanted all along. Go ahead." The words were like ashes on my tongue. I closed my eyes. "Kill me."

I could feel Michael's eyes on my face, his

expression undoubtedly as unrevealing as my own. After several seconds, I opened my eyes.

"You still won't. Why? What value am I to you?"

His composure was calm, perhaps too coordinated. And for once, I could see the effort it took. His eyes were a blank slate of black, but they were strikingly emerald at the core. At that moment, I realized, I had broken through.

"What do you want from me, Michael Moiré?"

"That depends. What," he whispered, playing into my game, his lips at my ear, "would you be willing to give?"

I leveled my stare. "You say it like I have a choice."

"You do, Leah Venn," he said, trailing the tip of the gun along my neck, making me shiver. "I'm just establishing your options."

My heart was very near pounding right out of my chest despite the fact that I had told myself I was in control. "And if I don't choose to bow down to you?" I retorted.

The aggression in my tone caught him off-guard. I wasn't sure, but I thought I saw his eyes narrow. "Then we go on as expected. You, the damsel in distress. Me, the cold-hearted killer keeping you prisoner."

His words touched something in me, first and foremost because there was no mockery in his tone, no sarcasm. Michael believed what he said.

It reminded me of Beau and his self-loathing again. But it was more than that. It was almost as if he had been marked as just that—the cold-hearted killer—for so long, that he'd eventually started to believe it, though it wasn't actually true.

But it was true. Wasn't it?

I thought back to the fights, the battles we'd had, the times he'd hit me harder than anyone ever had, harder than I thought I could take. He'd certainly beaten the ever-living daylights out of me, over and over and over without mercy—something no man could ever be commended for and that certainly affected me on many plains. Me, a fragile little girl.

But you're not fragile, the small voice inside of my head whispered. *And you're not a little girl anymore.*

Why had it taken this long for me to realize that?

Somehow, somewhere, in the back of my mind, I knew the answer had something to do with this man. My enemy. At the same time, something turned inside of me uneasily that snuffed out all of my malice, replacing it with emotions frighteningly different.

"And if I do?" I said, staring through the dark into eyes that were even darker. "If I could choose you? If you could choose me over this life? Over killing for these people, this organization?"

"Then I'd let you go." Michael removed the gun from my throat and released me abruptly. "Before either of us could be that stupid."

"Michael."

I reached forward to touch any part of him I could get, to maybe feel at least something, anything that could help me understand him, even if it earned me a violent retaliation—I didn't care anymore. I needed this, needed truth.

I had played every card in my hand and I longed to see what his were, but where I reached, my fingers touched only air.

I heard the door, very quietly, drift to a close. And I waited for the sound of the lock, but it never came.

COMRADERY

I DROPPED DOWN TO the ledge that was a small piece of metal bolted to the side of the apartment and then I reached up and pushed the shattered windowpane to a close, my fingers just barely reaching it. Steadying myself, I stuck my left leg out as far as it could reach until I felt the sturdy metal structure beneath my feet. Then I pushed myself over until I caught hold of the rusty bars that clung to the side of the building. Sweat building on my forehead, I climbed all the way down. Minutes later, my feet made contact with solid dirt.

I could've walked out the front door—Michael had all but left me that option, it seemed. But no matter how easy it would've been, I couldn't bring myself to do it. I had stood there, had stared at that door for several long seconds knowing that, if I had opened it and walked out with my own free will, it would've meant something. Something I wasn't willing to admit, or accept.

This was an escape, nothing less. An escape that would lead me to where I needed to go, no matter the consequences or the difficulty, away from a violent, unstable enemy.

That's what I told myself.

I turned one last time to survey the building to be sure that he hadn't heard my drop or noticed the absence of me in the bedroom he'd left me in only hours before, but the air was filled with a resolute silence. And then I was walking.

"I'm coming for you, Sean," I said softly, determinedly, to myself. *I will find you.*

I had been walking for what felt like hours, though it couldn't have been any more than one. My feet were tired from traipsing through the dirt. There wasn't any distinct road for me to walk on or any pavement to identify if there had ever been one. Once I had managed to get out of the inner-city, aiming for the sandy horizons far from Michael's apartment in the hopes of finding a roundabout way, everything changed. It was as if there were a divider, a physical line that cut right through the outskirts of wherever I had been. The urban atmosphere became a deserted landscape almost instantly, and more times than one I feared that I was too exposed to reach my destination—wherever that even was.

But I pictured Sean in my head—my memory of him, as well as my predictions for what was being done to him. And it was that which kept me going, kept me walking forward even when I felt like I couldn't.

The flash of lights that suddenly blinded me sent my whole heart racing, my mind automatically zeroing in on that "fight or flight" reaction people get when facing sudden danger, for my thoughts automatically went to the worst-case scenario.

A large, black jeep pulled up right alongside me, seemingly out of nowhere. I backed away several feet, but I was too busy staring frightfully at the giant machine that I didn't have the mind to run away. The engine roared for another second and then, surprisingly, it shut off. There were no tracks behind it, just miles of sand.

I was still standing there with my bottom lip on the ground when she asked me, "You lost?"

I tore my eyes away from the vehicle and the miles of landscape it had illuminated and was astonished to find the driver to be a short, small woman. She was around my age, I guessed, maybe a few years older—though I was about four inches taller than her. She was dressed in dark clothes that didn't reveal her figure, and her hair was a deep almond shade, chopped neatly just below the ears.

I cleared my throat, trying to remember what I looked like to this stranger and put on an apologetic smile.

Then her words registered. "English. Are you American?" I asked hopefully.

The woman eyed me up and down and then she took a few steps towards me. *"Puertorriqueño."* With a smile, she added, "English is not just an American language."

I grinned, embarrassed. "Right, sorry. I'm kind of new to...foreign places."

"I can tell."

"You can?"

She raised one polished eyebrow. "You look like a *turista*."

"Oh." I blushed, feeling like a child. "I guess I do."

"*Si*. Where are you headed? And might I ask why you are walking alone at this time of night?"

"Oh...well, I—"

"This isn't exactly the safest place to be wandering around in," she interrupted me, though her tone was light. "Especially for pretty young women like us, no?"

I smiled, unsure what else to say to that.

"Your destination?" she repeated, after concluding that I was going to be a total moron and forget that she'd asked me a question.

"I'm trying to get to this part of Ghazni...I mean, I was *in* Ghazni, but I left because I need to get to a different part of Ghazni...but I've no idea which way to get there. Do you...?"

"Know how to get to 'this part' of Ghazni?" She let out a light-hearted, breezy laugh and said, "Sure do. Hop in, I'll take you where you need to go."

"Oh, you don't have to..."

"I insist." She held out her hand to me just then and said sweetly, "*Me llamo* Rya."

I took her hand—it was ice cold, despite the humidity—and said with a smile, "Me llamo Leah."

As we shook hands, I thought I saw a calculated look in Rya's eyes that had nothing to do with my poor pronunciation of Spanish. But I was too desperate to think twice about it. I jumped up into the passenger seat of the jeep and she turned to flash me a reassuring smile. I smiled back at her, wondering, for just one second, if this was a sign that maybe things were going to go smoothly for me, after all.

"Welcome to this part of Ghazni," Rya smiled, as she pulled the jeep to a stop on the side of the road and unlocked the doors for me. She parked facing a huge structure, its giant, yellowish stone walls shining in the night. "*El palacio sultán masood,* and its beautiful gardens. What most *americanos* come to see, yes?"

My eyes zipped back and forth between the height of the palace, the antique design on the outer walls and the rush of a small stream into what appeared to be a fully-blossomed garden on each side. It was beautiful, unlike anything I had ever seen.

"This place must be ancient," I said absentmindedly.

"It was constructed in the very first century of time," Rya said, her eyes on me. "*El palacio* has soldiers' quarters, government offices and a throne room inside. But it is primarily for political and diplomatic frivolity of *embajadores*."

"Ambassadors."

"Very good."

I broke my eyes away from the building and glanced at Rya, thoughtfully, my eyes the feigned picture of innocence. "You mean the military does not actually meet here?"

She smiled the slightest bit. "No. The military base here in Ghazni is about a mile that way," she said, pointing her long, slim arm in the direction just beyond the Sultan Masood Palace. "But it is not a nice place for Americans, Leah. Whatever business you have there, I suggest you abandon it."

We made eye contact and finally, I saw an end to the façade we had both been portraying.

"Thank you for bringing me this far," I said, reaching into my pockets in the hopes to find some money. "I can…"

"*Por favor,*" she said quickly, reaching out with surprising speed to place her hand on mine. "I am no taxi. Just do me a favor, *mi chica*, and know where you are and what that means."

I looked up to meet her eyes, but she didn't pause long enough for me to question her remark.

The moment I was clear from its path the jeep shook as the engine roared to life. Without another second to spare, Rya floored it and drove off in the direction from which we'd come. For an instant, I questioned her intentions, but I let it go for now.

I turned and eyed the city we'd entered, this time completely bypassing the palace that stood tall in front of me and instead, to that which lay beyond it. The sight gave away little but the clustered blur of lights here and there.

Being that it was nighttime, there was just a shadowed silhouette of two lines of buildings that were separated by a small, undefined dirt road that ran right through.

As I walked it, I noticed that there weren't any people around. I distinctly remembered the time back in Kandahar when there had been no people around—right before all hell had broken loose.

So I was already on edge when I rounded the corner and saw them.

UNDER FIRE

FBI Headquarters
Washington, D.C.

"OKAY," JONATHON LANSFORD SAID, as he paced the length of the room quickly, his white dress shirt zipping back and forth, making him look like an apparition. "So this is what we know."

Thomas Lawton inclined his head, though his mind was off in a foreign direction.

"Joseph Locke is actually Beau Moiré, in real life," Lansford said. "However, the National Archives treats them as two separate entities. Locke doesn't exist in any archives besides the Army Enlistment he participated in, dated in 2016."

"The year of the draft," Lawton noted absently.

"The year of the draft." Lansford nodded, making a mental note. "Moiré *does* exist in the archives up until the age of seventeen. After that, all record of him is absent. Possibly even erased."

The more Lawton considered the conundrum, the more he was almost certain the information had been erased. To consider that the National Archives was as incompetent at keeping records as the CIA was at keeping a secret was just too much.

Lawton smiled at his own internal quip. *Conniving Ignorant Assholes.*

Anyway. The files had been erased. Lawton was sure of it. The million-dollar question was by *who.*

Lansford continued, "Mr. Vince contacted those in possession of the United States Army Enlistment records, and the files of Beau Moiré that have been erased from the National Archives, despite being lined up with his alleged enlistment date, were not tampered with by them. They have only the enlistment of Joseph Locke, the background of which was proven to have been falsified by Moiré by the Department of Defense in 2018 after he went Absent Without Leave. 2016 to 2018. So he'd gotten away with it for two years before he was caught."

"But he was only caught because he gave away his position first," Lawton reminded the young trainee. "Only when Moiré went rogue did the Department of Defense discover he'd falsified his enlistment alias. If he had stayed where he was and continued with whatever he was doing, perhaps we would not be having this conversation."

"So the real question is…what was he doing?" Jonathon Lansford nodded his head slowly as if he were conscious that the wheels turning inside would falter if he jostled them too much. His mouth was twisted into a frustrated line that Lawton knew all too well. He, personally, had exhausted his many years ago.

Lansford paused all of a sudden. As if a light had turned on in his brain, he asked, "Where was Locke deployed to, initially?"

"Sheberghan," Lawton recalled. "Capital of the Jowzjan Province in Afghanistan. The U.S. has a military base there."

"Had he ever been there before? Locke—or, Moiré, that is?"

Lawton pursed his lips. "I don't know. Why?"

John Lansford flipped through the pages of a folder he'd set precariously on the edge of Lawton's desk and slid his fingers up and down several pages, murmuring quietly to himself for an irritatingly long time. Lawton wasn't sure what the young man was reading, or if it even contained relevant information. He'd never seen the folder before. It was probably a *Playboy*.

"John?" Lawton prompted, adding a throat-clearing *hack* sound to make the prompting more official.

Lansford looked up. "Yes?"

"Why does it matter whether Moiré had ever been to Sheberghan before? Are we hunting down the man's lineage or solving this case?"

"Yes, right," Lansford closed the folder and tossed it back down on the desk with exhilaration. "Mr. Lawton, don't you find it odd that a young soldier with allegedly no terrorist connections would travel to the Middle East and decide, overnight, to switch sides?"

"There are two years of lost files," Lawton reminded him. "It needn't have happened overnight.

He had time."

"But why erase his files only up until the Army Enlistment? Why not obliterate Moiré off the map entirely?"

Lawton eyed the man with a measured look of curiosity.

"I believe something went wrong in Afghanistan and I'm going to see if I can find out what," Lansford decided solely as he shuffled his paperwork into a thin tan folder and shoved it into his tiny briefcase. The man had become so official in just a few weeks' time that Lawton wasn't entirely sure he was speaking with the same person.

Every time they met to discuss the case they were trying to solve under the FBI's radar, John Lansford had a new accessory. This time, it was the flimsy black briefcase and a silver wristwatch like the ones you'd see in the movies, paired with a strangely full folder and an increasingly can-do attitude that Lawton wasn't entirely sure he liked or disliked.

"John," Lawton said, before the young man could bustle through the door. "I have another area for you to look into."

Lansford paused. He evidently picked up on the implied part of the sentence that said this was a bit more sensitive and wound his adrenaline-fused youth back a notch. "Sir?"

"I want a full background report on the Democratic Nominee for President."

Lansford frowned, the request catching him by obvious surprise that he wasn't experienced enough to try and hide. "Tyler Millerton. Why? You think he's involved with this?"

Thomas Lawton thought of the media reports, the press conferences, the uncertainty and mistrust he sensed in the man's eyes and, above all, the way in which a woman named Savanna had called him into question. Her presence in his mind over their encounter, despite having taken place days ago, had hardly faded. And with that intensity came an entirely new train of thought, one he had yet to share with Lansford and probably wouldn't until he knew more, and one that, Lawton could already tell, held far worse consequences for the country than Beau Moiré, Justin Roland and Wesley Marshall.

Unlike Lansford, Lawton *did* know how to hide things.

"I think he deserves some of our time," Lawton said plainly, as he watched the wheels continue to turn inside the young man's head as if they never tired, never dimmed. "Besides, he may just be the next Commander-in-Chief. If we're to solve this, I need all of the pieces, John. All of them."

Jonathon Lansford smiled weakly before nodding his head. "I'll see how many I can find before I implode."

"Atta boy."

Before the door could close behind the whirlwind of thought that was the young FBI officer in training, Special Agent Thomas Lawton got to his feet and stopped it in its tracks. Peering out into the busy hall, Lawton cast a quick glance in either direction, waiting to see a wisp of fiery red that never came.

Thoughtful, he glanced at the clock across the room that told him it was half-past eleven o'clock in the morning, not the evening, and that perhaps her secret encounters were meant to be just that—a midnight secret.

While he was standing in the doorway, two agents brushed past him without a word or a glance in his direction. Oddly, one of them was Special Agent Logan Williams.

"Logan," Lawton said abruptly, slightly confused over the fact that Williams hadn't given him his typical smart-assed remark the way he had for the past ten years of their friendship and partnership on the same floor at the Federal Bureau of Investigation.

Williams turned slightly, caught Lawton's eye and spun around as if it pained him to do so.

"Tommy," Williams said after he made parting remarks with the agent he'd been walking with—a stiff-necked try-hard from the floor above, Lawton noted. "What's up, buddy? I thought you were out sick today."

Lawton frowned. "I can't even remember the last time I called in sick," he said, trying to decide whether there was an uncomfortable look in his partner's eyes or whether that was a result of Williams' inherent ugliness. It was a toss-up.

"Well there you go, that's probably why they said that, you could use a break, Thomas, take a vacation," Williams said, with a smile that wouldn't have fooled a toddler, and slapped Lawton on the shoulder. "It's nuts around here, you know? I don't blame you."

"Blame me for what? They said what? And who

are they?" Lawton felt like *he* may implode. "Logan, I apologize if this may seem forward, but what the actual fuck are you going on about?"

For the first time, Williams cut the shit and gave Lawton a look. Not just a *hey-how-you-doin* look, but a *look look*. Williams nodded his head towards Lawton's office and followed him through after closing the door behind him.

"What's going on with you?" Williams said the moment they were alone, ignoring the fact that Lawton believed he should be the one asking that question. "You hardly leave this five-foot square," he said, gesturing at the office, "and people are starting to talk about...what happened the other night."

Thomas Lawton immediately thought of his sultry encounter with Savanna the Somebody, and did his best not to sound guilty. "I'm not sure what you're referring to, but I can assure you, nothing—"

"Wait." Logan Williams' face was growing paler by the second and measurably more uncomfortably ugly. "You don't know, do you?"

"For the last time, know *what?*"

Williams glanced around the room once, let his eyes rest on the window, and then the door before he moved towards it.

"Follow me."

Lawton was beginning to feel the pulsating pressure of a workday-gone-wrong type of headache. Because he didn't believe he could form any more questions coherently without losing his mind entirely, he followed Williams to the tenth floor, which was one below the top level, and frowned at the *Special*

Security Clearance Required sign on the door to the room Williams finally stopped in front of.

Well, not necessary *stopped.*

Williams touched some numbers on a keypad under the handle of the metal door and then scanned the security clearance card he and Lawton both had possession of. The room was entirely accessible at all hours of the day to anyone in the building with an FBI clearance card. However, few knew they even had that right to exercise, which is what kept the FBI's famous shroud of secrecy alive.

Ha.

"Logan, what are we—?"

Lawton allowed his sentence to drift off. Williams was staring at him with an inquisitive look, for he had removed a particularly thick folder from the farthest filing cabinet in the room and placed it on the island-desk that separated them.

"What is this?"

Williams nodded his head toward the file, careful not to expose any more tension than was already in the room.

The encounter was strange, to say the least, and entirely out of Williams' character. Lawton felt like he was about to open the cover and see his own obituary.

He was wrong.

It was an obituary, autopsy report and case file for the death of FBI Special Agent Derek Vince. For the first time in a while, Lawton was speechless.

"They found him two days ago."

"How?" Lawton asked after taking a breath to ensure he wasn't about to join him.

"How everyone with classified information dies," Williams said. "Heart attack."

Lawton lifted his head. His neck felt like a tree-trunk that was just about to give out its roots. "I spoke with him three days ago."

Williams nodded slowly as he covered the file and replaced it back where he'd found it.

"I want that autopsy report."

"So does everyone," Williams said as he closed the drawer and locked it. "But there's a reason why I'm showing you this, Thomas, and you yourself just mentioned it. Consider this a warning."

Lawton frowned. "I don't understand."

"No one does, it doesn't add up, he was as healthy as an ox, so young, at the height of his career, no known genetic tendency for blocked arteries, etcetera, etcetera…" Williams eyed Lawton carefully. "There's only one thing the Bureau knows, Tommy, and it's that you were the last one to speak with him. He died in his car, didn't even make it home to his wife, his kids, hell, his fucking golden retriever didn't even get to see him but you," Williams pointed at him and shook his head. "You did, Thomas."

Shit.

"You know what that means."

The repercussions of the bone Williams was throwing him was not lost on Lawton. He nodded absently. He knew what it meant— that not only was he about to be the prime suspect in the possible murder of his boss, Derek Vince, but that someone had read the man's cards and not liked what he, or *she*, had found.

Lawton fought his mind's urge to panic and, instead, thought calmly about his next move.

Williams made a gesture toward the door for the security cameras, but as he moved toward the exit, his words drifted through the air, undetectable by anyone but Thomas Lawton.

"Whatever Vince told you, whatever you're working on—keep it to yourself before your job isn't the only thing under fire."

PROTECTOR

MY EYES WIDENED.

Down a long, shadowed alleyway, there were four figures standing about. Three of them were tall, burly and somewhat foreign men, all crowded around the last figure—a little girl.

"Where's your *mommy* now, *baby?*"

One of the other men let out a throaty laugh and then the man who'd spoken pushed the small girl up against the wall as he brought his face closer to hers. She mashed her eyes shut, her straight black hair falling around her tear-stained face as she lowered her head.

"Answer me when I'm talkin' to you, bitch!"

"Yeah, baby bitch!"

The girl started to cry, trembling horribly, the front of her brown shirt already soaking wet.

"I...I don't...know," she stuttered in a thick accent, her wide eyes pleading and desperate as she whipped her head around, searching for her parents, or, I'm sure, anyone at all.

That's when she first saw me and when her brown eyes first met mine. That tortured, overwhelmingly terrified child's gaze stared at me, locking me in place as I fought myself not to run to her aid.

"You *don't* know, *do you* baby?" the man snarled as he shoved her back against the wall again.

Suddenly, the girl reached out and smacked the guy across the face. It was a small, weak attempt at a slap, but it made me suddenly proud. Behind the fear, the weak exterior and those soft brown eyes, I could see a strong wall of defiance.

The man gritted his teeth, anger replacing shock. I cringed as he lashed out and slapped her hard across the face, the sound echoing off the stone walls of the alley.

"Baby thinks she's tough, doesn't you baby?"

Another man snickered and stepped forward. "Think we should see how tough baby is?"

"See what baby's made of, won't we?"

Then, sickening every part of me, the three of them started to tear at her clothes.

"Stop!" Before I could stop myself, I jumped out from behind the corner and took a few steps forward. "Leave her alone!"

The girl's eyes widened further, as if that was even possible, and the fear that had dominated her face was gone. Well, it wasn't gone. It shifted—to fear for what was going to happen to me.

All three of the men stopped, and, one by one, their eyes settled on me. My hands began to shake. Each of them looked me up and down and then, slowly, they started their advance.

"Now what do we have here?" the lead man smiled, and I noticed that he was missing a few of his front teeth. The two others fell in line beside him, all advancing toward me, their expressions lit with a cruel satisfaction.

I harnessed enough control to look past them, to the girl who was still standing with her back against the wall, her clothes tattered and wet, still crying as if frozen in place. "Go!" I shouted. "Run!"

The girl lifted her head and stared at me but didn't move.

"Get out of here!" I snapped, my tone loud and forceful with just a hint of desperation. *Please.*

She burst into a new fit of tears, but I didn't get to see her cry them because she bolted in the other direction and, within seconds, the girl was running out of the alleyway, out of sight. My heart soared with relief.

And then fell, with dread, because I'd blown my only chance at escaping, myself.

The lead man—the one who'd done most of the harassing—was the first to reach me. He grabbed me by the shoulders and slammed me back against the wall, shaking my vision and causing the head-ache I'd been fighting against to hit me full-force.

The man sneered—half his teeth were missing, and the ones that weren't were disgustingly rotted. He, along with his companions, all appeared to be in their mid-thirties and dirty, yet not incompetent. Ex-soldiers, perhaps?

One of them was slightly more clean-cut,

attractive even, with the build of someone who didn't belong in this crowd, but his eyes told a different story. Red-rimmed, as if he were on drugs, and infused with hatred and lust that matched that of his comrades.

He was the one who said something sarcastic at that moment, though it was hard to decipher, for the language he spoke just then wasn't English. I could hear the syllables, however, rushed together in a way that was faintly familiar, but shouldn't have been the tongue of a predominantly Persian-speaking area.

Arabic.

The man grabbed me by the shoulder strap of my shirt and spun me to the side where I landed with a sharp roll onto the thick dirt that crusted the floor of the alley.

As they laughed, taking their time enjoying the harassment, I pushed my palms against the ground and jumped up to my feet. As fast as I could, I dashed towards the lights that illuminated the main street. Towards safety.

A man grabbed me by the wrist, yanking me backwards so fast I lost my footing and stared to fall. Before I could, however, one of the men caught me. Instead of relief, my mind raced with panic. I jerked my arms away from him, twisting and turning out of his grip. Muttering under his breath, he pinned both my arms behind my back and turned me to face his accomplices.

"I think miss grown-up baby will be a lot more fun than little baby, aye?"

The two others laughed and I felt the man

behind me put his mouth close to my ear as he breathed, "How 'bout it? Wanna play?"

As fast as I could, I twisted to one side and dug the heel of my boot into his shin causing him to release me. I thought of the moves I'd used against Michael, all the tips he'd drilled into me. It didn't last, however, for one of the others was there to catch and subdue me before I could act on them.

You hesitate.

"Let go of me!" I shouted, this one's hot breath making my stomach turn. Then, as if I remembered I had a voice, I screamed. "Help! Somebody help! Pl— !"

The man in front of me stopped me from my last scream as he mashed his lips against mine, the force of it making me bite my tongue so hard I tasted blood.

"Mmmm, she kissed me!"

"My turn!"

I turned my head to the side as one of the others came at me. And the move cost me. The man behind me twisted my arms in a pretzel shape, punishing me for resisting.

You're weak.

I tried to scream again, but he threw me forward and I hit into one of the others, his chest like a wall. This one grabbed me and, just like I'd seen him try against the little girl, started to tear at my clothes as another sneered, "You'll find no American flag wavers here, girl. Scream away."

I felt helpless, thrown back and forth between the three of them, each one pulling at my shirt or my pants. I tried to flail my arms and legs in resistance, but each attempt only got me another smack in the face or a sharp blow to my stomach.

You're vulnerable.

"That's enough!"

The words soared in one ear and out the other; the voice didn't even register in my head. Tears blurred my vision, my eyes unable to blink them away fast enough. I was sluggish, tired. Defeated. Between Michael's fighting and this pathetic defeat, it was as if my body felt nothing but ache anymore.

The men dropped me.

I fell to the concrete, my clothes tattered, not noticing anything but the violent shiver that coursed through me and the quiet, desperate whimpering that I hadn't realized I'd been doing.

A gunshot sounded through the alleyway, forcing a scream out of my throat and me to scoot back until I felt the cold, stable surface of a wall behind me. The three men who'd attacked me all ran off down the other side of the alley and then I heard nothing but the echoing ring of the gunfire. Then, footsteps.

I pressed my back against the cement behind me and my palms tightly against the dirt below. I closed my eyes, my chest rising and falling so fast, so hard I couldn't breathe. And for a moment, I was lying on Beau's floor in a pool of my own blood.

Fire. A burning, piercing fire that emanated from the bullet in my side and the two that had skimmed other parts of my body. I heard Wes's scream, felt Beau's agony all over again and suddenly, I knew what it was like to relive, not just emotional but physical trauma, all over again.

The footsteps stopped. In a loud voice, a man said, "You're alright now, Miss, I won't hurt you."

I cringed and pressed myself close to the wall without realizing I was doing it. The picture was gone, the memory fading but still sharp, particularly in my left side.

I sensed him as he bent down to one knee and lowered his voice into a softer tone. "Miss, open your eyes. My name is Kyle Dellis. I am an American soldier. You're safe."

Hearing the familiar voice of an American, my eyes shot open and I found myself staring into the soldier's deep blue eyes. The word *safe*, however, didn't resonate with me in the slightest.

The soldier cautiously put his hand on my cheeks. "You're safe," he repeated, as if expecting me to believe him. His expression faltered, and then he added softly, "You saved my daughter's life."

"Y-y-your d-daughter?" I stammered. It didn't make sense. I had thought I'd heard a slight accent on the girl that was devoid of this man's perfect English. Besides, he looked to be about twenty-five, and the girl had to have been at least ten.

"Yes," he said without missing a beat. "She came home crying so hard we could barely understand her, but she told me what you did." Tears formed in his eyes that he didn't shake away. They seemed pretty real. "Thank you."

I shivered but managed a nod. "Thank you...too."

He stood back up and held his hands out to me. "It was the least I could do." Timidly, I placed mine in his and he lifted me up with the strength of a soldier. He held me in his arms until I could stand, and even then he kept a firm grip on me.

"Do you live around here?" he asked me as he guided me towards the end of the alley and back onto the street. I noticed that he kept his gun lowered, but readily accessible.

I shook my head and said quietly, still shaking tremendously, "I was...looking for..."

"Looking for who?" he asked. "I patrol these streets regularly—I know mostly every American. Do they live here?"

"I-I...don't know...Sean's a...soldier."

"A soldier," he murmured. "Tell me, what's Sean's last name?"

"C-col..."

"Collins?"

I gasped, hearing the recognition in his voice as he assumed the correct soldier. A piece of my fear diminished, and I didn't even stop to question how he could've known.

"Sergeant Collins is an acquaintance of mine," he continued. "I've only known him for a short while, but he's a good man, Collins is." Dellis eyed the jewel around my neck, the heart shaped necklace that Sean had bought me, with one small addition. Before I had left California, I'd strung my mother's wedding ring onto the necklace. It was a simple ring, but a noticeable one.

"Is he your husband?"

I started to shake my head. Then, suddenly, I thought twice about it.

"Yes." I cleared my throat, trying to sound calm despite the fact that I was anything but. "He, um, told me only to come if it was an emergency. D-do you know where I can find him?"

At my mention of an emergency and the chance to help me, Kyle Dellis perked up. "Of course. He should still be at the base. He had a meeting on level seven—with Warrant Officer Bryant. I'm sure if he knew you were coming, he would have made sure to send word."

"Base?" I asked, my throat feeling suddenly tight.

"The U.S. Army base here in Ghazni. Technically, it isn't protocol to bring civilians into the base without necessary cause, but...well, I'm sure Sergeant Collins will demand the General make an exception for his wife. Besides, I owe you at least this much."

"The..." My heart was falling fast. "General?"

"Yes, Mrs. Collins," Kyle said, his expression depicting a hint of confusion. "The General oversees operations here in Ghazni. Surely your husband has mentioned that?"

I hesitated. "Anyway," he said, his attention diverted as he helped me into a small, old black car across the street. "Sergeant Collins, even though he is new here, is well respected, particularly by the General himself. His wishes will be acknowledged. I'll make sure of that myself."

I nodded slowly, my mind still trying to process

the situation and my blood still thick with adrenaline, partial relief and a growing sense of fear because my plan was a go—even though I was almost certain I would've been safer with the vile rapists than where I was headed now.

TRAPPED

D79 Headquarters
Ghazni, Afghanistan

"MY...WIFE?"

The man nodded and said, "Forgive me for arriving unannounced, and with a civilian, sir, but I knew you would want me to bring her to you straight away."

Sean eyed the corporal with a frown, then dropped his army pack to the floor. He'd been in the middle of final preparations for his newly assigned departure when he was interrupted with the news. "Are you sure you have the right person, Kyle?"

"Yes, Mr. Collins. She was adamant of that; inquired about you immediately. Said it was an emergency." Kyle glanced down briefly. When he lifted his head, there was a sly smile in his eyes. "You didn't tell me you were married, Sean. And to a gorgeous girl, at that."

Sean's eyebrows shot up. *Apparently, I forgot to tell myself.*

He studied the man again, suspicious, wondering if it were merely a joke the guys were pulling on him. But Dellis's face was as serious as Sean had ever seen it. Not to mention, it was against protocol to bring civilians into the base, and even more so to escort them directly into the tunnels that ran below the main base in Ghazni, Afghanistan. Dellis was either positive on this woman's identity or he knew something that Sean didn't.

Sergeant Sean Collins shook his head.

"All right, Kyle. Please escort in...my wife." The words felt strange on his lips.

Dellis didn't notice. He saluted, then exited the room to carry out the request. Leaving the twenty-six-year-old soldier to his confusion and downright curiosity.

I CONTINUED TO GLANCE over my shoulder, desperately wishing that Kyle Dellis would hurry. So far, we'd made it past the security and the outer guard without any problems or questioning. Maybe this would work...

My head snapped up as the man who'd escorted me here came walking back down the hall in which he'd left me, a small smile on his lips as he said, "This way, Mrs. Collins."

I hesitated, shot a final look behind me and then followed him.

"I have to say, your husband did seem a little surprised at your visit," Dellis commented. "He was partially...taken aback."

"Oh," I said tightly.

We reached a thick metal door and the man turned towards me as he lowered his eyes, looking suddenly sort of embarrassed. "I'm sorry for what happened to you, Mrs. Collins, and I apologize for not being there sooner. If you ever need anything, come find me. I owe you greatly."

I gave him a weak smile and then glanced at the door. "Thank you, Mr. Dellis."

He nodded his head and then turned to go.

"Kyle." He stopped as I turned to give him a look. "Tell your daughter I said thank you...She saved my life too."

Dellis gave me another small smile, this one devoid of any tears or sadness. Just a small, simple smile. And then he disappeared off down the hall, leaving me alone.

Alone to face my husband.

I took a deep breath, and then another. Slowly, I pushed the door open and stepped inside.

Sean was wearing a pair of desert camouflage pants that were baggy on his slim figure and a tan t-shirt underneath a camouflage jacket that matched his pants. I could see a thick scratch on the side of his face, but there weren't any other injuries on him, so I figured it must've been from training. He looked just as boyish and handsome as ever. But the warm, friendly smile that used to always be in his eyes wasn't there. And that should have been a warning sign.

I heard a gun click and my breath stopped as soon as I saw the barrel that was suddenly resting on my chest.

"Who are you? And what gives you the right to

lie to the United States Army and call yourself my wife?"

I fought the urge to close my eyes and, instead, I lowered them to the floor. It was his voice. His words. But it wasn't his tone.

"Sean, I—"

"How do you know my name?" he snapped, jamming the barrel of his gun into my chest harder, pushing me back a step.

"Sean!" Tears ran in streams down my face. "Sean it's me! It's—"

"Silence!"

I clamped my mouth shut, trying to quiet my sobs as they became more and more distinct. Sean didn't recognize me, and it dawned on me that I was probably covered in dirt and grime from being tossed around back in the alleyway. I felt it all over my body and all through my hair. I realized that he couldn't see me.

"Sean, its L—"

"*I said silence, woman!*" Sean dropped his gun and slammed me back against the door with both of his hands against my shoulders. I was stunned. Sean had always been strong, but his grip was suddenly much more powerful than ever before, devoid of concern.

"You will speak when spoken to, understand?"

I bit my lip in utter dismay and disbelief that my cousin, who I'd walked hours for, had chanced being raped and killed to come and rescue, was ordering me around like I was a captive.

Like I was nothing to him.

"Do you understand?" he repeated harshly.

"Yes," I whispered through the pain and the tears as I looked up for the first time and met his gaze. And there it was—that same look. Those same brown eyes, staring back at me. Except this time, they were dark and filled with anger.

Anger that flickered as shock replaced it. I watched his eyes widen, and then they narrowed. Without comment, Sean lowered his eyes down my figure and then back up as he eyed me intently for a long moment. His hands started to shake. He lifted one of them and brushed it across my cheek. He did the same on the other side and then he did one final sweep across my forehead.

I watched as he pulled away and studied his hands, now covered in a thick layer of dirt. He let his eyes reach mine again and then I saw tears start to well up in his.

"No..." He was shaking his head. "It can't be..."

"It's me, Sean," I whispered desperately. "Leah."

"No," he said, staring into my eyes and trying to find deception. "It can't be."

"Please." I took a step forward. He backed up one. I took another towards him. Again, he backed up.

"It's not possible," he breathed, still moving away from me.

The wall was behind him now and he had nowhere left to escape to. As I took the last step forward, he took the last one back.

"Please," I whispered. "Please, Sean, this is real. I'm here."

He started to close his eyes as he shook his head—but then he stopped, and his breath stopped and if I had to guess I'd say his heart stopped too. All because his eyes had halted at my chest, and even covered in dirt, he recognized it.

Sean's hand reached up to my neck and he traced his fingers over the small diamond heart necklace I had always worn around my neck, with my mother's wedding ring. The necklace he would remember, because it had been a gift, a birthday present, from him. The ring he would know, too, if only in a fleeting, distant memory of my parents.

His lips shaped the word "impossible" but the sound didn't follow it. "Leah?"

I nodded quickly, biting back more tears as I wrapped my arms around his neck and hugged him tightly without his approval.

"Leah," he repeated, as if saying it would make it more real. Sean tightened his arms around me. "I can't believe it's you."

I nodded weakly and clasped his shirt between my fingers like my life depended on it. "I'm here, Sean. It's so good to see you."

Slowly, Sean loosened his arms and pulled me out so that he could see my face. There was a questioning look on his as shock fell away. "Leah...what are you doing here?"

I inhaled, feeling like it was safe enough to breathe for the first time in forever. "I came to rescue you, Sean. You're in danger."

There was something different, something strange about the way he looked at me, almost as if his eyes were calculating. I expected him to ask me how I got here, or how I found where he was stationed, or why I'd made a special trip overseas to see him or even why the hell I was covered in dirt.

He didn't ask any of those.

"Are you alone?"

I hesitated. He was my cousin; this was Sean. If there was anyone I could trust, it was him. Right? I remembered the way I'd suddenly begun to doubt and question and undermine everything I thought I'd once known as truth; how awful it felt to have a mind devoid of trust, of certainty. Sean was a breath of fresh air from the necessity of that.

"Yes," I said. "I'm alone—I came alone."

He narrowed his eyes at my words, but didn't comment. Sean turned and studied the blank stone wall for a moment, his hands clasped stiffly behind his back, toying with each other.

"Are you still with him? Moiré?"

"Yes." I couldn't deny that his words were troubling. "Look, I know you've probably been told a lot of terrible things about Beau, but they aren't true. You have to trust me, Sean. He's a good guy. But these people—some of the soldiers, in Division-7-9— they're the bad ones. That's why I came, to get you out of here. And we have to go before anyone recognizes me or tries to stop us—"

"Where is he now?"

I frowned. "Beau? He was in Kandahar, but they're probably in Zaranj by now. That was the plan, anyway. But Sean, you're not listening. These people you serve are part of an organization that has infiltrated the American government. They're terrorists. You—"

"I believe you." Sean turned towards me, his expression similar to what I remembered—light, easy, reassuring—no matter how strange his tone was.

"You do?" I asked, my eyes sparkling.

"Yes," he said. "Now what did you say about this...plan? Whose idea was it and what does it involve?"

I opened my mouth to speak, then closed it slowly.

"Leah." Sean stepped towards me, his voice soft but urgent now. "I've known the truth for a while. I just haven't had the chance to do anything about it or escape to find you."

I stared at him. He glanced around, as if to see if anyone was around to hear, and took my shoulders. "Now's our chance, Lee."

My heart soared at his use of my old nickname.

Sean continued, "I need you to tell me what Beau is planning and who's helping him. I can help you, help them, but you must let me in on it. You have to tell me what the plan is."

I searched his eyes and nodded. "Wes and Matt—they're on our side too—came up with it. They plan to attack Zaranj and burn it to the ground after we've taken what we can of D79's weapon storage there. After that...well, I don't really remember the second part. Beau and I had gotten into a fight and I—"

"Burn it?" Sean's eyes were wide. "How would they manage that? Zaranj may be a very valuable hit, but it is heavily guarded for that very reason. Did they specify *how* they were to achieve this?"

I hesitated, something itching in my head.

"Leah, I can't help you if I don't know how."

"Wes has built a bomb," I said quietly. "I know it doesn't exactly sound humane, but…it's the best chance we've got."

Sean stepped back, his expression thoughtful. He glanced at me, then averted his eyes for a while. I didn't know for sure, but the look gave the impression that he was conflicted. As if he was fighting some huge battle inside that finally gave way as he said, "Okay Leah. Come with me."

I took his hand as he extended it to me, but it didn't immediately register that it was shaking. He pushed against the thick metal door, the hinges scraping against concrete as it swung outward. Sean rested his forehead against the door for a second, his eyes closed.

And I recognized that look. I'd seen it too many times before.

"No," I whispered, my eyes swelling with tears. "Sean, please."

"He threatened to kill you," Sean whispered, "if I didn't obey him. Leah…I had no choice."

"We always have a choice," I said sharply, angrily. "*You* have a choice. Right now! You're *choosing* to sell me out. Me, your family!"

At my use of his old phrase about choices, Sean sighed. His hands shook, his eyes closed harder, his face became more ghostly pale.

"I didn't choose this."

I fought to pry my hand out of his, but Sean's grip was tight. He pushed the door open and pulled me forward—into a group of five soldiers, all armed.

I spun and touched my free hand to his chest, right above his heart. "Sean, please. I know you're scared, but submitting to them isn't the answer. Come with me. Beau will help you—"

For the first time, hatred flashed in his eyes. Hatred I had seen before, just never on him. "Beau Moiré and those traitors are the reason for all of this. If you knew what was good for you, you'd turn on him before he gets the chance to turn on you, because he will. That's what a traitor does, Leah, that's what he is!"

I shook my head. "They're controlling you. Please, Sean. Don't do this. I'm your cousin, your family, don't *do* this to me!"

"You're too naïve," Sean said quietly. "You always were."

"Please…"

"You'll be safe, Leah," he said. "He promised to keep you safe." But the look on his face proved how little his certainty was.

Sean released me and backed away from my outstretched hand. His brown eyes never left mine, however, as two of the soldiers came forward and took hold of me. The look on his face deteriorated everything that made him who he was. Everything that reminded me of the sweet, funny, charming cousin I grew up with.

I couldn't see him as the caring guy who used to tuck me in every night because I didn't have anyone else that could, or would. Or the protective guy who used to tell anyone off that tried to hurt me or make fun of me or take advantage of me. Or the understanding guy who wouldn't turn me away when it was thundering outside and everything inside my childhood dreams was out to get me—instead, he let me crawl into his bed until I felt safe again, no matter how late it got or how early he had to be at work the next day. The guy who never required a thank you, or even asked for appreciation for always giving me someone I could lean on, no matter what the situation.

"Sean," I whispered. "Please, let me save you. Please. I love you."

His eyes were closed again. And as the men led me away, down further into the tunnels, deep under the ground beneath Ghazni, he stood there. For the first time, Sean didn't come to my rescue.

"I love you too," he said, almost too quietly for me to hear, to believe he'd even said it.

OUT OF THE FRYING PAN

I BANGED MY HEAD against the wall of my cell in the underground tunnels of D79's Headquarters in Ghazni, too tired and drained and defeated to care about the pain it caused me. I slid my feet out from under me, stretching my legs across the cold, concrete floor of the cell to release the cramp that had been building for the past hour or so.

I knew it was only a matter of time before someone important heard about my capture here. And when that happened, he'd know.

The General.

I closed my eyes, allowing the pain from Sean's betrayal to sting me so badly I wanted to cry out. It was all I could do to stay quiet, calm, submissive. What choice did I have at this point?

A door creaked loudly, the deadbolt's resistance proving strong, even for a key. I heard a slot slide open, closed, and then the metal door to the cell room swung open as it granted the outsider access.

My breath picked up, my chest rising and falling faster. My lips started to quiver, but I clenched my fists in defiance.

"That's the spirit."

I sighed, my fear declining just a bit—which, three weeks ago, would've seemed immeasurably absurd.

"You got far. I'm impressed." I opened my eyes and glared at him, his sharp face smug, his blond hair disheveled and his outfit irritatingly similar to before. "For a woman."

Michael Moiré knew how to bring my blood to a boil.

"You followed me?" I challenged, lifting myself to my feet for the first time since the soldiers had thrown me in here.

"I thought I'd give you a head start." Michael lifted his left hand into the air, a ring of keys jingling in his grip. "You got farther than I expected. Pretending to be his wife. Clever."

"How did you know that?"

Again, he shrugged.

I eyed the keys in his hand. "Are you going to let me out?"

"That depends." Michael's eyes narrowed. "Are you going to come willingly and *not* try to defy me again?"

I hesitated. If I stayed here, captive in Ghazni, chances were probably good that the General would either kill me, or use me to kill Beau and *then* kill me. If I went with Michael…

"Trust me," he said quietly, like he knew just

what I was thinking. "You'd rather die by my hand than his. The General is merciless."

I stepped forward, inches away from the bars, which were inches away from him.

"And you're not?"

He stared into my eyes, the hint of a smirk in his. He didn't reply. I heard the locks on the gate click and then the bars slid aside.

"Try to keep up."

Michael pocketed the keys and then walked to the door, his eyes forward. He didn't even scan the corridors before he stepped out into them, didn't hesitate for a second.

"Michael."

"Be quiet."

"If I go with you...will you answer me one question?"

He glanced over his shoulder, eyebrows raised. "By saving you, I somehow owe you something?"

"Is he in danger?" I stared into his dark gaze with uncertainty. "If I escape, will Sean face the consequences?"

Michael studied me in return, his expression unyielding. Finally, he looked away.

"No." In a low voice, he added, "But if you don't leave, he will—and he won't be the only one."

He didn't give me any further explanation. I didn't ask for one.

I walked forward, brushing some of the dirt off my arms, still aware of the ripped state my clothes were in. Michael didn't seem to notice. He reached his hand out to me, his eyes watching for soldiers now that I had stepped out with him.

I hesitated. Michael rolled his eyes and grabbed my left wrist, his touch making the rifts in my skin burn—but I bit my tongue and followed after him, unwilling to let him know the pain I felt because of him or to stay here another second longer.

After walking for about three minutes down a long, shadowed corridor, we stopped in front of a big metal door, lined all the way down with a thick, heavy dead-bolt like none other I'd ever seen.

"What kind of lock is that?"

"Quiet."

Michael pulled a thin little chip out of his pocket and slipped it against the wall in three presumably random places. I frowned, confused. Evidently there was an invisible scanner that sensed it for, within seconds, the metal door clicked, the locks—each and every one, one at a time—slid down, over, and then down again. A small square slid out, directly where the last scanner had been. Michael set his hand on top of it, paused, then lowered his mouth close to it and breathed out. Something beeped. The metal door swung open.

"X1-2200," he said under his breath to me. "Division security advancement. Ask Wesley about it sometime. It was his idea. Let's go."

Michael jerked me forward, the heel of my boot almost tripping over the concrete path that led out of the hall. He glanced over his shoulder once and then closed the door. The locks slid back in place, beeping once, twice, a click, and then silence.

This was completely different from where I had

entered at. We came to what looked like an abandoned shack. Michael jerked me forward, his grip harsh as we walked up a dusty old staircase and through a small, tiled walkway. He slipped his card through another seemingly-invisible scanner and pushed his way through another metal door. This one, however, wasn't as complicated as the last and we were through in a matter of seconds.

As soon as we passed, we came to a long, dark alleyway. The dim lights a distance away let me know that we were back where I'd started, above ground, in Ghazni.

Though this area was different. Despite the late hour, the streets were lined with people—most with head coverings or bandanas, dirty and garbed in simple, ripped clothing. A few caught my eye, but the majority of them carried on with their business, walking with their eyes downcast, an almost dejected air about them. The place was bleak and musty everywhere my eyes settled.

This was the poorer side of Ghazni. What better place for a secret underground security exit?

"Stay close and be quiet," Michael snapped, yanking my arm when I stopped to discern where we were.

I glared at him, but he didn't care. He pulled me down the alley, steering clear of the poor, until we reached the main road—which wasn't much finer than the alley. Unpaved and rugged, we crossed the main road and headed down another alley.

This one, at least, was familiar.

I froze, causing Michael's hand to jerk me

forward from the abruptness of the halt. But my legs completely stopped moving, so this time, he was forced to either drop me or stop.

"What?" he demanded, his eyes fierce.

I cleared my throat and said, "Can't we take a car, or...? Do we have to go through...here?"

He saw the fear on my face, heard it in my tone, and frowned. He pursed his lips and, for a second, let his eyes drift down my body to see the dirt that covered me for the first time.

They narrowed. "You were jumped."

"Not exactly, but..." I shivered. "I was attacked by some men. Soldiers."

If the information affected him, he didn't show it. In a flat tone he asked me, "How many?"

"Three."

"How did you get out alive?"

"Another soldier with a gun. Kyle Dellis. Do you know him?"

Michael didn't answer. He looked me over one last time and then nodded towards the road that was just visible in the distance. "This is the quickest way to my apartment from Headquarters, but not the other way around. You took an unnecessary detour down the most dangerous part of this city. It's a miracle you're even alive."

I opened my mouth to speak, then closed it slowly, stung. Had the woman I'd met, Rya, really led me astray? Had she known?

Did it even matter?

Still, I glanced around fearfully. Michael rolled his eyes.

I jumped as a gunshot went off. Michael slung the cartridge of his gun chamber back, reloading it. Several of the beggars on the street raced off in a terrified frenzy. He lifted his eyes to mine again, and in them was a solid confidence that dared me to challenge his ability to make it through. I tried to convince myself that I wasn't afraid of the darkness, the alley or the gun in his hand, and then I let him lead me forward again.

Within five minutes, we reached a smaller alley that was covered in shattered glass. I walked precariously, but Michael tromped straight through with assurance and, just by his attitude, I knew we'd arrived. Tucking the gun back into his jacket, he stood in front of the door for a second too long.

He pushed the door open, his hand still gripping my right arm and my body very conscious of it and all that had happened between us in the past few days. I followed close behind him as he led me through the doorway, unwilling to admit how glad I was to be back inside, in this place, with these four walls and Michael himself.

With all of the anger, pain and adrenaline, there had also grown a twisted sense of security.

However, as we walked through the door, there was an aura about him, something that felt different than before. His body was very tense and alert. I wasn't sure when the mood had changed, but there was definitely something off about the way Michael was acting when we entered the building. A cool, calculated acceptance over trouble that was about to go down.

I looked up and immediately understood. My body stiffened, my jaw dropped, my eyes widened and my heart froze solid—because, after everything I'd been through this night, he was the last I had been expecting.

"Beau," I whispered.

BROTHER

BEAU STOOD IN THE center of the room, his arms folded tightly across his chest. He wore dark camouflage and a black t-shirt that was abnormally loose against his chest—had he lost weight? He looked thinner, less threatening and more broken-down than I remembered. His brown hair seemed darker somehow and there were bags under his eyes—which were sharp, piercing and fixed solely on Michael.

I barely felt Michael's hand slide off my arm as I bolted towards Beau. Beau didn't so much as shift his eyes, but he opened his arms enough to catch and hold me tightly when I crashed into him.

I threw my arms around his neck and pressed myself as close as possible. "What are you doing here?" I whispered, tears in my eyes. It had been just short of three weeks, yet I felt like it had been years. "Are you okay? How did you get here? Beau?"

I lowered myself back down and moved back enough to study his expression. Something was wrong. I could tell just by the feel of his hands around me and the stiffness of his body. I started to pull away, but he tightened his left arm around my waist and kept me wedged in his hold in a way that was blatantly possessive.

The door slammed shut and then I remembered. I remembered where we were and why Beau was here. The whole situation crashed over me like a tornado and I knew, without a doubt, that things were about to spiral out of control like one.

Michael folded his arms across his chest as he leaned back against the doorframe. Like Beau, his eyes were locked onto his brother's without blinking. His body language was calm and relaxed, yet there was that chilly calculation in the way he conducted himself. I felt the air get tenser, though I didn't think it was possible at this point.

"*Ahlan, akhi al sagheer.*"

"*Ahlan.*"

"I'm impressed." Michael's eyes burned bright with amusement. "Four years. I'd expect at least a slight mispronunciation."

"Why'd you do it?" Beau's voice held the same dark, angry tone as the last time they'd spoken, over the communicators.

"You're going to have to be a little more specific."

"Why did you kill my uncle?"

"*Our* uncle." Michael shrugged. "What makes you think that was me?"

"I know you're the one appointed to kill me."

"Actually," Michael said, "that honor no longer

belongs to me."

His eyes flashed to me. I narrowed mine. The fact that I even knew whom he was referring to was painful; the image of Sean's new attitude was just salt in the wound. Beau didn't notice the eye contact between us, for he was far too enraged. His grip on my arm became tighter—whether he meant it to or not.

"What makes you think I believe a damn thing that comes out of your mouth?"

"What makes you think I give a shit what you believe?" Michael replied coolly. I could see the barrel of his pistol positioned just inside his jacket, very accessible. It would take him milliseconds to have it out and ready to fire.

"Stop it," I said quietly.

Michael didn't shift his eyes from Beau, but he winked for me.

"Beau," I whispered. "Let's leave, now. Please."

"I'm not finished yet." There was a heavy threat to his tone and, though he aimed the explanation at me, he glared at his brother.

Regardless, Michael's stance, attitude and tone did not change. If anything, he became more relaxed, more amused. The edge of his mouth pulled up into an unnerving smile.

"Beau, he's dangerous." I squeezed his right arm and tugged on him. For the first time, Beau turned his head towards me. Our eyes met and in his was a look I'd never seen before. It was anger that surpassed loathing, a deep-seated hatred that was sincerely boundless. It was an undying thirst for revenge.

Revenge that he would die for.

"Please," I begged.

Out of the corner of my eye, I caught the movement. A small shift, a single flash. A breath later, Beau whipped out his gun so fast that I gasped. His fingers dug into my skin but I was too terrified and anxious to notice. My eyes shifted to the door but, surprisingly, Michael hadn't moved. His eyes glittered with amusement.

"Paranoid much?"

My eyes dropped to the floor and I saw that it was a piece of split dry wall that had fallen off the wall behind him.

Michael's eyebrow was raised derisively. "For the record, if I wanted to kill you, you would already be on the floor."

Without lowering the gun, Beau grabbed me with his other hand and pushed me behind his back. "Don't move."

"Beau—"

"Leah."

There was no argument in his tone. I pursed my lips and didn't fight him. Beau walked forward until he was just close enough to rest the barrel of his Colt against Michael's forehead.

Michael did not resist it.

"Taking her from me was just about *the stupidest* move you could've made," Beau said. "Second to shooting at Wes in California and killing Raymond in Kandahar, *of course*."

"Perhaps she is not yours to be taken from and I told you already, *yakhara*, that I did not kill my uncle."

Michael's tone, despite the gun to his head and the murder in Beau's eyes, was calm. And I realized that all the arrogance he'd displayed over the past three weeks, all of the control, wasn't a façade at all. He was just that confident.

Beau's eyes narrowed into slits. Instead of addressing the remark, he held out his other hand and said, "Give me the knife."

Michael smiled. "Maybe you did learn something from me after all." He lifted his left hand and in it was a switchblade I hadn't seen him take or conceal, but recognized. He raised the knife level to Beau's outstretched hand but let it fall to the floor.

The second it hit, Beau slid his hand into his belt and brought out a knife similar to the one Michael had just surrendered. Except this one was larger, deadlier, jagged and covered dark red with—

Dried blood.

I cupped a hand over my mouth. *Luke.*

"You arrogant sonofabitch." Beau slashed the blade across Michael's chest so fast I didn't see it happen until I saw the blood in its path. He cut a slice over six inches long in a diagonal over his chest, then pointed the blade at Michael's face. "He stood no chance against you and you *knew* that."

Michael's smile faded into a frown, but he showed no sign of pain or surprise at the wound. "Luke should have known better than to challenge me. As should you."

"You're in no position to threaten me."

"That's a matter of perspective."

Beau had the knife up again and this time he

drew a similar slash across Michael's chest on the opposite side, digging in deeper. There was now a bloody, six-inch X right over his heart.

"There," Beau smirked—as if he were *enjoying* this. "To fill all that empty space."

Michael's hands were clenched into fists. I could tell he was weakened this time just by the brittleness in his stance. His shirt was shredded into two separate pieces that flapped open, exposing the wound and the streams of blood that covered his torso.

And yet, he'd let it happen, without so much as a flinch.

You never hesitate. Ever. Why now?

"Why are you still here?" Michael's tone was flat. He nodded towards me. "You have what you came for."

"Not yet."

Michael's mouth twitched, the ghost of a smile on his lips. "You think you can kill me, Beau?"

"Absolutely." Beau lowered his knife but didn't re-sheath it. "We've fought before. You've never beaten me."

"I've never tried."

Instantaneously, Beau swung his fist out and punched his brother across the mouth. Michael stumbled back, his hand instinctively reaching up to hold his face.

"Bullshit," Beau replied.

Michael spit a glob of blood right onto the floor, his lip split and bleeding in two places, though it didn't seem to bother him much. He shook his head as if unimpressed.

"Nineteen years," Michael said quietly, "yet here you stand just as foolish as ever."

"Twenty," Beau corrected him. "And you're one to talk, aren't you? Giving yourself to people who'd turn on you the second The General commanded it? Killing people who deserve to die ten-times less than you do?"

"But you can sympathize with that, can't you?" Michael retorted. "You may project those angel-white-wings to appease her and your own conscience but you and I both know how you really feel, Beau."

"Don't profess to know me, Michael. You gave up that right a long time ago."

"That doesn't make it any less true. I may deserve to die, but you, Beau Moiré, are no saint either."

"I'm not the one on the bad side, now am I?"

"*Khara*," Michael spat in Arabic, shaking his head. "Why is it always about *sides* to you? Don't you get it? There is no such thing as *sides*. And you're a hell of a lot stupider than I thought you were if you still believe that there are two sides to this game."

"This isn't a game anymore, Mike! It's a fucking war!"

"Since when?" Michael challenged, voice rising. "Since when did my irresponsible little brother decide to grow up and be a man?"

"When you and your *allies* started murdering *everyone* I care for!"

Michael laughed bitterly, still shaking his head. "If I had a dime for every time you were dead wrong I'd be a godforsaken millionaire."

Beau clenched his fists, his eyes narrowing further.

"Stop!" I said quickly, but it was too late.

Beau threw his knife straight at his brother, its blade spinning fiercely through the air. Michael dodged it easily. Beau hadn't used it as an attack, though, but as a diversion, for as Michael focused on the knife, Beau charged at him and sent his fist, with a terrifyingly strong speed, into Michael's stomach.

Michael hit the wall and then the floor hard, his head smacking the concrete first from the sheer ferocity of the blow. I watched his gun topple out of his jacket, landing just out of his reach. Though he didn't even try to go for it.

I cringed as Beau kicked Michael in the side, making his entire body shudder. He closed his eyes, wincing from the pain, his bloody lips parted the barest width and his chest exposing more blood.

"Get up!" Beau shouted, eyes on fire.

When Michael didn't comply, Beau kicked him again, this time harder. Gritting his teeth, Beau reached down and grabbed Michael by the split remains of his shirt, tearing it further. It took effort, because Michael did none of the work, but Beau managed to lift his older brother to his feet. As soon as he was up, Beau shoved him back against the wall. Michael smacked the wall hard, his eyes closing to hide the pain I saw in them as he finally hit his knees.

I didn't understand. Michael was stronger than this. I knew it, had seen it. Why, then, wasn't he fighting back?

Beau stood in front of him, his own chest

pulsing quickly out of rage. I had never seen him look so intimidating, so *angry*, before.

Michael struggled to his feet as Beau drew his Colt and, sliding the cartridge into place, cocked it and aimed it against his brother's chest. His finger touched the trigger, poised and ready to shoot.

And he would have done it.

"STOP!"

Beau paused at the sound of my voice—loud and desperate. But he recovered after a second and reached again for the trigger of his gun, this time with even more certainty.

My heart was pounding, my blood soaring through my veins so fast I felt lightheaded. And, as quick as I could run, I stepped in-between the two— uncontrollable Beau, immobilized Michael—in front of the aim of the gun. It happened so quickly, Beau didn't have time to shift it. From where it had been aimed at Michael's chest, it rested firmly against my forehead.

Our eyes met. In his, I saw shock, anger, but most of all, betrayal. In mine, there was only determination.

"Move," Beau said.

"No," I replied.

"Leah." Beau narrowed his eyes, his fists shaking. In a low, stern voice, he ordered me, *"Move."*

"Shoot me."

Beau slammed his fist against the wall so hard it shook me, shook the wall, shook the whole room, in fact. He glared at the ceiling for a long moment. Then, finally, he turned away and tucked the barrel of the gun into his waistband.

"She just saved your life." His tone was ice. He walked forward and retrieved the knife that he'd thrown as a distraction, then spun in our direction without looking at either of us. "Don't think it'll happen again."

Beau tossed the knife at Michael, who caught it by the hilt. I don't know how he did it, it didn't matter. He probably could've caught it by the very blade without spilling a drop more of blood. That was the point, wasn't it?

Michael's lip was still bleeding profusely and there was an ocean of blood on his bare chest from where Beau had sliced a deep X. But despite his injuries, despite the fact that he'd just lost to his younger brother, Michael never looked stronger.

He was, again, shaking his head. Disappointed. Why?

Beau didn't look at me, but he turned his back and headed for the door. He paused there, obviously waiting for me to follow. I turned, still against Michael's chest—his blood on my arms—and met his eyes. He met mine too and there it was again. Strength.

I gave him a pleading, questioning look. It was quite clear what I was asking, but he averted his eyes and never gave me an answer.

I lowered my head and walked, with Beau, away.

It was the longest, most unnerving drive of my life.

Beau sat a few feet to my left, his hands gripped tightly to the steering wheel of the old, rusted car he'd apparently commandeered and driven through the dunes all the way to Ghazni. I stared out the window into darkness, watching the silhouette of mounds of sand and broken buildings pass by—though I hardly saw any of it.

I'd already tried talking to him three times, all of which he'd thoroughly ignored. Ever since, I'd been as quiet as a mouse; only glancing at him when I was positive he wasn't looking.

It took us roughly three hours to arrive in, what I assumed, was Zaranj. The clock on the dashboard was faded, but functional.

5:17am.

Beau pulled the car off the road and drove through barren land for over two minutes. The old car shook, rattled and clanked the entire ride, only serving to unhinge my nerves further.

Up ahead, I caught the sight of a small, square building; a shack, perhaps—there were plenty of them in Afghanistan. It was illuminated by a soft yellow glow, candlelight. The single door and all three of the windows I saw were sealed shut.

Beau killed the engine. We sat there for a long time, the headlights no longer giving me anything to see by. I glanced beside me, saw the faint outline of his handsome face against the dark and exhaled. He wasn't watching me. He was staring straight ahead, past the shack, beyond anything I could have seen.

Slowly, he shook his head. I reached my hand out to touch his wrist, gently, trying to make at least some sort of amends. He pulled it away just before our hands could touch.

"Figure out whose side you're on."

With his left hand, he jerked his door open and stepped out, all in one fluid motion. He didn't slam the door but I wouldn't have heard it anyway. I closed my eyes for a long moment, stung.

But I did not cry.

NEW INTELLIGENCE

FBI Headquarters
Washington, D.C.

"MR. LAWTON?" JONATHON LANSFORD asked, for what had to have been the six-thousand, seven-hundred and fifty-fifth time in the past eight minutes. He yawned. "What are we doing again?"

Special Agent Thomas Lawton made a *shushing* motion with his hand because he wasn't sure he could respond like a civil person otherwise. After yet another long stretch of inactivity, he dared to take his eyes off the apartment complex that stood diagonally across the street for one split-second to give the young trainee seated beside him a drastically inquisitive look.

"Right, sorry, Mr. Lawton, it's just that—"

"Thomas."

John Lansford's expression was stunned for quite a long moment. "Sir?"

"Call me Thomas, John," Lawton said as he returned his eyes back to the residency. In doing so, he missed the flash of excitement and awe that crossed the young man's face just then, sparing himself the guilt he'd been harboring at not coming clean—on several fronts.

Thomas Lawton was not an idiot. The FBI were gearing up to pull the rug out from underneath him that he knew had been placed there by Derek Vince, his boss and—however unwittingly—his friend. He knew that the case of the missing fugitives was one that had slid off the desk of almost every elected official in the executive branch. How it had come to land on Vince, and then his, desk was what the world yearned to know and what Lawton knew he would never quite understand. How, then, could John?

Truthfully, the last words of the man who'd died not seven days prior still rang in Lawton's ears along with everything else. Words he'd never shared with John or anyone. Words he couldn't even bring himself to speak, but that swirled around in his head like a constant stream of a separate, living consciousness.

"The time's gonna come when all of the pieces fall together, and unfortunately, you're it, Lawton, Vince had told him, just before the pair had departed from the J. Edgar Hoover building precisely one week ago. *"You're the one who's gonna see the shitstorm that this country's been waiting for, and God willing I won't be around to see that. It's not a coincidence that this case began with you, Thomas. But I'm afraid it has deeper implications than you or I could have ever foreseen. Trust no one but yourself, your experience and..."*

Lawton studied the apartment building in the distance through the foggy glass window beside him, slightly tapping his finger against the part of his cell phone that displayed the time: 5:57 a.m.

The street lights were on, shedding artificial light every few feet where the early-morning darkness was concentrated. A full cup of coffee sat in the divider between Thomas Lawton and John Lansford, untouched and growing colder by the hour.

Lansford yawned again.

Retracting his anxiety, frustration and focus for the first time since the two had set out at 5 a.m., Lawton felt a growing sense of respect for the man who'd practically dropped everything to accompany him on quest after quest since this case began. Even when, like right now, Lansford had no idea what the subsequent quest would bring.

Before Lawton could say anything too sappy, the streetlight on the closest corner to where their car was parked flickered once and then died. The flash was followed by the dying light of the next corner, the next and then the next until, almost instantaneously, it was light enough that the last lamp gave way to the morning.

Not long after, a door opened above one of the ground-level suites. Just as Lawton had guessed, the woman who'd privately visited him in his office at the FBI Headquarters stepped out into the misting morning. Dressed in a black pantsuit that was much more professional this time, the woman, Savanna, got into the driver's seat of a 2011 Ford Focus and drove off down the street at a quicker-than-average-speed.

Lansford perked up at the development, but he held his curiosity, surprisingly, when Lawton put the car into drive and followed the woman down several streets, across blocks until, finally, she pulled into the lot of the Office of Public Affairs in Washington, D.C.

Fuck, Lawton thought to himself.

"Fuck, fuck, *fuck!*" he said aloud, because a silent curse was far from sufficient as he pulled the vehicle to a stop in front of the building that belonged to none other than the Central Intelligence Agency. Savanna walked up to the entrance, flashed an identification badge and strutted through the door like the Conniving Ignorant Asshole that Lawton suddenly felt like.

Jonathon Lansford looked more lost than ever, but again, and as he'd learned since the very first day working with the peculiar Special Agent, he asked no questions, only shared acquiescently in Lawton's frantic obscenities.

"Fuck," Lansford said, nodding like a bobble-head.

Lawton couldn't take it anymore.

"Come on, John," he said as he put the car in reverse and thought of all the mistakes, all the false intelligence, all the lies and all of the death that lay in the rear view. More importantly, however, of all that lay ahead.

Trust no one but yourself, your experience and Jonathon Lansford.

"Once again, we have a lot to discuss."

BEAUTIFUL CONTRADICTION

"YOU'RE ALIVE," I WHISPERED.

Luke smiled wryly and leaned his head back against the wall. "How many times are you going to say that?"

"Until I believe it."

He sighed. "Come here."

I lifted myself off the floor and stood beside the cot Luke was lying on. I studied the stark-white bandage that covered the majority of his bare torso and hesitated. "Are you sure…?"

"That I won't shatter into pieces if you look at me too hard? Yes," he said flatly, "I'm sure."

"I don't want to hurt you."

"Or my feelings—which you *will* be hurting if you don't get your pretty little self over here and hug me."

I sighed and crawled up onto the unsteady cot with him. Luke shifted over to make room for me, his face a twisted grimace. I moved as cautiously as I could and lay as far on the edge as possible, but he reached a hand around my waist and pulled me against him so that we were lying on our backs next to each other with our shoulders touching the slightest bit.

"Ah!"

"Sorry, sorry!"

Luke chuckled. "I'm joking, Leah. Seriously. Relax."

I restrained myself from punching him in the shoulder and leaned my head against it instead. "I can't believe you're alive," I said again, my eyes beginning to tear up.

He sighed again, but didn't make a smart comment.

"When he…and you…I thought…" I closed my eyes. "There was *so much blood*."

Luke studied the ceiling for a while. "I'm sorry you had to see that. If I would have known it was him…"

"Can I ask you something?" Luke nodded. "Have Beau and his brother ever…fought? Like, physically? For real?"

Luke hesitated before he said, "I didn't know either of them until they joined the organization—and even then, I didn't see them much. They were my brother's friends, not mine. Beau was always cool with me, but Michael…I didn't like him. So I did everything in my power to annoy him, piss him off." He laughed. "Anyway, when I saw them together, I always thought there was something strong between the two of them. Michael seemed *so* protective over his little brother, and Beau, he practically worshipped

Michael, the *a'askari*—the soldier—even though he likes to claim he hated him. They were competitive, always, but they were close. So no, I never saw them fight."

"He trained you, didn't he? With a gun." I thought of the night Wes had told me about his younger brother, Luke. All he'd said was "he learned from the best," which hadn't made sense, until now.

Luke nodded once without looking at me. "Michael taught me how to hold a gun, how to aim and how to pull the trigger."

"Do you know what happened?" I asked, my voice quieter than a whisper, though Beau and the others were outside, far from hearing. "What changed? How did Michael betray them?"

Luke shrugged. "No one really knows. At least, I've never heard Beau or Wes talk about it. They were the closest to him, so if anyone knows, it's one of them. Wes, probably."

"Wes?" I frowned. "I thought Beau was the closest to his brother before…"

"No," Luke said firmly. "Beau and Mike were close, but like I said, they were competitive and I think the animosity between them had to do with their parents' deaths. I don't know—they're a weird dynamic. No, my brother and Michael were best friends. Closer, even, than Wes was to Beau."

"That doesn't make sense," I said. "Michael called Wes out the night he captured me, and he tried to shoot him in California. Why would he do that?"

"Because. There's something you keep failing to see." Luke's body was tense. Obviously he didn't

183

approve of this topic. "Michael has changed, Leah."

"What do you mean?"

"He was always violent. I don't know why, but it was almost as if he couldn't control himself when it came to fighting. He was good at it, but it was like it just...took him over." He paused. "But when he wasn't fighting, he was relatively normal. He cared, sort of, and had a heart—at least for the people he loved. Ray, Beau, Wes, Rya—"

I froze. "Who?"

Luke turned his head, studying my expression. Then he pursed his lips and murmured, "Nevermind."

I held my tongue, though I did not forget about it. Could he have meant the woman I'd met on my way into Ghazni? For some reason, my mind went back to that evening on the beach in May, back before reality had set in and complicated our lives, Beau and I. Before the truth, or at least the twisted parts. Before the pain, the heartache and the love.

"Have you ever been in love?"

"Once. But it was a long time ago, and it wasn't real."

Luke continued without noticing my reverie, "I don't know what changed him—Michael, that is—but once it did, he stopped caring. He betrayed his friends, killed anyone and everyone in his way. After we left the organization and went back to America, Wes kept tabs on them. Michael lay low for a few months, but then he went right back at it. The missions, the fighting, the killing. And somehow, Wes could spot a job Mike was on—just by how bloody the casualties were. Not just the targets, *the civilians*. He slaughtered them all. Mercilessly."

"Why?" I whispered.

"Because," Luke said coldly, "he's a monster."

I closed my eyes. Why did I feel like contradicting him? Defending Michael, just like I had back in Ghazni when he'd been at gunpoint. Would the world honestly be better off without Michael Moiré? Was he really as evil as Luke, as Beau, as everyone, even himself…made him out to be?

If he was so terrible, so heartless, so bloodthirsty, why had he kept me alive when he didn't need me? Why teach me to fight when I was supposedly his enemy? Why rescue me after Sean didn't, in Ghazni?

Why let Beau beat him while he lay there, taking the pain, from someone he supposedly did not care about anymore?

It just didn't make sense.

"You don't even consider it a little bit strange that he allegedly changed overnight, for no reason?" I asked. "That Michael respected and loved his brother and your brother and then, all of a sudden, out of nowhere, he betrayed them?"

Luke sat up at once, forcing me to sit up as well. I began to protest and croon over his injury, but his expression silenced me. His eyes were dark, his mouth a hard line. "Don't," he said.

"What?"

"Don't defend him. He doesn't deserve it."

I bit my lip. "Luke, you don't understand. I saw—"

"You saw exactly what he wanted you to see. Don't you get it? That's what he does, Leah. Michael p*lays* people. He'll say what he needs to, be all charming and smooth, and then he turns around and stabs you when you least expect it, where it hurts the most. He kills people and he hurts *everyone*. Trust me, Leah. If you'd have seen some of the things he's done, you wouldn't be so quick to fall for him."

My jaw dropped. "I am *not* falling for him!"

"Good." Luke gave me a sharp look and then moved to lie back down. "Because he's evil. One-hundred-percent. I do not approve."

"Don't worry," I said, smiling faintly. "He's the one who shot me. And stabbed you. I haven't forgotten that."

Luke rested back down and I set my head back onto the pillow. For some reason, I felt guilty. In the back of my mind, I still believed that Michael wasn't who he wanted everyone to think he was. He was hiding something.

And now so was I. Because, even for just one moment, I had seen something in him that disproved everything everyone told me I was supposed to feel.

"CAN YOU BELIEVE HER?"

"Honestly?" Justin hesitated. "Kind of."

Beau glared at his older cousin threateningly. "How can you even say that?"

"Beau," Matt warned, his hazel eyes concerned as he watched Beau pace the sand; Justin, seated beside him, held a similar look; Wes, also part of their group outside of the shack, sat expressionless. "I realize the anger and resentment you feel over the situation, but we are not against you."

Beau opened his mouth to retort but he bit his tongue and stared off in the distance. Finally, he sighed.

"The only reason I say that," Justin said calmly, "is because...well, you know Mike. He can be very persuasive when it suits him. Not to mention he's your brother. Basically your twin."

"But the evil one," Matt interjected, smiling at Beau.

Beau rolled his eyes. "Dually noted. That does not, however, give her the right to do what she did."

"Which is?"

"Trust him."

The group fell silent.

"Well," said Matt, "on the bright side, you rescued her—however unwillingly. She's alive, and you're alive; not to mention we're all prepared for the plan to proceed tomorrow night."

"My brother," Justin sighed. "Forever the optimist."

"God knows you *need* someone like me," Matt replied, defensive. "With all this pessimistic brooding, you're lucky I'm here to balance you all out. Honestly, what would you *do* without me? Besides murder Beau in his sleep, of course, and wander around the desert with your noses in the sand, that is."

Justin and Matt laughed, even Wes cracked a smile. Beau shook his head, fighting a smile of his own. They could always do that—make him forget his worries, no matter how drastic, or simple.

"So," he asked, as the mood inevitably grew solemn again. "When do we go?"

"Tomorrow night," Wes reiterated. "We depart at ten, arrive at Zaranj's base by car around eleven, enter and wire the bomb in their intelligence unit by eleven thirty after we've retrieved what we can of their weapon supply and be ready to retreat before midnight."

"That's when the MP run their patrol," Justin added. "If we time this right and not make much of a commotion, we should be able to flee just after the fire ignites, before anyone is prepared to stop us."

"The detonation will, obviously, alert them of our arrival," Beau mentioned.

Wes shook his head. "It will alert them that someone has attacked, however, they will not know who or with what or how. We should have approximately five minutes after detonation, during which they will be in a chaotic frenzy trying to discover the source of the attack. Our escape route is quick and straightforward, and we'll have already displaced the weapons. We'll be miles away before that time is up."

"How will we get to the weapons?"

"I know where they are," Justin said. "I worked with a guy who was part of the artillery unit. I can get us inside, but we'll have a very small window."

"They'll know it was us," Beau said softly. "They

always do."

"All it takes is one time when they don't," said Wes, drawing an acquiescent nod from Beau, which he returned.

"We won't be able to carry all that weaponry," Justin noted.

"We'll have to stash it somewhere nearby," Wes agreed. "Hidden, but accessible to us once the smoke from this attack clears."

"I have a feeling it won't," Matt said quietly, "for a while."

Again, they fell silent. A fire crackled at the center of their half-circle, the coals underneath what little brush Justin could locate were red-hot and blazing. The core of the tiny inferno was reflected in each of their eyes—rings of black smoke, orange-yellow flames and crimson red coals.

"We're really going to do this," Beau said softly, his eyes alight with the spark of the fire he stared into. None of the others commented. What was there to say?

They sat in an uncomfortable silence for nearly an hour. Finally, Matt stood up, bade them all good night and went inside. Justin leaned back against the wall of the shack, his eyes drifting to a close and his head jerking forward a few amusing times before Beau encouraged him to retire also.

Beau sat on one side of the fire, Wes on the other.

"Do you think it'll work?"

Wes didn't take his eyes off the sky. "It has the potential to work. Yes."

"But it also has the potential to fail."

"Failure is always a part of the equation, Beau."

"Do you remember what I said the day you first proposed it?" Beau asked absently as he crossed his hands behind his head and leaned it back against the sand like Wes had done.

"'We're hypocrites. We discuss the murder of hundreds of soldiers as if we were planning a trip to the grocery store. We say the preservation of one innocent life doesn't measure up to the death of three guilty ones. What makes us any better than them?'" Wes sighed. "I remember it every day."

Beau nodded. He still felt unsettled about what they were planning to do. At the same time, he knew it was what had to be done. *So why,* he questioned, *do I feel this way?*

"I'm not the man I used to be," Beau said quietly, answering his own question out loud. "I've changed."

"Love does that, Beau. It changes us."

"Wes." Beau lifted his eyes and met his friend's with a sudden, sincere look. "Why did you stay? You knew she wanted to go home, and you knew what D79 was. Why? Why put her through that?"

Wes was quiet for a second. "Laci never came right out and asked me to leave…but I knew it was what she wanted. I don't know why I pretended not to see that, but that's what I did. Denial."

Wes snorted. "You ask me why I stayed with Division and didn't leave while I had the chance? Trust me, I ask myself that every second of every day and I will for the rest of my life. Looking back, I know that my decision to stay was selfish. But, at the time, I thought I was doing what was right, fighting for a necessary cause, to preserve my county. To hell that all went," he remarked, shaking his head.

"Unfortunately, Beau...you get a different perspective when it's all said and done. The circumstances you face, the choices you make, the love you lose...it changes you. Suddenly, you don't see things the way you once did when you were optimistic. When you had hope."

It was quiet for a while. Finally, Wes stood up and walked to the door of the shack, silent, where all the others were sleeping.

The night, as well, was dead silent.

"Wesley."

Wes paused at the door; a hint of reluctance.

"Thank you. For your wisdom, your guidance, your trust. I know you think me irrational and reckless—you've always told me so, even without directly saying it. I want you to know that you have my trust and my respect. If it weren't for you, I would have died many times over and I know that. For standing with me, in possibly the worst of times, I just want to say thank you."

Wes didn't turn back around, didn't face him. By the low set of his friend's shoulders, Beau could sense an unexplained contriteness. For what, however, he had no idea.

"Don't thank me," Wes responded finally, his voice quiet. "When all of this is over...just remember that I was always your friend."

Beau frowned as Wes walked away without the

barest hint of an explanation.

Beau stood up and walked, not towards the shack, but away from it. He had little light to see by, not that he cared. The moon was bright through the clouds; the stars were hidden by them.

Beau exhaled, frustrated. "Ray," he whispered as he stuck his hands into his pockets, standing in a particularly thick pile of sand. "Why did you leave? I swear I need you now more than ever."

I'm always with you, that little voice whispered in the back of his mind, the one he'd always ignored. *You'll find me, if you would only stop worrying, stop arguing and listen. While there is foolishness in words, there is wisdom in silence.*

"How do I keep the people I love from getting hurt?"

You ask the wrong questions. You've always looked at things the wrong way.

"How then?" he demanded, frustrated further and angered by the fact that he was denounced to talking to himself. *I must be insane.*

Perhaps just in-tune with yourself. Beau suddenly pictured his uncle Raymond, wise-eyed and smiling with paternal, loving condescension. The thought saddened him beyond compare.

You are a man, Beau. You cannot control anything other than your own path, and even then, only the way you perceive the world around you.

Beau tried to decipher the meaning of that. He knew the answers weren't really coming from Ray; they were just his conscience trying to reason with him, in the best way it knew how.

"Then how do I protect them?" Beau whispered.

Is it protecting your family that has your mind so troubled?

Beau lowered his head guiltily. Despite all of the severity of the situation, the consequences of the chaos he was about to cause, Beau knew where his heart was aching the most.

"I love her too much."

There is no such thing as too much or too little love. There is only love, and how we choose to respond to it.

"I don't think I'm responding very well."

Ah. You've never been very sure of yourself when it comes to love, and women.

"For trying to help me," Beau said coolly, "you sure seem to enjoy pointing out all my mistakes."

"Raymond" chuckled. *I'm not trying to help you, Beau. You need to help yourself. You see, wisdom isn't about being perfect or figuring out the best course of action to take at all times. Wisdom, as your friend Wesley has come to realize, is about making mistakes and learning from them. Building yourself up with the new knowledge you learn every day, not tearing yourself down with the failures and faults of your decisions. There will always be failure.*

You ask why you have changed so much, so quickly, recently? It is because you have finally done what I have always tried to get you to do, son. You're starting to forgive yourself. And that, Beau, is the first and hardest step towards finding the peace you crave.

Now all you need to do is...

"What?" Beau opened his eyes and glared at the sand, at the sky, at the moon and the absence of the stars. "What do I do now?"

Silence.

Angrily, Beau moved away. He knew that the answer wouldn't come that easily; mostly because everything the voice had been telling him was knowledge he'd already gained and understood.

It just seemed so simple when Raymond said it.

Fine, he thought. *Maybe I just need to work this out myself...phrase it right...maybe then I'll understand. Ray always said the answers were there...*

"If forgiveness is the first step, what is the second?"

Silence.

"Why does every step I take seem like I'm heading in the wrong direction?"

Silence.

"Damn it!" he shouted. "Why won't you answer me?"

Because I am you, and you don't know the answer.

"You knew the answer to that one."

That was a simple question.

Surprisingly, Beau found himself laughing at his own sheer absurdity. "I've finally gone insane. Haven't I?"

No. Yours is a rare case. You see...you were never sane to begin with.

"Maybe that's the problem," he said dryly.

Or part of the solution...

"You're not making any sense."

Beau didn't need the voice to remind him that it wasn't the one who was speaking on its own accord. He sighed.

"What about Leah?" he asked, solemnity

returning as quickly as it always did. "I feel like I don't know her anymore."

Maybe you don't.

"Or maybe…she's changed."

Ah. Now, I believe, you've begun to make sense.

Beau stared at his hands, conflicted. Leah used to be timid, fragile. She was passionate when she wanted to be, but there was a certain reserve to her. But now? Now she didn't even break eye-contact with him when he was angry with her. She didn't walk into a room as if she were the physically weakest, or even like she was afraid. Beau couldn't explain it well, but she'd grown…bold.

You're overreacting, he told himself immediately, dismissing the idea. Leah had been a captive; one enslaved by someone who probably degraded her every chance he could, made her feel as trapped and cornered as possible. The situation couldn't have had a positive effect on her. She couldn't have changed that much.

You did, that voice in the back of his head whispered.

"I'm losing her," Beau said absently, his words almost inaudible. "More and more every day."

Maybe…

"Yeah. I know," he said, turning in the direction of the shack. "Maybe it's not too late to do something about it."

I LOOKED UP AT the old, wooden ceiling, my eyes staring but not necessarily seeing. My mind, for the first time in days, was completely blank. I closed my eyes. It had to be early morning and everyone else was asleep. I lay on the hard, uncomfortable cot in one of the three secluded rooms, tired but unable to fall asleep.

So I was wide awake and alert when the door opened slowly and I heard the rough, grating sound of his army boots slide across the floor as he stepped into the room. I knew it was him just by the calm, unhurried pace that an ambusher couldn't have mimicked.

My heart started to beat faster—whether with resentment or with nervousness, I didn't know—but I stayed where I was and didn't turn, unwilling to let him tear my guard down so easily.

But he did it anyway.

Without a single word, without any indication of what he would do, without so much as a warning, Beau leaned down and kissed me. I suddenly realized that there was too much tension between us, so many things we needed to talk about. At the same time, I found that I didn't know what I would say, if given the chance. It all seemed too overwhelming for words that would only trap us further.

And already I was lost in the kiss. I lay my head back, the tension in my body starting to drain away as he rested both hands against the sides of the cot, locking me in place. It had been too long since we'd been like this, wrapped up in each other's arms. I slid my hands onto his chest and up around his shoulders where I wove my arms around his neck, pulling him closer to me, deepening the kiss.

I barely noticed as he pulled away, for my mind—still impossibly numb—was behind, entranced. My eyes fought me when I tried to open them.

He didn't seem to mind. He leaned down and kissed me once, lightly, but with the ghost of passion still lingering on his lips as they lingered over mine. He slid his hand down my arm and over the back of my hand and then, slowly, he withdrew.

"Come with me."

Without pausing to catch my breath, I sat up and moved off the cot. Beau took me by the hand and led me, quietly, out of the room and out of the shack. I didn't even think about the fact that I wore only a thin t-shirt and rolled up shorts, or even that Beau was fully dressed in jeans, a sweatshirt and boots. At least, not until we were far enough away that, when I looked back, the shack where the rest of our group was sleeping obliviously was nowhere in sight.

"Beau," I said abruptly. "We're not…leaving, are we?"

He turned towards me, his eyes distracted. "Hmm?"

"I know things are difficult and frightening, and I'm just as overwhelmed by all of this as you are, but we can't—"

I stopped as Beau pressed his lips against mine harder than before, almost hungrily; not only my words but my mind paused. He pulled away slowly and kept his forehead lowered against mine.

"You think I would abandon them so easily?" he asked after a moment, eyebrows raised.

I blushed. "I…"

"We'll be back before the sun comes up. Which, of course, you would've figured out if you'd have only trusted me."

"I do trust you." I took a step towards him, clasping the strings of his sweatshirt as I stared into his eyes. "I'm sorry."

The look that crossed his face let me know that he understood the deeper meaning in my words. He turned his head for a moment, then looked back at me, his eyes even more troubled than before. "Come on," he said, taking my hand again.

We walked for at least another mile or two; I stopped wondering whether Beau actually had a destination or if we were just walking.

A half-hour later, we reached another small, abandoned shack. This one wasn't as big as the other, and it was falling apart in many places. The wooden door that spanned the front was half off its hinges, but Beau didn't pause to inspect it. He walked with the grace of familiarity.

"We used to come here a lot when we were stationed in Zaranj," he explained, and pulled me through the doorway after only pausing for a moment. Even though I was a head shorter than him, I still had to duck to get through the entrance. Inside, it was much less furnished than the other shack, though there was something different about it. Something…odd.

I glanced at the walls and realized what it was.

"You did all of this?" I asked, my eyes wide as I took it all in. On just about every inch of the wood, there were carvings. Words. Fragments and phrases and drawings. All etched into the walls, the floor, the small pieces of wooden furniture that remained. All in clear and perfect English.

"Not exactly," he said, leaning back against the side of the wall next to the entrance, his arms crossed and his eyes on me. "When we first discovered this place, there were a few carvings in it. We thought it was…inspiring. So we came back here, every time one of us was in the area, and we wrote down whatever came to mind at the time, like a getaway. We never told anyone this place existed. We were afraid to compromise our secret or, worst of all, to lose it."

I tore my eyes away from the etchings and asked, "We?"

He stared at me for a moment, then nodded his head towards one particular spot beside the door, a few feet from where he stood. I walked over to it, eyes searching for some sort of explanation. And I found it, very near the bottom. Two initials:

B. M.

"Beau Moiré," I said.
He nodded. Beside it, two more initials:

J.R.

"Justin Roland."

G.S.

"Gabriel Schrader."

H.B.

I frowned. "H.B.?"

Beau stared past me, out the small window on the other side of the room where the sun was just beginning to peak out from beneath the sky. "Hunter Blain," he said quietly. "He was a comrade of mine, though he was closest to Gabe. He threw his lot in with the General from day one, so he never would've escaped with us. He's ruthless, very skilled and a Captain we will face, should things go wrong tomorrow. He's stationed in Zaranj."

I lowered my head, then lifted it one last time to see the final two initials, etched just beside the first two. Just beside Beau's.

M.M.

Michael Moiré. I stood up and turned away, catching Beau's eyes for a brief second before I stared at the farthest wall, trying desperately to lose myself in a random soldier's words:

My name is Jordan Lovett, US Army Private. I am twenty-seven. Today is my birthday. Probably my last.

And below it:

Will Vaunt. My wife called today. She told me Lila, my daughter born two nights ago, has my eyes. Maybe soon, I'll confirm it for myself.

I shifted my gaze to another, my heart growing more and more dense with each passing second.

Goodbye Cole. As soon as I find him, I'll give that damn terrorist who shot you a reason to remember your name. You were a good man.

I'll write to Rebecca for you.

I closed my eyes, tears sliding down my cheeks.

"Why?"

"Why what?" I whispered.

"Why did you defend him?"

I shook my head, not bothering to cover the tears or stop them from spilling down my face. Right then, they just didn't matter.

"He showed me how to fight," I said. "Taught me that no matter how weak or vulnerable you are, there's always a chance if you're strong enough to find it." I turned and met his eyes. "He's strong."

Beau studied my face. "You think he let me win?"

"I think it wasn't about winning or losing. I think he was trying to prove something to you."

Beau pulled off his sweatshirt, his t-shirt, let them both fall to the floor and stood up to his full height. My eyes went right to the black, spiraling tattoo on his shoulder, just as he expected.

"Tell me what this means to you."

I stared at it, let the black and red ink wash through my mind, discerning every detail, every mark, every symbol of the words that were written there and the depth of the promise he'd made.

I looked up to his eyes. "It means you were tricked into something that you didn't understand, but not something you couldn't handle. You're alive. You're a survivor. It doesn't mark you as one of them, but something else. It proves that, even though you didn't have many choices, you had one: to do the right thing. And you did. You *are*."

Beau stared into my eyes, his unreadable. "My entire life, I blamed Michael for our parents' deaths. But even when I hated him...I loved him more. I respected him, envied him. He was my older brother and even then, as you say, Michael was strong. He always has been. We joined the Army together, promising that we'd *always* fight for one another, and we did. I did, he did. Even when he excelled, caught the attention of every commanding officer, he looked out for me and he promised me that family would always come first to him."

Beau smirked, his eyes evidently lost in a memory I couldn't see. "We were both good, but Leah, Michael was *great*. The *a'askari*, many called him. The—"

"The soldier."

Beau studied my face for a moment before he nodded. "But there were others, those we didn't realize were affiliated with the organization, who called him by a different name and who still call him by it. *Almasih."* His expression was solemn. "Razer."

Destroyer, I identified silently, having heard that word only a few times before, but understood wholeheartedly, nonetheless.

I didn't say anything, wary that if I spoke, he would stop speaking. And this was a story I needed to hear.

"Michael grew close with a few soldiers who knew what was going on with Division," Beau continued, his shoulders tense. "I told you several weeks ago how Wesley found out about the organization's deception; what I didn't tell you was that Michael was there with me when Wes sat us down in a café in Iran and told us everything. But he was the one who destroyed the trackers on us. He knew. Even before Wesley told us what we were involved in, somehow Michael already knew."

Even though Beau's voice didn't change pitch, I could tell he was grasping for the strength to say the words. "The night we left the organization, when the alarms began to sound after our attempt to erase their database failed, Michael turned on us."

I looked up. Beau's fingers were balled into a fist so tight it was like the blood in his hands was suffocating.

"He fought beside me every day right up until that very last time. He watched out for me, despite the fact that I was three years his junior and always getting myself into trouble, Michael protected me. The day we left the organization, Leah, was the day Michael broke his promise. The day I finally dissolved everything and let myself hate my brother was the day he chose them over me."

"When we left," Beau said, his eyes dark and his voice hard, "Michael stayed. You claim everyone has a choice, well, maybe you're right, and he made his. He didn't fight for me, Leah, he fought *against* me. When the odds were stacked against us, when we needed every ounce of strength we had, every piece of loyalty we could muster up, he chose to defend them. He chose to stand with D79. He chose to turn his gun on *me*."

After several long seconds, Beau's fists came loose, unclenched and uncaring—a mirror for the way his voice changed just then.

"And the worst part?" He shook his head, but there was no bitterness. Just acceptance over a story he was all too familiar with. "I should have known. Mike was the one who talked us all into it. When Division-7-9 considered us for recruit, he convinced Justin and I to join. He loved what he did, gave everything to them. I should have seen it coming, should've realized just how deep they'd hooked him. But the hardest betrayal is always the one you never expected."

"Trust me," I whispered. "I know." Sean's betrayal still cut me, like a piece of glass pierced deep into my skin. What was worse, I still believed in him. I still loved him, still wanted to save him. Like Sean was cutting me with the glass and I was cheering him on.

Looking into Beau's eyes, I saw a similar look of pain, one that could only be caused by a betrayal of someone close to you, like Sean was to me or how Michael had been to him. But it was also different;

something that, I understood, proved it to be too late for the two of them.

While there was pain in Beau's eyes, there was no forgiveness. He had given up on his brother a long time ago.

Something, I promised myself, *I will never do to Sean.*

I turned and met Beau's eyes. I wanted to tell him I was sorry for ever making him believe that I was questioning my love or my loyalty to him. That I was angry and hurt and betrayed at what Sean had said and done to me and that that was why I hadn't tried to find my way back to him sooner. That I was scared for Luke, for Justin, for Wes, for Matt and for Beau, who'd all become so important to me. That I still grieved for Raymond and his wisdom. That I was confused and scared over the sudden connection I felt with Michael because, at the same time, I was beyond grateful to be back in Beau's arms again. The arms of my soldier, my protector and my very best friend.

How do you put something like that into words?

"I love you," I said.

He didn't pause to study my eyes or scrutinize my expression. And somehow he knew; he understood everything I didn't know how to say, just by that one simple truth. Right now, it seemed to be the only one that mattered.

Beau took me in his arms and then I was crying again. How many times had I done that in the past twenty-four hours? I leaned into his chest and he held me there and I cried because I was angry that I'd let so many things, so much heartache, bring me to this.

"I love you, Leah," Beau told me. "I'm sorry for

letting you go."

Beau retracted his hands from around me and used them to tilt my chin up so he could kiss me. I slid my arms up onto his chest, pulling myself closer, fitting perfectly into his embrace as if we were two puzzle pieces of the same complimentary design that had been separated for entirely too long.

"I'm sorry for not finding my way back to you," I whispered.

Beau brushed the back of his hand across my cheek. "You did," he said sincerely. "And even when you don't, I'll find my way to you. I'll find you, Leah, and I'll fight for you. I promise."

I lifted my eyes to his, my heart prepared to fall like it always had with those words but for some reason, it lifted by the look in his eyes.

I met Beau's lips for the kiss that was a long time coming, that was always soft and hard at the same time, fragile and dangerous and exhilarating. He kissed me back with everything he had. My head spun so fast I forgot how to think or how to breathe, my pulse racing and my heartbeat sounding very loud in my own ears. I still felt tears on my cheeks, but I'd forgotten the reason they were there or if, perhaps, these were new ones. Life was such a blur I didn't know.

There was no furniture to rest on, no beds, no chairs. Beau laid me down on the floor, the move so fluid our lips continued as if nothing had changed. The room danced around me in a cadence of rhythm and time and unspoken words. His hands traced the contour of my sides, my hips, and I breathed in as he kissed my lips, my neck, my chest. I slid my fingers across every inch of his skin, the defined muscles that bulged underneath, while he worked my shirt up over my head and kissed every inch of my bare skin.

His fingers were on the tip of my pants when I stopped, suddenly, and bit my lip. Beau instantly slid his hand away, unabashed, and pressed his lips against my forehead in a peaceful surrender.

"You don't have to stop," I said suddenly, the words rushing out of my mouth as if spoken directly from my heart, breathlessly before my head could catch up. But even when it did, there was no protest, no fight left in me for this particular battle.

Beau's eyes were intense, honest and inquisitive, but not proud or victorious. "Are you sure?" he said, and meant it.

I did too as I smiled and whispered, for the very first time, "Yes."

And maybe that's what makes life so beautiful. Maybe it's that one moment where, despite the danger, the heartache, the loss, the pain and the chaos, you can let go and embrace love. The one moment that is so powerful that every infliction of pain seems worthwhile.

We were still at war. We were still fighting, still in danger. But that didn't stop us. I let Beau take me, and I let the world go for just one moment to be with him on our own. Where everything was simple, everything was safe, and everything was easy.

✦　　✦　　✦

PART THREE

CHAOS CONSUMED

"There's a saying that goes: 'the exercise of power is determined by interactions between the world of the powerful, and that of the powerless; all the more so because these worlds are never divided by a sharp line. Every man has a small part of himself in both.'

Whoever wrote that knew more about my life than I ever did, for I never quite understood just how sickeningly true it was, or how close to home a divisive self-loathing like that could hit. With every death that happens around me, I realize something. Manipulation has its enemies, the first and foremost being love. And when love crumbles, so does loyalty.

A woman named Rya Ivrea taught me that."

August 20, 2018
Three months after The Breach
Location: Ghazni
Entry: Nine

STRATEGIES

Zaranj, Afghanistan
August 7, 2020
11:23pm

"HOW MUCH TIME NOW?"

I glanced across the seat at Luke, sitting with his feet up on the dashboard of the stolen car, his head reclined back and his eyes closed. His face appeared calm and relaxed, but I noticed the way he was tapping his fingers against the side window, anxious. I fought the urge to do the same.

"Thirty-five minutes," I told him. My eyes caught sight of a blue piece of cloth lying discarded on the floor and I frowned. "You really should put that back on."

Luke snorted. "What's the point?"

"Matt said—"

"Leah," he said, in as calm a voice as he could manage, "shut up."

I waited a few seconds before I continued, "If it wasn't important, he wouldn't have insisted that you wear it."

"See, that's where you're wrong. Matt is *relentless*

about stupid shit like this. Besides, I don't need that irritating little contraption."

"Your sling," I enunciated, "is supposed to help. But there really isn't much it can do lying on the floor, now is there?"

"Don't baby me."

"I'm not."

"Yes," he snapped, "you are. Stop it."

I studied Luke another second longer and then sighed. Dressed in light brown camouflage like the others to match the sandy terrain, he appeared to be perfectly healthy. His pants were looser than they should have been, since he'd been too weak to eat for days at a time after the injury, but otherwise he looked like a strong, capable soldier. He wore a tan shirt under a gray vest that contained bulletproof material, adorned with small, easy to reach weapons such as his slingshot, multi-tool and various knives. Around a leather belt at his waist were two pistols and a carrying cartridge. Every color on him was of a light shade to avoid detection against the landscape.

Zaranj, as I had been previously instructed, was light colors that could blend with the shifting sand and cloudy sky alike. Ghazni, with its pitch-black tunnels that ran below the city and occasionally exposed pathways above ground that flooded the corridors with night, would be the opposite—dark greys and blacks. Though I tried not to think about that.

One step at a time, and the first step was Zaranj. Tan it was.

But at a closer look, Luke's skin was paler than

normal and, every so often, he would shudder away a wave of pain. I knew that beneath the camouflage tan, his stomach wound was wrapped tight with bandage that restricted his lungs and caused his breathing to be somewhat inconsistent. With the lack of sleeves, the white bandage around his left arm from the gunshot wound was visible, though Matt had done his best to rewrap it with gold-tinted tape.

"Would you stop?"

Breaking out of my reverie, I looked up to Luke's face to find that his eyes were open and he was watching me study him. I tore my eyes away from his body and gave him an innocent look. "Stop what?"

"Stop gawking at me like I'm about to turn to dust."

"How do you know I'm not just drawn to how devilishly attractive you are?" I said lightly, using his go-to description for himself.

He wasn't fooled. "And what do you find most attractive, then? The four-inch stab in my chest or the giant gaping hole in my arm?"

His sudden bitterness caught me off-guard and I turned away. The horrifying memory of Luke lying on the ground after those injuries brought tears to my eyes—both caused, no matter how indirectly, by me.

I felt his warm fingers on my wrist, but I didn't face him. Not like this. Not with tears of regret and weakness on my face.

He sighed. "I'm sorry, Leah. I know you're just worried about me. I shouldn't have said that."

"It's okay."

Luke slid his hand into mine and laced our

fingers together. He squeezed my hand. I lifted my head and met his eyes.

"Come here," he said, tugging on my hand to pull me over to him. I hesitated, but as he insisted, I lifted myself across the seat divider and slid my legs over so that I was facing him, pressing the side of my knees against his leg, and rested my head cautiously on his chest.

"Am I hurting you?"

"Yes." Instantly I started to get up, but he held me where I was. "But I don't care."

I sighed again and closed my eyes as I returned my head to his chest. I listened to his heartbeat for a long time. The consistent, steady rhythm was enough to calm me, soothing my nerves so deeply that I almost forgot all about the current situation.

"Beau, please!"

"No," he'd told me, earlier that morning, his voice stern. We were alone inside one of the small rooms in the shack, Beau standing with his back to me, facing the window. He was dressed head-to-toe in desert camouflage, a baggy tan T-shirt tucked in to a belt adorned with various weapons, the foremost being his 1911 Colt. He was handsome and deadly, all at once. He didn't just look like a soldier, he looked like *the* soldier.

"The answer is no."

I jumped up off the small, rickety cot and moved behind him as if I stood even a fraction of a chance against him. "You can't expect me to sit back and wait for you to die, and I will not."

"Don't be ridiculous. I'm not going to die."

"You don't know that! These people are dangerous—everyone, including you, has said so."

"Yes," he agreed. "But I have no intentions of confronting them. We've been over this, Leah. We get in, plant the bomb, retrieve their weapons and get out. No fighting, no dying."

"You expect me to believe that? Let's say it does work. You're telling me you have absolutely no intentions of confronting them if you get the chance?" I challenged. "I know you, Beau. I know you want revenge, and I know just how far you're willing to go to get it."

He didn't deny it. He simply replied, "I would never jeopardize yours or anyone else's safety for my own personal agenda."

"I don't believe that."

"Then maybe you *don't* know me."

Handsome, deadly and *frustrating.* I set my jaw and wedged my body in-between Beau and the window, despite the obvious fact that he was trying to avoid me. I was not going to let this go. The risk was too high. I had to talk some sense into him, because I knew that none of the others would. They wanted this almost as much as he did.

Men.

"Beau," I said softly, changing tactic. "Look at me." Reluctantly, Beau lowered his head and locked eyes with me. I could see the intensity in them, knowing full-well the reason for it all. And he knew that I knew.

I slid my hands up onto Beau's chest, my fingers

grazing over the necklace he wore beneath the fabric of his shirt. He didn't fight it. Instead, he closed his eyes and took a breath that was heavily weighted and highly overdue, allowing his guard to come down for just one second.

That was all I needed.

Standing on my toes, I leaned into him and he put his hands around my waist and pulled me closer. There was no space between us this time, no hesitation or unfamiliarity. The proximity was entirely different in a way that brought a slight blush to my cheeks as flashes of the intimacy we'd reached the night before crossed my mind and, I'm sure, my face.

I took a breath and the moment was over.

"I know what I'm doing," Beau said quietly. He released me gently and his guard went right back up. But he stared past me just then, his eyes fixed out the window, and it was like I could *see* the bloodlust, see right through his transparent sense of self-sacrifice.

"You can't take them all by yourself," I said softly, angrily. Didn't he understand that there was so much more to this than just him? That if I lost him…

"I have to try." Beau sighed and met my eyes. He brushed his hand down my cheek and pressed his lips to my forehead as he said, "I don't expect you to understand, my love. I just need you to trust me, and trust that I'm going to keep my promise."

I stared into his eyes, trying to wordlessly plead for him not to do this. But all I could see was a blazing wall of anger and determination that I knew I could not penetrate. Nothing I could have said or done would've changed his mind. Once he had his heart set, Beau would not so easily concede.

That is, after all, one of the reasons I fell in love with him.

I sighed, too and surrendered with, "I trust you."

"Leah."

Luke's voice brought me back to the present, shaking me out of the soft, carefree world created by his familiar warmth. I opened my eyes and glanced around. We were still in the stolen car, parked in the shadows, in a cave-like mound of sand a mile outside of the base in Zaranj. My eyes shot to the dashboard. 11:30pm.

Reaching into my pocket, I retrieved the communicator Wes had given me in advance, considering that mine had been destroyed. At the same time, Luke held the control for the bomb Wes and Matt had spent weeks constructing. The plan was simple—the group would get through the gate and into the base by eleven, plant the bomb by eleven-thirty, break into Zaranj's arsenal and contact us to detonate it while they made their way out with the weapons by midnight. The thought was that, even if they were captured, or worse, Luke and I could still set it off and deal a blow to the organization that would leave them reeling for at least a little while. We were the final line of the offense, the last-ditch effort and the safety net, all at once.

I studied the communicator restlessly. Seconds passed, followed by minutes. My uneasiness grew and so did Luke's anxiety.

"What's taking so long?" I said finally, unable to

refrain any longer from asking the question we were both dying to know.

"I'm not sure," Luke said. His eyes passed over the control every few minutes, though he tried his best to do it inconspicuously. Unfortunately, he failed.

"What if...?"

Luke squeezed my hand and pulled my head back down against the side of his shoulder. "Don't say that. They're fine."

I bit my lip, but sat still and didn't press the matter further. Luke was right. He had to be. They were okay. Beau was okay.

He *had* to be.

I closed my eyes and tried to convince my heart to relax but for some reason, the itching, nagging feeling wouldn't let up. It dug and picked and clawed at me until I couldn't take it anymore.

"Luke," I whispered shakily. "Something's happened."

He didn't respond. I lifted my head off his shoulder and slid back over so that I was in the driver's seat. My left hand clasped the door handle at the same time that Luke grabbed my right forearm.

"Wait. I can't let you leave."

"We have to do something! We haven't heard anything from any of them and we should have by now." Besides, if they had been captured, it wouldn't be long before we were found here, too.

Luke's eyes were troubled, fingers twitching. I knew he was anxious enough already; his mind was undoubtedly leading him to a similar conclusion. It wouldn't take much to push him overboard.

"Beau strictly told me not to…"

"Since when do you ever take orders from him?"

Luke pursed his lips, his expression remained uncertain.

"We'll go quietly, just to see what's going on, and then we'll come back," I urged. Just to push him further, I added, "They would've done it for us and you know it."

He studied my face for a long moment. Finally, I watched as the indecision in his eyes turned to determination and my heart sang triumphantly.

"All right. I'll go—but you stay here," he declared, opening his door and stepping out of the car with the remote-control to the bomb, leaving me jaw-dropped and appalled.

Like hell I am.

I jumped out of the car and followed him. Before I could get two steps away from the car, he realized I was tailing him and turned back around. Despite his injuries, Luke was still stronger than me. He shoved me back with resounding force. "I said you're staying."

"I'm coming with you."

"No, you're not. I promised him I would protect you."

"And you can't exactly do that by leaving me out here to fend for myself, now can you?"

"I sure as hell can't do it by taking you in with me," he retorted.

"Luke, please! They'll find you, and you're going to need someone on your side—"

"Leah," he said sharply. "No."

Exasperated, I shoved him back twice as hard. "I am *so* tired of you selfish, *arrogant men* underestimating and discrediting me!" I snapped. "I left my home so that I could be with Beau and help you guys, the whole time being called a weakness and a vulnerability for it. I gave up everything to be here in this psychotic environment! I spent *weeks* being a stupid captive, thinking that I had no chance and that you were *dead*. I've been pushed around since we left California, since I met Beau, since before you were *even born* and I've dealt with all of that, Luke, and I am *still here*. So I am going in with you because I am just as much a part of this team as you are and *you have absolutely no right to tell me I can't.*"

Luke's eyebrows were raised, his hands hanging limp at his sides. After he deduced I was finished and recognized that to continue to resist was entirely futile, he shook the dumbfounded look off his face and smiled his dimpled smile. "Now that," he said, "is an argument. Come on." Luke held out his hand to me.

Without hesitation, and with a tiny sense of gratification, I took it.

11:23pm

BEAU LOWERED HIMSELF TO the ground as he used the strength in his arms to drag his body through the dirt and under the electrically charged gate. He could hear the subtle snap of the voltage that kept him pressed flatly to the sand until he was clear.

He got to his feet and shot a quick glance at the others. Wes and Matt had veered off to the left to shelter behind what appeared to be an offhanded lean-to, though it was probably a small outer weapons storage for the MP—Military Police. The building they were after that housed their head command center (H-Comm) was one just like it, on a larger scale. Wes determined it would be in the south section of the base, which, from their position, was on the very opposite side and ran right through the base's core.

Justin had paced to the right and was currently ducked behind a large building that was just one of the many barracks in the circle that was D79's primary base in Zaranj, Afghanistan.

Beau scanned his surroundings quickly to detect any movement. Seeing none, he took off after Justin and, a second later, pressed his back to the wall just as his older cousin did. Beau waited as Justin peered out around the building and then reigned his head back in as he got down to one knee. Beau mimicked the action and raised an eyebrow in an unspoken question. Both were breathing hard.

It was completely silent, so they did not risk talking. Justin held up his right hand and showed three fingers, then did a walking motion and jerked his finger towards the right twice. Beau understood: *There were three men, walking at angle from the left, towards them at the right, and they were not at a close distance.*

Beau tapped his finger to the M-16 strapped

across his back and raised an eyebrow again. *Armed?*

Justin shook his head.

Beau didn't need any hand signals for this one. He stared into Justin's eyes, the look on his face leveling out into a flat, calculated consideration as he asked with his eyes: *Should we kill them?*

Justin turned to the side, lowered his palms down onto the ground and peered around the corner. It was a few seconds before Beau received any signal of response. And then it came, as Justin's entire body stiffened. Beau got up onto both knees and moved closer to the corner. He tugged on the back of Justin's camouflage jacket, but nothing happened. Alert and on-guard, he did it again, suspense and adrenaline driving at him to know what his cousin was seeing.

Justin flung his hand back and smacked Beau in the face, though he used the end of his sleeve so that the sound wouldn't be as loud. Beau suppressed a groan and slid back down the wall as he held his left hand to his cheek and rubbed the dirt from his now-irritated skin.

After another second, Justin crouched back down next to Beau and pressed his back to the wall. He instructed him to do the same.

Beau fought the urge to roll his eyes. This was a waste of time. Sneaking around undetected wasn't exactly his style. He preferred to confront his enemy head-on, fair-and-square, and either won or lost by his own merit—not by his enemy's ignorance.

But accepting the fact that he was outmatched this time was something Wes had lectured him on, continuously, before they even arrived. And it had already been drilled into him that he was to follow Justin and listen to the more experienced one no matter what.

At least, he thought, *until I get my chance.*

Beau slid his fully loaded M-16 off his shoulder and took it in his hands. Beside him, Justin frowned.

Don't even think about it.

Beau rolled his eyes. He mouthed: *We're wasting time we don't have.*

No. If you fire even once, our position is compromised and we lose the element of surprise. Minimal confrontation, remember? Justin shifted eyes to the corner of the building where approaching footsteps could be heard and instructed: *Get out your knife, and don't move until I tell you to.*

Reluctantly, Beau slung the gun back over his shoulder and took out his old Army knife from its place on his belt and unsheathed a similar, yet less familiar knife. He raised his brows at Justin.

Three are within fifteen feet of us. No MP—so far as I can tell. But I'm sure we will run into some sooner or later.

Beau nodded solemnly. Their best chances of success were if they didn't have to face armed soldiers. Fortunately, Military Police were the only ones permitted to carry on-site here. The rest of the weapons would be in the artillery range.

Beau got into a readier position, planting his combat boots square with each other, lifting himself on his toes so he could jump to his feet without having to shift anymore, and wielding one knife in each hand. Set, sharp and ready to kill.

He felt the force of the memory slam into his

consciousness, almost knocking him over.

It was three years ago. Beau was almost eighteen, though he had already been serving in the U.S. Army for over nine months. He was in a similar position to the one he was in now—crouched behind a building, hiding from enemy soldiers, his comrade Justin to the right, guiding and giving him direction as bombs exploded all around.

He remembered the sound. The loud, bursting *bang* that sounded through the air and the loud ringing bell that struck his ears shortly after. But the worst of it was the heat. They were concealed behind a cement wall, but the height didn't go up very far—ten feet, at most—and they were near the edge, just as they were now. The flames licked around the sides of the wall and enclosed them in a thick, heavy gust. Beau felt every square inch of his body subjected to the inferno, and suddenly, he was on fire...

Justin shoved Beau back against the wall, knocking him out of the reverie. His vision returning, Beau grimaced and glared at his older cousin. But Justin was already moving. As soon as the soldiers rounded the corner, he sprang to his feet and dug the knife in his right hand deep into the chest of the man on the outermost side. Beau acted one second delayed out of confusion, but because he was well-versed in improvisation with a knife in combat, his skill made up for the delay.

Beau was on his feet in an instant and slashing his knife through the neck of the soldier who'd been on the right in the next. The D79 patch on the fallen soldier's shoulder would've made it easier to accept any other time, but right now, Beau was too focused to feel the guilt. Instinctively, he whipped his head around to find the last man who'd had an extra second to prepare for the ambush than his fellow soldiers lying face-down, bleeding in the dirt.

Beau felt a cold metal barrel against the back of his head and froze precisely where he was standing. *Found him.*

The third soldier was tall, lean and muscular. Dressed in a dark gray uniform adorned with metallic buttons and patches, this man was clearly an officer. From the classifying symbol on his breast pocket, Beau recognized him to be a Sergeant First Class.

Even so, Beau realized with a sinking feeling, *he shouldn't be armed.*

The sergeant's rifle was aimed at Beau, while Justin's Ak-47 was, in turn, aimed at the sergeant.

"Drop it," the soldier ordered.

"You first," Justin said.

Beau made sure to keep very still, but he closed his eyes and counted to ten, preparing for the shot. When his lips mouthed *ten,* he spun on his heels and clipped the soldier at the elbow, knocking his grip on the gun loose. The sergeant recovered a second later, which turned out to be a second too late. Justin fired one clean shot, hitting the sergeant square in the chest and knocking him backwards.

He dropped to the sand, dead. Beau and Justin had perfected that technique.

Beau wiped the blood off his face and commandeered the man's rifle, strapping it across his back, and then turned towards Justin with a derisive look. "What happened to the element of surprise?"

Justin shook his head. "In case you didn't notice, that man was not MP. Something's up."

"Just because he was carrying doesn't mean he anticipated an attack." Beau gestured at the two dead soldiers. "His buddies didn't."

"No, Beau. You need to pay closer attention." Justin moved to one of the soldiers and knelt on one knee. He flipped the man's hand over and in it was a black walkie talkie.

The light was on and blinking red. "Sergeant?" a stern voice came through the device. "Have you apprehended Marshall?"

Beau and Justin shared a look. *Marshall?*

Justin smashed the device. Beau's eyes widened.

"Shit! They're after Wes!"

"Beau, the walkies are being tracked! *Hurry!*"

Beau ran to the other dead soldier, kicked his hand upright, and stomped on the blinking, active device that flew out of it. "Shit! Shit! They knew we were coming!"

"Which means they know we're here," Justin said as he crushed the other soldier's walkie with definitive force. He stood and glanced toward the gate. "Forget the weapons. We need to find the others and get out of here. Now."

"Oh, I believe it's a little late for that."

Beau spun. His M-16 was slung across his back and out of quick reach, but if there was one thing he'd learned from his brother, Michael, it was to never be caught without more than one weapon.

He aimed his Colt at the voice, but it was

useless. Standing less than three yards away were six soldiers—each garbed in charcoal grey Division-7-9 camouflage with the signifier of Delta Victor One. Each armed with a semi-automatic rifle.

Five of the men were plain soldiers. One of them was an officer. But his tall, burly features marked him as *the* officer. Beau's hands clenched into fists and his eyes narrowed menacingly.

"Blain," both Beau and Justin said through gritted teeth.

"Hello again, boys." Captain Hunter Blain smiled darkly, his eyes bright in the caramel-colored moonlight. "You've kept me waiting."

✦ ✦ ✦

11:35pm

"HURRY!" I WHISPERED LOUDLY. "And *stop* messing with it!"

Luke, some forty paces behind me, was clutching at his arm and mumbling under his breath. Before I could protest further, he ripped the sling off his arm and buried it in the sand with his boot before catching up to me and ducking behind the mound I hid behind. I glared at him fervently. He shook his head.

"Give me your knife."

I unsheathed the blade from my belt and handed it to him. Luke studied me up and down for a moment, then shook his head again.

"What?" I demanded. There was a quiet smirk

on his face that I realized was aimed at my outfit.

I was wearing a pair of tan-colored pants with brown high-kneed boots over top and a golden-brown long-sleeve. On my hands were thin nude gloves that Luke had lent me, which were almost too big, despite his thin fingers. Justin had thought he would be funny and use my eyeliner to draw football streaks on the tips of my cheeks on the ride over—he'd told me that it would help me look more "fit for battle." My cheeks felt rough and sticky from where I'd involuntarily smeared the chestnut color all over.

While they all looked like desert warriors, I knew I looked like a caramel-covered mess.

"Stop smirking at my face," I said sorely.

"I wasn't." He used my knife to slice off the remaining heavy bandage around his arm, keeping his eyes on his work.

"Then what?" I challenged.

Luke discarded the bandage and hid it in the sand. He walked up to me, standing close, and pressed the hilt of the knife into my hand. "You look like one of us," he said, nothing but sincerity in his tone, before he stepped past me.

I smiled. No one had ever said that to me before.

Sliding the knife back into its place at my belt, I spun and followed him with an electricity in my bones that reminded me, however unwittingly, of every encounter I'd faced with Michael.

We got no more than three steps before the gunshot sounded.

Luke turned and our eyes met. In his was

suspicion, but in mine was flat-out fear. I immediately raced forward, spying the gate only a few yards and several mounds ahead. My body was tired from having to scale the five-foot deep mounds that had been dug around the base like an intricate pattern of moats, but with all of the strain I'd been put through over the past three weeks, my legs had become more solid, allowing me to climb and project my body easily. I lunged forward, dug my feet into the side of the last mound and pulled myself up. Sweat dripped down my face and was cool against my back. Behind me, Luke was catching his breath.

I reached the gate and, to my surprise, there were no sentries, no guards, no one at all. I almost reached out to push on the gate to see how sturdy it was when Luke grabbed me by the waist and yanked me away from it the moment he caught up.

"Careful," he said briskly, between breaths. "I bet that fence has every bit of five-thousand volts. Listen."

I didn't have to strain my ears to hear the loud *snap* that pulsed from the fence. Luke had most likely just saved my life.

"Will you at least give me the chance to protect you, instead of always running to do everything on your own?"

From the adrenaline, I was breathing hard. I pushed Luke's hands off me. "By all means," I said, gesturing at the high voltage fence.

He grinned and reached a hand towards it. I gasped and snatched his hand out of the air, pulling it towards me and as far away from the fence as possible like a mother would.

Luke chuckled quietly. "Good to know you care." Still smiling, he gestured towards the bottom of the gate. I followed his gaze and noticed a small valley in the sand. This must have been how Beau, Justin, Matt and Wes had entered the base.

Too easy, I thought, frowning as I surveyed the over fifteen-foot tall electric fence surrounding the compound. A guard tower stood to the right, but it was vacant, allowing anyone with a reasonable build to slide right under and into the compound with minimal duress. The gate might as well have been open.

It's almost as if…

"Come on. Let's go before we're spotted."

I nodded and Luke held my wrist as I ducked down and slid on my stomach under the gate. He did the same and, once we were in, Luke helped me to my feet and kept me behind his back while he surveyed the area. I itched to step out in front of him, to stand my own ground instead of allowing him to act as my shield. The urge caught me off-guard, at first, before I dismissed it. To our surprise, however, the area appeared even emptier than the entrance.

Luke held a pistol in his hands, more than ready to aid the others, protect us from enemies, or both. But as we walked further and further into the base, past the barracks and the police quarters, the more puzzled we became.

Something's wrong, my instincts screamed.

A hand touched the back of my arm and I started to scream but the person slapped another hand over my mouth before I could do so. Luke sensed the additional presence a second after I did. He spun around with his gun raised and ready to fire.

"Would you mind lowering that?"

Matt.

Luke removed the barrel of his pistol from Matt's forehead and opened his mouth to speak. Matt, still holding me tightly, shook his head and motioned for the three of us to veer off from the path of the entrance and into the shadows near the outer fence.

As soon as we were hidden, Matt released me. My breathing was now ragged and inconsistent from the shock of the unexpected arrival, and Luke was favoring his left hand the slightest bit. To be honest, we looked like two twins—our stark blonde hair evident and matching—who didn't belong here at all.

"What on earth are you doing?" Matt challenged. "I was under the impression that you were to guard Leah *outside* the perimeter."

"Have you *met* Leah?" Luke snorted. "She's not exactly the easiest person to baby sit."

"I don't need baby sat!" I snapped at them both. "What's going on?" I asked Matt. "This place should be ashes by now."

"I know," Matt said quietly. "Nothing went as planned."

"Obviously," Luke remarked.

I sent him a dark look and said, "What do you mean?"

"As soon as we arrived, Wes and I realized something was out of the ordinary, but it was too late to fall back. Beau and Justin split off to the right and went to silence any patrol that might prove to cause us problems. Wes and I went left, crossed between the barracks and proceeded to the designated place within their head command center where we were to set the bomb, but it was crawling with soldiers." Matt shook his head. "I don't know how, but they knew we were coming. They were *waiting* for us at the target site."

"And Wes?" Luke's expression tensed. "Where's my brother?"

"He's all right," Matt reassured him. "We decided to try and find a new location for the bomb that would produce the same results—our goal was the communications and networking tower—until we heard gunfire. Your brother sent me to find out who fired it and, better yet, who it had been fired at."

Luke and I exchanged a look.

"And Beau and Justin?"

Matt shook his head. "They may be retrieving weapons, I'm not sure. I heard a noise and thought it was them. But it was you two."

Worry began to tear at me. In a stiff voice, Luke demanded, "Why didn't someone contact us?"

Matt retrieved something from his pocket and held it up. His communicator. He pressed his thumb against the side. The device should have made a *click*, but nothing happened.

"They're ineffective here," he said solemnly. "I don't know what it is about Zaranj's Intel system, but something in their network is conflicting with our signal."

"Coincidence?" I asked.

"Perhaps." Matt shrugged. "Perhaps not. I cannot say."

"But, wait. Isn't the signal—?"

"What I'd like to know," Luke said abruptly, "is how our element of surprise was broken."

"Unfortunately," Matt said, "I don't believe we ever had it. The soldiers appear to be prepared, the majority of them are clustered at the base's core and I imagine the rest are positioned strategically also. There's nothing we could've done differently. They were alerted to our plan prior to us following through with it."

Luke's eyes narrowed. "A traitor?"

Matt shrugged and stared out across the base. But just before he did, he glanced at me with a look that held the tiniest bit of uncertainty. My eyes narrowed incredulously at the slight accusation, and then, suddenly, they widened.

Matt was right. There was a traitor.

"Get down!"

Two shots went off just as Luke grabbed me by the wrist, Matt by the arm, and pulled all three of us down. I landed a few feet from the other two, my knees skinned up and my arms covered in dirt—not sand, but thick, clay-like dirt from where the sand had been tempered and unearthed. I got to my feet just as quickly as we'd fallen, hurrying after Matt and Luke who'd headed off towards a particularly high mound of cover near the outer wall of the base.

Before I could reach them, a band of soldiers cut me off.

"Leah, RUN!"

More shots went off and I knew my choices were slim. I was caught in the cross-fire between Luke and Matt, who'd begun to fire, and the soldiers of the base, who were firing back with heavier artillery. Reluctantly I spun and dashed away from the direction of the other two, my destination simple: anywhere but here.

All around me, soldiers began falling into place as if it were an ambush. It was getting increasingly closer to midnight and I realized, with a sinking feeling, that we were running out of time, if we hadn't already. The base was large enough that a confrontation could be had without raising total alarm, but for how long, I couldn't know. All I knew was that I was alone again in a very bad place with nothing but a knife at my waist. Luke was my gun, and he was gone now. Finding him would be nearly impossible, not to mention dangerous.

I unclasped the knife and tightened my fingers around its hilt. Adrenaline, fear and the burning desire to help my team was what kept me upright and ultimately what fueled me forward, dodging men at every turn, all the while keeping my eyes peeled for that one specific soldier.

I was about fifty yards from the entrance we'd crawled through, weaving diagonally behind buildings and keeping low to the ground, when I saw him. Standing in a crowd of roughly twenty soldiers, he was garbed in his official military uniform, a gun in his right hand and a wild look in both of his eyes that stopped me dead in my tracks. Matt was right, he was positioned on the outskirts of the very core of the base, calling out orders to the men around him not fifty feet from me. Suddenly, he looked in my direction where I was crouched down behind a stone barrier. I froze. Our eyes met.

And then I was running.

11:41pm.

The place was bustling with soldiers in uniform now. They flooded the compound like a colony of ants, and it was impossible to discern which were Division soldiers and which were innocent Americans. I wasn't entirely sure there was a difference anymore.

I'd been separated from Luke and Matt, left to find cover on my own for what felt like hours but should've only been several minutes, at most. Before anyone could spot me—clearly an outsider—I had run to the very edge of the closest corner of the base and ducked behind a brick building that looked identical to every other structure. I tightened my fingers around the knife in my hand to center myself as my control waned and the adrenaline, but mostly fear, tilted me off balance.

What am I doing here?

The communicator in my pocket was dysfunctional, and I hadn't heard a word from Beau or Justin or Wes since they had entered the base at eleven, and now I was completely separated from both Matt and Luke. My heart cinched with an overwhelming sense of worry—though, shockingly, not for myself, but the others.

For Wes, who was on a mission that would

render him vulnerable. Matt, who was used to helping people, not hurting them. Luke, a minor with major injuries that he would undoubtedly downplay until it cost him again. Justin, who would fight and die for any one of his brothers. Most of all, for Beau, a man hell-bent on vengeance that left him unpredictable.

Where *was* he?

My head started to spin and I knew it was because I was trying too hard to figure everything out in my mind when nothing made sense to me in reality. I knew nothing of this terrain, no one besides my team and no idea how to traverse this place without running into trouble with either. I took a breath and closed my eyes for just a moment, expecting to see more fear rebounded off the backs of my eyelids but instead, I saw flashes of something else.

The map of Zaranj. The structure of the base laid out and broken down by Wes only hours before.

The heat of the moment had led me to believe that I was lost without the others. That I was on my own now, with nothing and no one to rely on but myself. And maybe I was, after all.

Maybe that wasn't necessarily a bad thing.

Soldiers walked close by, and the sound of crumpled static interrupted my thoughts just then.

"Copy that. All plain soldiers have been given the order to protect head command, and all MP have been instructed to protect the armory with every ounce of firepower we've got."

I closed my eyes again once the voices stopped and tried to picture the crumpled sheet of cardstock Wes had used to diagram the city of Zaranj.

Narrowing the scope, I focused on the outline of the military base. Even though I couldn't draw specific lines, I knew which buildings were the important ones—head command center, communications and networking tower and the armory—and where they were located. Luke had assumed control of the detonation remote, so I had no way to assist in the planting of the bomb, nor did I really believe I could be of assistance there anyway. At this point, confrontation was a must to get anywhere close to the core, and that wasn't why I had been separated. My advantage was in that no one knew where I was. That was also my disadvantage. I had no way of knowing if and when the bomb would go off—though I tried not to dwell on that.

I had managed to finagle my way along the outskirts of the fence, behind stone walls that rose approximately three-feet at random intervals to protect the soldiers from incoming fire. There were trenches dug around them, but even these were shallow and weren't meant to conceal as much as they were to aid in soldiers' defense. I sank to my stomach several times when a soldier would cross by, but for the most part, the men were preoccupied with the gunshots that seemed more sporadic than they were concentrated in one area. I wasn't sure whether that was a good thing or a bad thing.

Focus, Leah.

My mind was racing ten-fold and my heartrate soared every time a shot was fired, but I knew that this was where Beau needed me, where Matt, Justin, Wes and Luke needed me.

Buildings sprang up ahead, and I traversed behind them carefully. These were the barracks, I recalled, which meant I was on the left half of the base if you looked at it from the gate we'd entered from. Up ahead would be the artillery field where weapons were tested and training drills occurred, Wes had informed us. And, directly adjacent from that, would be the armory which was undoubtedly crawling with soldiers on guard.

Soldiers on guard.

I froze where I was standing as the first clear thought reared its head amidst the haze in my brain. Then I covered my mouth as I let out an involuntary gasp for another reason. Footsteps echoed across the grounds, sounding especially loud since there were no soldiers in this part, or at least there hadn't been, until now.

"Yes, General."

My heart skipped a beat and then ascended. I lost all train of thought except for the fact that I had to find Beau and tell him what I had discovered. But with each word I heard just then, my chances of doing so lessened rapidly.

"Indeed, sir. They are here, right on schedule. I will send word when Marshall is apprehended and Moiré is dead."

That voice. I couldn't take it. The words were a knife in my chest, worrisome and deadly, but the voice made it so much worse. Taking a deep breath and burying my inhibitions, I stepped out from behind the building and faced him.

Them. They were close, within fifteen feet—two

soldiers, both garbed in U.S. Army uniforms hedged with a Division-7-9 touch. But I addressed only one. I knew only one.

My heart bled for just one.

Tears streaming down my cheeks, I shouted, "Why, Sean?"

✦   ✦   ✦

WARNING

4 hours before

Ghazni, Afghanistan
August 7, 2020.
7:57pm

THE SUN SET EARLY for an August evening. As the giant, powder-like clouds passed over the horizon with rushing, rumbling speed, denser ones took their place, casting darkness over what had just been light only moments before. Within minutes, the sky was opening up, spilling fat water droplets over and across the dry, dusty landscape that spanned for miles into Ghazni, Afghanistan.

Rain, rare for the time of year and the region in general, yet consistent for how it had been recently, brought with it a depressive mood that sulked in every corner, every alleyway, blanketing the city. The thick, looming fog that came with it was even more concentrated as the altitude curved down into what most American travelers would consider the slums.

Michael Moiré stared idly out the water-stained window like he'd done so many times during the past two years. He tapped his fingers impatiently.

Moments later, static echoed throughout the room.

"Captain?"

Michael lifted the blinking walkie-talkie to his mouth, numbly. "I assume you were successful?"

"Yes, Captain," the soldier on the line replied, voice hushed. "I've located the target you requested. It appears Sergeant Sean Collins is en route to our military base in Zaranj, sir."

The news did not surprise him. "Alone?"

"Negative. Sergeant Collins departed from HQ at 0900 hours this morning with precisely eleven soldiers from Quadrant D79-03, sir."

This, however, did. "Greymarks. He's sending a soldier to lead an assassin's task?"

"I am not privy to the specifics of the assignment, Captain," the soldier replied. "But if I may speak freely, I say there is more to it than that, sir."

"Speak freely, Lieutenant."

"Collins confided in Corporal Hauk that it isn't just a killing mission this time." The soldier lowered his voice. "The General has ordered for the capture of a specific target in Zaranj. He believes Collins may have an advantage."

"Interesting," Michael said, though the information was not new or interesting, for he'd heard it all long before Sean Collins had been given the assignment and, apparently, blabbed about it.

A light began blinking on the device inside of his pocket. "That will be all, Lieutenant," Michael said, reaching for it. "Report back if your scouts come across anything particularly suspect."

"Yes, Captain."

There was a message on his personal cell phone—the one he'd kept secret from the leaders of the organization, though the General had eventually tortured its location out of him. He'd managed to get it back, though it had taken him weeks to maneuver his way around the detection and surveillance software that had modified it. Personal phones were highly discouraged in the organization Division-7-9. They led to privacy—one of Michael Moiré's favorite things.

He typed a brief message and closed his phone without rereading it. It was a warning, a message with the instruction of avoiding the military base in Zaranj on this particularly stormy night.

The light flashed again. *Too late,* was Rya Ivrea's response.

Michael felt his patience wearing thin. Before he could act on it, a ringing sounded throughout the room, one that was unfamiliar and coming from his walkie. His head was beginning to spin with all of the echoing sounds in this tiny space. He recognized the voice on the line when he answered. What puzzled him was that the man contacting him had never, ever used that avenue of communication.

It meant something that set Michael's senses alert.

"Michael."

With a flat-stare at the half-crescent move above, Michael said, "Speaking."

"What is your location?"

"The City of Hell."

The cold, careful voice on the static-filled line was silent for a few seconds. "I haven't received any word on the man I asked you to win to my allegiance. Christian Stubler. Where is he?"

"I don't know."

The man paused again. When he spoke, surprisingly, it was without malice. "You don't know? *You* don't know? Michael Moiré, the man who enlists the world to do his bidding…has no idea."

Michael did not respond.

"Tell me something, Michael," he said, shifting gears entirely. "What significance does your brother play in all of this?"

"What difference does it make?"

"Because I'm going to kill him tonight."

Michael paused. He glanced at the crackling walkie in his hand, then studied his apartment, his eyes resting on every surface, spot and crevice. Casually, he said, "Then you'd be breaking our accord."

"Yes, yes, our agreement that Beau was yours to kill when the moment came, blah blah," the man said dryly. "Unfortunately, I've struck many accords, Michael, and I believe we both know that ours is beginning to wear its course."

"I can change this. I just need—"

"More time? More time to do what, Mr. Moiré? To draw more attention from the organization?"

Michael narrowed his eyes, fighting the urge to glance out the window where he would undoubtedly catch a glimpse of at least one or two sentries of Ghazni, eyeing his whereabouts at all times.

"You think people wouldn't notice that blonde number edging her way into the proximity of headquarters? That it was a coincidence she found her way to her snotnose cousin? Or do you honestly believe that The General has no idea what you're up to."

"Believe me," Michael said softly, twisting his security access card between two fingers, lifting it up to his eyes to study it, mockingly, "I am fully aware that he does."

The man on the line was silent for a long second. "Interesting. Perhaps you can follow orders, my friend. The General's, at least."

"Yet you continue to doubt me."

"I doubt your loyalty," the man replied, "not your capability."

"Loyalty means nothing anymore." Michael said. "And capability? Spare me. I've been sitting in the crosshairs of this fucking mess you call a plan for over six months now while you've been hiding out in America doing absolutely nothing." Though the words would have risen an octave coming from anyone else, Michael's composure, and his tone, remained the same. "It's easy to be dead, isn't it, Wyatt?"

The man ignored that, though his voice took on a note of repose. "How much longer will The General continue to trust you?"

Michael opened the door to the small porch that was connected to his apartment, half-expecting to see a body, but it was empty. He stepped out into the harsh wind. "Until I have to lie to him again."

"Then don't lie."

"Every word I say to him is a lie," Michael said, placing his ear away from the device, listening to the echo it reverberated in the small area. "You should know that by now."

"Ah, yes," the man said at last. "The infamous *razer*, the ruthless Michael Alexander Moiré. Cheater of the cheaters, and liar until the end. D79's finest, standing on the edge of the blade that will one-day bridge the shallow distance to slit the throats of every American man, woman and child." The man paused. "Or is he?"

There was a whistle in the air, soft and eerie in the evening wind. It was then that Michael realized there was no static on the line, no disruption that always permeated the distance between his walkie and the next. Distance. Location. Proximity. All words *he* had used.

Fuck.

"Fair's fair, Michael, so I'll cut to the chase. You're either with us, or you are against us. I'll wait patiently for your decision."

Michael dropped the device to the concrete floor of the porch and smashed his boot down on top of it, killing the power instantly.

With his other foot, he kicked the door to his apartment open, sending it crashing back against the frame.

Wyatt Vendelle was seated at the half-broken table in the living area, feet crossed casually on the surface, precisely where Michael had been standing only moments before.

"Just remember," Vendelle said, studying the device in his hand before lifting his smiling eyes to Michael. "We all have a choice. And every choice has a consequence. Pretty soon, Division will learn that. The only question is…where will you be standing when they do?"

LOYAL TO A FAULT

Zaranj, Afghanistan
11:41pm

BEAU DUCKED TO THE ground, his knees burying themselves into a pile of sand and trapping him from making as quick of a turn as he'd needed in order to avoid the hit. When it crashed down over his head, he sank straight down into it further, inevitably swallowing a huge gulp of grainy sand that stuck like muck in his throat.

Captain Hunter Blain stood to his full six-foot-five height, all two-hundred and fifty pounds of him packed into one aggressively hulk-like body that loomed victoriously over Beau in the sand.

Each had disarmed the other long before, their fight turning into one of pure strength that Beau was losing horribly.

Luckily, he wasn't alone. Justin Roland came out of nowhere, a heavy object that looked like a sedentary rock in his hand, and kicked Blain in the backs of the knees as he smashed the rock over the D79 soldier's head.

Beau instantly got to his feet and spit the glob of sand and saliva out of his mouth and onto the dirt beside where Blain's head had landed. He straightened his jaw, which he was almost positive had been somewhat dislocated, and glanced at his cousin, Justin.

"Where the hell have you been?"

Justin rolled his eyes and pulled out his knife as he kneeled next to Blain's limp body. "I suppose that's sort of like a 'thank you'."

"Thanks for letting me take all of the heat so you can charge in and save the day, J," Beau said dryly as he positioned himself on the other side of Blain, parallel from his partner.

"I'm sorry, would you like to me to hold your hand next time?"

"Let's just finish this so we can find everyone and leave," Beau said gruffly. While Justin took Blain's weapons, he clicked the button on the side of his Bluetooth that was linked to the communicator at his belt. "Wes? Matt? Leah? Luke? Can you hear me?"

"Give it a rest, Beau," Justin said, lifting his eyes to survey the grounds. There were five soldiers that had been travelling with Blain, four of which were lying in separate places, bodies contorted, dead, and one of which had escaped before Justin had chased him down and killed him, too. "If the communicators haven't worked since we got here, they're not going to magically begin to."

Beau held up his hand instantaneously. "Do you hear that?" They both listened. The sound of gunfire was audible in the distance. Beau pinpointed it to be coming from the southwestern side of the base, close to the gate.

Close to Leah.

Beau got to his feet only to be high-kicked square in the face and sent spinning to the ground by the force of it. As his face smashed against the ground for what had to be the tenth time in the past ten minutes, Beau realized that Justin was on the ground too, and Captain Hunter Blain was on his feet again, standing shoulder to shoulder with the new arrival who'd sent them both to their knees.

The sight of her sent his mind soaring back in time.

"I honestly don't know what the hell she sees in him," eighteen-year-old Beau Moiré said irritably to his cousin, Justin, both garbed in post-training gear.

Justin smiled his big, goofy grin and slapped a hand on Beau's back. "I think she's cool. Good for him."

"No, you think she's hot."

"So do you," Justin said slyly, eyeing his younger cousin as Beau was eyeing the two love-birds walking back from a scouting mission that The General had sent them on so many hours before. He didn't venture a guess at what had taken them so long to return. Michael Moiré had his hand on Rya Ivrea's back, his touch soft against her caramel colored skin that Beau had all but memorized in his time here, stationed in Zaranj, from afar.

At that moment, something Michael said made her turn and smile. Her eyes flitted past her companion's, however, resting instead, for a moment, onto Beau's. The smile that made her sharp face lovely faded slowly, replaced by a quiet, alluring smirk.

Beau—a reckless teenager who'd sworn off emotions since the death of his parents all those years ago, sworn off rules of decency and all that came with the code of women and therefore unaware of the damage a girl like Rya could cause a soldier like him—smiled back.

"Beau Moiré," Rya purred, drawing Beau back to the present once more, that same smirk etched across her face. "Hello, *mi querido*."

"I see you boys never learned how to get yourselves out of trouble and stay there," Hunter Blain said, the barrel of his M-16 aimed at Justin, who'd risen to his knees and was gritting his teeth, fighting to restrain himself from doing something impulsively Justin-like.

Beau's mind was racing. It appeared that Justin had enough glares for Hunter, so he shifted the aim of his glare onto Rya.

"What are you doing here?" Beau shot at her. "Wesley told me months ago you left this place, left the organization."

"Oh how I adore you Moiré boys," Rya chuckled, her long, slim fingers positioned delicately on the revolver she had aimed at Beau's heart—not for the first time. "So handsome and valiant and *estúpido*."

"Things have changed," Beau said through his teeth at the sound of his brother's name.

"Have they?" Rya tipped her delicate shoulders up, her knowing eyes warm and amused. "Both still fighting over which is the most daring, still playing ruthless games of chance. Oh, and both still pawning after pretty girls."

Beau furrowed his brows at her, his fingers pressed tightly against the blade end of the knife at his side. It cut into his skin the slightest bit, but at that moment, Beau was too angry to notice.

She read his mind easily. Her smile widened. "Pretty girl, indeed," she said, her devilish voice matching the twisted look of mockery on her face. "Michael sure seemed to fancy her. *Lay-uhh.*" Rya tossed her hair. "She must be *quite* something; your brother never really did have a thing for blondes. Until now, that is."

Beau's fingers tightened into a fist. "My brother never had a thing for decency, which is why he wanted you."

Rya bit down on her teeth as her finger hovered over the trigger guard. "*¡Cállate! Que ignoréis—*"

"Enough," Hunter cut in, his gruff voice rising over Rya's heightening threats. "Enough banter, enough *fucking Spanish*, enough games and enough breathing from these two. Ivrea," he snapped without sparing Rya a glance. "Find Marshall and bring me his head."

Justin and Beau exchanged a look. Even Rya hesitated. Her gun swayed slightly in the air with uncertainty and an abject confliction. "But... The General—"

"That's an order, soldier."

Without another word, Rya holstered her gun. She never did have much care for the chain of command. Sparing a wink for Justin and blowing a kiss at Beau, who spit on the ground in response, Rya slinked past them and headed back towards the center of the base where soldiers were beginning to disperse from.

Hunter eyed her silhouette briefly before he turned his disgusted demeanor back to the two ex-soldiers.

"I see The General has you on a short leash, Blain," Beau chided, brushing the sand from the stubble on his chin as his pulse began to increase.

"Subordinate bastard," Justin snarled.

Hunter Blain shrugged, his ripped and scarred face twisting into a feral grin. "I'm afraid The General doesn't run things here, boys. This is Zaranj, remember?" he said coldly, gearing himself for impending offense. "Here, *I'm* The General."

I HELD MY HEAD high, fists clenched to stop them from shaking.

"How could you, Sean?" I said, my tone as broken as I felt. The soldier that had been walking with him was directly behind me, my hands twisted tightly in his grip as he held me to face my cousin.

Sergeant Sean Collins studied me plainly, his brown eyes hard. "I could ask you the same question, Leah Rae."

"So much for family."

"Family? What about honor?" Sean spat, breathlessly raising his hands into the air like he'd done so many times when we were younger and I had gotten on his boyish-nerves. "Standing with ex-soldiers who aim to murder service men and women of the United States military? That doesn't sound like a member of *my* family."

"Then you must be brainwashed to think the men you serve still protect people," I replied sharply. The soldier restraining me twisted my arms into a pretzel, drawing a groan from my lips but nothing more. The harder he twisted, the more I fought to subdue the pain and disguise it from my face. If there was anything I'd learned, it was that these soldiers seemed to feed off weakness like wolves toying with injured prey.

"Enough, Jax." Sean raised his hand into the air. The soldier stopped and looked up. "She's not a prisoner to be tortured."

"Really?" I snapped, jerking my arms away from the soldier—who was young, not much older than me—my eyes on fire.

"Really," Sean said, tone laced with authority aimed at the man, Jax. "She's my relative, and I'll have her on the first flight back to California in the morning. See to it that she's kept somewhere safe until then."

Jax reached for me again, only to receive an unexpectedly harsh slap across the face. Before he could recover, I dug my knee straight up into his groin as hard as I could. He doubled over immediately, spitting loud curses in a shocked, rushed, practiced Arabic tongue.

I squared my shoulders and faced my cousin, who seemed just as shocked. "I suggest you keep your new friends away from me. I'm not leaving Beau to pick up the pieces of the mess I caused because of your selfish betrayal."

Sean's expression quickly turned to outrage. He ran a fierce hand through his twisted brown hair, rising up and down on his toes, looking like a madman. "Still infatuated with that piece of shit, I see."

"Beau's a good man," I retorted. "So are his brothers, and his uncle too until your men killed him."

"Brothers?" Sean scoffed. "You mean Justin and Matthew Roland, his cousins, and Wesley and Luke Marshall, his random affiliates? If you ask me, they're all traitors. Moiré's only the worst because he's somehow managed to trick a civilian into thinking she's a soldier. Tell me, Leah, when exactly did you become so pathetically gullible to the ways of men?"

"Yesterday in Ghazni when I trusted you."

Sean narrowed his eyes. The soldier, Jax, was getting to his feet, still spewing curses at me. Sean didn't seem to understand them nor did he care to acknowledge them. His eyes, riddled with malice and frustration, were focused on me and getting darker by the second as his emotions soared to heights that were new for him. Sean had always been an easy-going, carefree sort of guy. Not now.

"Come with me, Leah," Sean said, lowering his voice as if pleading with me for the last time. "I can still get you out of this, The General will still offer you sanctuary if you denounce these traitors and realize which side is the good one in all of this."

"I'm beginning to think there are no good sides

to this," I replied, shifting away from Jax, who circled me for a second before moving to stand with Sean. They looked eerily similar, both shooting daggers at the girl standing only feet from them. The girl.

"You're not a soldier, Leah. You don't belong here."

"Neither do you, Sean," I said, the girl disappearing once more as I took her place. "You're a lawyer."

"Not anymore," he said, his face a blank slate. "I am a soldier, and I am ordering you to *come with me* now before it is too late."

"It's already too late," I said softly, pained. I gestured at the base, a flooded influx of military men and women; at the sky, a dark cloud of gun smoke forming; at the shifting sand that threatened rain but was holding back a torrential storm as another took its place. "Look around you. Look what's happened here, Sean, what this organization has done to us, to you, to all of these people. Fighting and killing and dying and for what? What purpose?"

"Protection," Sean said, right on cue. "And loyalty to a cause that is greater than everyone here. Greater than me, and you."

"What's greater than *life*, Sean?" I whispered. "How many people have you killed for them?"

"How many people have died tonight at the hands of your *boyfriend?*" he spat back at me. "This is a defense against the war *they have brought upon themselves.* Besides, you of all people shouldn't preach to me about life, Leah, how many times have I found you on the edge of it? *How many times did I pull you back?*"

Sean's breathing was harsh and ragged now. As he slowly lost control, he simultaneously chipped away at my heart, taking piece by piece with him.

"Every time," I said numbly, "except one."

Sean met my eyes, his fueled with all of the emotion I was losing. "He is a coward! He lies until he gets what he wants, and even then, he doesn't know when to quit! How many more people have to die because of *Beau fucking Moiré*?" Sean was pacing now, his boots cutting into the sand with every sharp movement. "What has he done to you?" he demanded, his fingers curling in at his sides as he went over the edge. "What *the hell* has Moiré done to win your loyalty to him over me? Lie to you? Threaten you? *Sleep with you?*"

I opened my mouth to speak, then closed it tightly, stung.

Sean's eyes widened, shock replacing anger entirely for one split second, only for his anger to return ten-fold.

"You've got to be *kidding* me!" Sean bared his teeth and unclipped a device at his belt, right next to his gun. Before he lifted it to his lips, he said to Jax, "Find Beau Moiré and kill him. Now!"

"No!" I shouted, striding forward to try and stop the soldier from leaving. Before I could reach him as he turned, however, I felt a hand shove me to the ground with a force that rattled me backwards.

Sean stood over me, his face red-hot. He pressed a button on the side of the walkie and snarled, "Brian."

There was a pause, then a voice replied, "Sean?"

My pulse spiked and then dropped all in the same beat.

"Report to the southwestern corner of the base."

The man on the line replied affirmatively. My elbows gave in and I struggled to keep my body from lying flat against the sand. My strength was drained. Something was very, very wrong.

Sean confirmed it with the look on his face. Startlingly, it held only a sliver of satisfaction as time passed slow and fast all at once. The rest was laden with a slight regret I would have recognized anywhere.

I wanted to jump to my feet, to clamber however possible to my knees and to get as far away from this spot as I could. But somehow, without anyone restricting me this time, I was entirely subdued. My heart was pounding faster and louder than it ever had before, so much that my breathing picked up and I suddenly feared that I was about to go into shock.

Sean's eyes were lost, his fingers tapping the walkie he'd replaced at his side. Would he cancel the demand? Get me to sanctuary as he'd promised? Or was this man coming to deliver me a death sentence at Sean's order?

Somehow, it hadn't sounded like an order given from a soldier with a higher rank. It sounded like a request from someone he knew quite well. Someone who took it with the grace of an officer that had been in the ranks too long to recognize soldier from officer from ally. Or perhaps, a title much worse than any of the three.

Steel-toed boots scraped across the unearthed

clay of the outskirts of the base. They sounded like death grinding against the teeth of its victims, sharpening its blade for the next contestant.

Before long, a soldier came into view, and with each step he took my heartbeat dropped slower and slower until I was sure it had quit. I saw nothing but his eyes. Not the tousled blondish-brown and graying hair on his head, the limp in his stride or the hard line of his mouth. Only his eyes. Emerald colored, but drastically unlike Beau's or Michael's deep tints of black that had the tendency to drown out the green whenever they were angry, or scared. Until now, I hadn't seen a difference, but there was one, a drastic one.

They were pure, solid emeralds.

They were my eyes.

11:49pm

BEAU WAS UP TO his knees in sand, hands stiff at his sides, staring straight into the barrel of a gun thinking that maybe there was no way out of it this time.

Justin, of course, was not willing to accept that.

"How did you know?" he asked, his eyes forward. Beau could see the wheels turning inside of his head as he sought to stall for time.

Captain Hunter Blain averted his eyes from Beau, though he did not remove his finger from the trigger. "Know what, Roland?"

"That the General wouldn't order everyone in Ghazni to kill you the moment we left that night."

Beau glanced sideways at his cousin, then at Blain, who appeared to be just as caught off-guard as he was by the question. Hunter Blain shifted his attention, and the aim of his gun, onto Justin. His lip curled up at the edge. "Because I was standing right next to him."

If the response caught Justin Roland by surprise, he didn't show it. "You gutless coward."

"What did you expect? That I would run to your side and spend the next two years running for my life?" Blain scoffed. "That's no life at all. No, I alerted The General of the breach that night. I warned you to be cautious with your decisions. And you chose wrong."

"Does this seem right to you?" Justin challenged.

"Easy," Blain said, taking a step towards Justin with his gun raised eye-level. "I'm not the one murdering innocents here."

"No, you've already done your fair share of that," Beau chimed in as the distant sound of gunshots rang through the air. He eyed the rooftop of a building nearby, gauging its height from the ground.

"It's sad when the number of families you've slaughtered is higher than your IQ, right Cap?" Beau remarked, egging him on. "Orders before honor, just like Gabe used to say. Too bad your partner's rotting in the ground right now."

Blain's teeth were bared, his eyes low and squinty as he visibly attempted to maintain his composure. "Watch your tongue, Moiré, before I send you to the grave without it."

Beau could tell he was pushing him close to the edge, and Justin was looking at him sideways. Beau spit on the ground at Blain's feet and drilled the nail into the coffin. "Good thing I'd still be better looking than you without one, you charred son of a bitch."

As expected, Hunter Blain snarled and shifted the aim of his gun onto Beau, his sausage-like fingers snaking between the trigger and the guard with every ounce of the ferocity Beau remembered him capable of. A millisecond before he could pull the trigger, one decisive bullet sank past his face, exploding his right ear to pieces in a gruesome shower of blood and cartilage. Justin dove in the opposite direction as he searched for the gunman on the roof of the building, his eyes eventually making contact with his brother, Matthew Roland, who was loading another one into the chamber, and who Beau had spotted a few moments before.

An array of bullets wiped the smirk off of Beau's face as he rolled to the sand and stumbled low to find cover. Justin did the same, the two finding their weapons in just enough time to see a band of soldiers cresting a nearby mound, all armed with Ak-74s. As they began to unload, peppering the area and lighting the darkening sky with a mix of smoke and dust, a siren began to sound.

Justin and Beau made eye contact, both wearing expressions laden with concern.

Hunter Blain was nowhere to be found, having fallen after Matt had missed his forehead and shot his ear clean off instead. Beau glanced up, but from where he had just been perched, Matt was gone now too.

Beau tapped his fingers on his gun, his mind racing a mile a minute as his head ached from the sharp, piercing alarm system. All around them, soldiers were closing in.

Shots fired from behind them and both Justin and Beau hit the sand at the same time. The bullets, however, soared past them in a frenzy that picked off the men who were advancing on them, one after another after another.

Except for one that hit Justin in the leg, skimming the tip of his kneecap and burning through the topmost layers of flesh like a bolt of lightning. Justin roared in pain for a few seconds as the gunfire rang out and then ceased.

Beau ventured a look behind them and, approximately twenty-five yards away, realized that Luke had fired the shots. For some maniacal reason, Beau had the urge to laugh at the absurdity of it all.

Luke hopped to his feet and jogged over to them, coughing on a billowing cloud of gunpowder. His bright blond hair was a twisted mess. "You know, for how many times I've saved your asses in the past two years, you can't help but wonder why The General doesn't try to kidnap *me*." Luke glanced at the wound in Justin's leg that had begun to bleed, his baby blue eyes alight with energy. "Geez, Justin, why are you always getting shot??"

This time, Beau did laugh, if only for a moment.

Justin gaped at him, his face as red as a tomato.

"*Are you serious?* You—! You did that on purpose!"

"What?" Luke feigned incredulity, covering his ears as if he just noticed the loud, piercing sound of the siren echoing across the grounds. "No I didn't! I was saving your life!"

"Funny how I wasn't shot until you came along!"

Beau ignored them, his eyes focused again with the inevitable expectation that more soldiers would arrive within minutes. Sliding the knife he'd grabbed into the sheath at his belt and shouldering his gun, Beau paced over to a building that appeared to be a previously emptied barracks—somehow they'd shifted from the right side of the base to the left—and put his back against the wall as he peered around the edge. Ahead, he saw nothing positive. A few seconds after the bickering ceased, Beau felt Justin and Luke's presences behind him and they caught sight of what he did.

"It's surrounded."

"What do we do?"

Beau's eyes darted around, frustrated. From his vantage point, he could see bands of soldiers flanking the communications and networking tower that Wes had aimed for after abandoning the head command center.

Despite the fact that he wanted nothing more than to fight his way in and protect him, knowing now that Wes was the organization's primary target, Beau conceded that there were just too many men congesting the area. He had to find a way to lure them out, get them to disperse, but he was having trouble thinking with the deafening wail of the siren...

All of a sudden, Luke took off running in a different direction, drawing Beau's attention and his fury. He realized, however, that Justin had turned and followed him, both sprinting with a sudden urgency that puzzled Beau, but, after several seconds and the sound of gunfire, sent him sprinting after them.

Within minutes, Beau caught sight of a valley that was slightly cut-off from the rest of the compound, only yards from the artillery field. And, crouched within it, was Matt.

The moment his eyes zeroed in, Beau breathed a sigh of slight relief that began to wither away the closer he got, replaced by a pang of adrenaline that kicked up instantly.

For, on the other side of the vantage, facing two tall men garbed in D79 camouflage, was Leah.

It took everything in him not to burst forward and slit the men's throats.

Grudgingly, Beau ducked down beside the others who were eyeing the situation with distaste, a solemn look of uncertainty on each of their faces, concerned. What startled him wasn't the look Matt gave him once he eyed Beau and the others' arrival, nor was it the silence that pervaded the group or the fact that the siren had all of a sudden stopped, intensifying all three.

What startled Beau was the way in which Matt was poised with his gun oddly in his hands, rather than in the air aimed at the men who were obviously threatening Leah's life.

At a second glance, Beau realized who was in

front of her.

Sergeant Sean Collins, the organization's newest recruit.

"Matt, Sean's not a threat to her, but I want you to aim your gun on that other soldier," Beau said quietly, pointing. When Matt didn't respond or shift his position, Beau insisted, "Matt, I don't want her out there blind with an enemy three steps away."

Again, nothing.

"*Matt.*"

Finally, Matt lowered his head for a long moment and then looked Beau square in the eyes. "I can't."

Beau frowned. "What the hell do you mean you can't? It's—"

"You don't get it, Beau. That's not just a soldier." Matt returned his eyes to the man in uniform. His face, like that of the others once they had also found out the terrible truth, was as solemn as the day Raymond had died.

"That's Major Brian Venn," Matt said.

Beau's heart stopped beating.

"That's Leah's father."

11:59pm

"HELLO, LEAH," HE SAID.

My throat was as dry as the burnt air fused with

acrid smoke and the bitter taste of gunpowder. As the world around me erupted into chaos, my heart was simultaneously battling its own version of Hell that left me incapable of sound reason or solid emotion.

"Leah," he said again, but I hardly heard him this time. Everything had slipped away from me—pain, confusion, anger, fear. Even the ability to comprehend what was directly in front of me, footsteps away, vanished. My head, like my heart, was empty.

"Leah Rae Venn."

And then it all came back one harsh syllable at a time.

Sight. Smoke danced all around, but I saw him clearly. He stood with his feet set measuredly apart, shoulders squared and his uniform, adorned with gleaming silver strikingly bright in the moonlight that was fading behind the ever-darkening clouds. A light in the darkness. He was the picture of strength and beauty of age.

Sound. "Listen to me," he said, his voice low compared to the gunshots and clambering that was happening around us, but his words drilled their way into my ears, through my brain and right back out again, distorting into a distant memory that somehow didn't seem to match this one.

Confusion and chaos at the sudden realization that this wasn't a fallacy but a reality. My breath was ascending as blood rushed its way through my body attempting to bring life back that had been lost but only seemed to amplify my injuries and nothing else— leaving me bruised, scarred and weak within my body that was slowly giving in to a form of panic I had never known in this lifetime and, therefore, had no idea how to control.

Major Brian Francis Venn took a step forward, his pure emerald eyes a mirror for my own, though bearing a different reflection that I was too terrified to witness. He took another step forward and then stopped, just out of reach.

"I'm not your enemy," he said. "I'm your father."

I had the urge to run, to fight, to cry and to melt right where I was standing, all at the same time. Instead, I was frozen amidst the frenzy of active capabilities that ultimately left me motionless as his words multiplied in my head, attempting to break through, and failing.

Like all of the years I tried to break through to my mother, distant and alone, and had failed.

I'm not your enemy. I'm your father.

I'm not your enemy. I'm your father.

I'm not your enemy. I'm your father.

I lost all association with either of the words. Enemy. Father.

Beside him, Sean looked as broken and lost as I was, standing as still as a toy soldier. And when the bombs began to go off around us, he fell like one, too.

11:59pm

BEAU WAS SHAKING his head, adamantly trying to comprehend as the weight of the situation fell onto him. "That's not possible, her father was killed, years ago. Why would he send word back that he was dead if he were actually alive? Unless..."

Matt and Justin shared a look. "Unless he had no choice," Justin said, his mouth formed into a decisive line. "Instead of erasing his existence the way they tried to do to us, maybe The General thought it would be easier, more believable this way. Killed in the line of duty in the middle of a war. No cover story necessary."

"But what is the coincidence he'd be here tonight?"

"It's no coincidence. The General's playing us." Matt stared straight ahead. "All of us."

Beau felt a pang of emptiness he hadn't felt in a long time as he returned his gaze back onto the scene ahead, unsure how to proceed, or, honestly, if he were even capable of taking another step forward.

The unspoken question of *What do we do?* hung in the air over them for several seconds, leaving the group in an unsteady dismay.

"We need to leave. Now."

Beau, Justin, Matt and Luke all turned abruptly at the sound of the voice the moment they realized to whom it belonged.

Wesley Marshall stood behind them, his pants splattered with blood that didn't appear to be his own, his ever-straight golden locks twisted atop his head, partially covering eyes that were simultaneously wild and calm, speaking as if he knew precisely what the others had been thinking.

He opened his mouth to speak again, his lips framing the words *the bomb is set,* when the ground several yards behind him exploded into a new cloud of dirt, dust and debris that shook each and every member of their team. Another explosion erupted fifty yards down, followed by another and another and another, all running along the lengths of the fence surrounding the base.

In its wake, each bomb tore deep down through the earth, leaving an unsurpassable valley that, Beau realized, was sealing the perimeter at each and every pass—the look of shock on Wes's face reinforced the knowledge that this, at least, wasn't part of their plan.

We're out of time, Beau thought, turning back to find Leah, Sean and Major Brian Venn nowhere in sight as the central building of the base—the communications and networking tower that *was* their target—shook like an earthquake, erupted like a volcano and sent sand and shrapnel flying like shooting stars that lit every surface in the Middle Eastern heat, ablaze.

LET THEM PLAY

D79 Headquarters
Ghazni, Afghanistan
12:00 Midnight

"ZARANJ IS BURNING, GENERAL," Aziz Hassan said solemnly.

His pale face never looked so cracked, worn and aging before, The General thought to himself. Aziz looked troubled, angry, scared and, above all, shocked beyond compare.

The General felt none of those things.

"What would you have me do, my old friend?" The General asked kindly, turning to face the floor-to-ceiling window directly behind his desk at one of his many offices in Ghazni. Outside, rain crashed against the dark glass, some drops splattering, others breaking and sliding down and, still others, keeping form. And yet none of them were able to pierce through even a section of the glass no matter how hard they fell. The General smiled. "Snuff out the fire?"

Aziz did not respond. His legs were trembling the slightest bit, his wrinkled fingers stroking the lengths of his silver beard frantically.

"Perhaps you could—"

"Perhaps I could fly to Zaranj, or catch a train, or a bus, or walk. Perhaps I could send every branch of this organization that has been bestowed upon me into battle against a group of three, four, five, six children with petty pistols and hand grenades. Perhaps I could send a drone strike that would draw every media station on the east and west coast of the United States and Europe to our doorstep. Perhaps, perhaps."

The General turned back around slowly, eyes hard once more. "Or perhaps I could let this spark of flame snuff itself out, in time."

Aziz bowed his head apologetically. "Forgive me, my General. It's just…all those men…"

"Men die," The General said shortly, turning away. "And men live. But, as I've said time after time after time, my very old friend, these are *not* men. They are children. They play, and then they lose."

"Yes, General."

"So, what shall our orders be?"

"Let them play," Aziz said, bowing his head in surrender.

"Let them play," The General agreed, his steely smile returning as he studied the water droplets' inevitable defeat. "That is, after all, what pawns are designed to do."

PART FOUR

INFERNO

"I loved her. With every breath in my lungs and every strength in my bones, yes, I loved her.

But the problem when a man loves a woman is that, unlike the antithesis, vulnerabilities mean so much more. Women live for love. Men can only die for it.

For Rya, I would've left the organization that you will come to know. I would've broken every vow, every promise that kept me in Ghazni—the City of Hell. I would've died for her. I would've, and did, kill for her.

And, in return, she did what any reasonable woman would've done in her shoes, if given the chance. She fell in love with my brother, and then she broke his heart, too.

I will say it a thousand times if that's what it takes for people in the future to listen, to learn this lesson of the past.

Loyalty is *everything,* and nothing.

All at once.

July 1, 2018
Two months after The Breach
Location: Ghazni
Entry: Eight

TO THE LAST SHOT

Zaranj, Afghanistan

BEAU WAS ON THE ground, his ears ringing.

The first and worst part about opening his eyes was the sandstorm that struck him like a wave of fresh salt, burning every surface of his exposed skin—the cuts in his long-sleeved shirt, the tear in his pants that was just below the right knee, the back of his neck and his entire face. The second was the fact that he had been knocked so far and so hard on his back that every breath he drew was suddenly painful.

The third was sitting up to find Justin on his back beside him, eyes closed with a piece of metal sticking out of his left thigh, and no one else in sight.

Grunting loudly, Beau slid his feet under him and got to his knees, his legs trembling though he couldn't figure out why. A quick once-over told him that he hadn't been shot, scraped or struck by anything that could've caused the sort of lethargy he felt now, but it dragged him down almost as much as the fear for his cousin picked him back up and kept him going again.

Beau assessed the wound in Justin's leg. Despite the size of the piece of metal, there wasn't much blood and he didn't appear pale as if he'd lost a lot, either. Justin's eyes were closed and his breathing was shallow, but to Beau's relief, he was alive.

Beau pressed his forehead against Justin's chest and took a breath. Lifting his head, he surveyed the area, hoping to find Matt, Wes or Luke who could help him carry Justin to a less-exposed area, but there was nothing but bodies and the distant sound of footfall. Two buildings—barracks, perhaps—had been struck by debris from the explosion of the organization's control tower, so he had some cover until the rest of the soldiers who'd survived came looking for him ready for a firefight. Besides, he was in the section of the base that sloped down into a slight valley, more secluded, having followed the others to where Matt had been, and Leah.

At the thought of her, Beau's pulse picked up a beat and gave him the energy to get to his feet. It wasn't that he'd forgotten her; his fear and frustration at not being able to protect her while they were so dangerously close to the enemy was a battle he knew he couldn't win. Beau channeled it, instead, into determination and strength to stand and search for a way to get his wounded cousin out.

Once Justin was safe, then he'd be free to find Leah and silence anyone who stood in his way. Especially—

Blain.

The soldier stood directly ahead of him, blocking Beau's view of the artillery range that was visible in the distance as if he were its guard dog, and a feral one at that. Hunter Blain's ear had been poorly patched with a piece of his uniform, which was also ripped and dirt-covered, but blood still seeped from the wound Matt had inflicted, cascading down the right side of his face where it stained his desert-colored uniform. Beneath his scarred face was a look of pure hatred. If death had a face, Beau mused, it would've looked a little something like that.

And for the third time tonight, and the first night in a while, Beau was absolutely terrified.

Blain was armed with no weapons, but he charged forward with a ferocity that said he wouldn't have used them even if he did. Beau twisted out of the way just in time, but Hunter kicked his foot out and clipped him in the shin hard enough to knock him off his feet again. Beau hit the sand and rolled as his attacker advanced on him without hesitation, wailing a fist straight for Beau's face that he barely dodged. Beau rolled several feet down the sloped terrain, losing sight of Justin and Hunter both until the latter jumped over the embankment and followed him.

Good, Beau thought to himself as he struggled to his feet. He knew that he had to keep Hunter away from Justin as long as possible, but Beau also knew he was fading fast. This fight would be the last bit of strength left in him if he didn't end it swiftly.

Beau breathed with precision as he circled Hunter in the valley, keeping his focus split between the enemy before him and his cousin's limp body that lay at the top. Hunter didn't waste a second of the diversion, lunging forward with wrists crossed like a club that he brought down forcefully over Beau's head.

Beau staggered for a second before he fell. Hunter dug his boot under the sand beneath him and flipped Beau's body over with ease. Beau smacked his head off the dirt again, his vision blurring for one split-second that was enough time for Hunter to grab him by the shirtfront and lift him entirely off the ground. Defenseless, Beau instantly began to panic. And, like a bear trapped in a fence, it was the worst thing Blain could've done.

Instinct drove him to action and a new bolt of energy coursed through him, though he knew it would be short-lived. Beau dug his thumbs into the shattered mess that was Blain's ear, causing the soldier to bring his head down fast. Anticipating the reaction, Beau met Hunter's head with his right knee. As jaw collided with bone, both soldiers toppled to the ground. One in pain, one in a desperate frenzy for escape.

Beau searched with his eyes and his hands for his weapon, or any weapon for that matter, but the wind had picked up and it meant that everything had been covered by layers of shifting sand. Beau knew he was running out of options and time. He also knew he could not beat Blain with sheer strength.

If he didn't find a weapon, and soon, he would die right where he was and the sand would cover him like it covered everything else eventually. His Colt, Justin's M-16, Justin himself—

Suddenly, Beau jumped to his feet and made a mad dash for the top of the valley he'd fallen into. As he crested the mound and caught sight of his cousin, still lying unconscious on his back, Beau dove to the sand just as Blain came barreling after him. It was his last move, and as Beau dug under the sand beneath Justin's body, which was twice the size of Beau's thin frame and only half the size of Hunter's hulk-like build, his fingers made contact with the hilt of a knife at the same time Hunter flew through the air like a missile braced for impact. Beau had just enough time to snake his fingers out from under Justin's weight before Hunter crashed down on top of him.

And, consequently, on top of the knife that was still crusted with the blood of Division soldiers like Captain Hunter Blain.

Beau had a hold of the knife with two hands that were caving in as Hunter jerked wildly, blood dripping from his lips from his inability to breathe as the knife had undoubtedly punctured one of his lungs. The weight prevented Beau from breathing either, and while Hunter took longer and longer to die from asphyxiation as he drowned in his own blood, Beau felt his life slipping away simultaneously. He had used every bit of strength left to lift his hands to his chest in the right place just in time to cause the right amount of damage that he had no back-up plan, no escape route to save his own life.

Beau's head hit the sand at the same time that Hunter's body gave its final jerk and fell limp. Because he was balanced on a body that was much smaller than his, Hunter slid off with a *thud*.

Dead.

Minutes, maybe hours passed before Beau came-to.

He didn't know which. The first breath he drew caused him to choke, bringing him upright despite the effort it took. The sky was a hazy gray that matched his thought-processes, and several buildings Beau could discern in the distance were on fire.

"Easy, Beau," a voice said.

It took him a moment to realize it was the man who'd, shockingly, saved him not once, but three times this night.

"Matt," Beau choked out gruffly. He glanced to his left and saw Hunter's lifeless body, then to his right and saw Justin, who still hadn't risen since the blast. Panic brought Beau out of the rest of the haze he felt as he dropped the bloody knife and grabbed Matt by the shoulder. His shirt, too, was ripped and looked slightly singed.

"Help me get him up," Beau said, with difficulty he tried to hide. Matt saw straight through him.

"First we need to get you up," Matt said, pushing him back down. "Lay back and breathe steady. You're wheezing."

Beau resisted the urge to shove Matt off of him and tell him there was no time, but he knew he didn't have the energy to be stubborn. Beau lowered himself back down, grimacing, and took several deep breaths until his chest didn't feel like it was caving in on him anymore. He felt far from well, but it would have to do. They were farther still from safety, and now his team had been separated yet again.

Matt didn't fight him this time as he sat up and then got to his feet. Matt stood as well, carrying the M-16 Justin must have dropped, which was slung across his back. He did, however, put his hand out when Beau took a step toward Justin, who twitched.

"I can handle this, he seems to be on the brink of stirring and I can get him out of the base before more soldiers come," Matt said with confidence. He reached behind him and pulled out a familiar weapon that brought a wave of relief to Beau.

Matt handed Beau his Colt and nodded toward the artillery range. "Wesley and Luke went that away, after Leah."

Beau's pulse picked up and so did his anger. He nodded thanks to his oldest cousin, who bent down and lifted Justin's head. His eyes were open now and his chest rose and fell with definitive motion that told Beau he would be okay.

It was a fate that Hunter Blain didn't have the fortune of sharing.

As Beau pocketed his weapon and the knife that was still coated in fresh blood—the blood of a man who, like Gabriel Schrader, had once been his friend, until the organization had driven a wedge between them, too—he couldn't help but picture soldier after soldier, man after man, dead on the ground like their Captain before them.

It was a gruesome, ungodly image, but it was the fuel that kept him moving when he didn't think he could press on. That, and the inclination that the battle had only just begun.

Honor and peace only go so far, the voice in the back of Beau's mind whispered, though it held no trace of Raymond's tone.

I'm going to find you, Leah. I'm going to find my

brothers. And then I'm going to burn this place to the ground until there's nothing left.

✦   ✦   ✦

HOLD ON

Zaranj, Afghanistan

HE WAS DRAGGING ME. My feet scraped off of every rocky surface they touched, powerless against his pull like I had been the evening that D79 soldiers broke into Beau's house in California and yanked me away from the house, away from Wes who I'd grown close to and then taken a bullet for, all those weeks ago.

He had me by my wrists, his thin, grimy fingers fitting perfectly into the blood-crusted rivets that had been worked into my skin from the ropes that reminded me of endless captivity—of the frustration and anger that powered me to stand up to Michael, over and over until he beat me back down again and again.

Jax had come out of nowhere and seized me amidst the chaos of the explosions—one, two? I didn't know how many times the ground had shaken and the sky seemed to open up to allow the ringing of the insurmountable blasts to unleash upon the earth or who, exactly, had orchestrated them. All I knew was that my team was suffering, this place was quickly descending into Hell, and I was being dragged right down with it.

I tried digging my feet into the dirt to stop him, but the shifting sand only moved aside and alerted him of my rebellion. Jax would twist my body around until I was forced to quit. A quick glance at my waist told me that I had lost my belt, to which my knife had been clipped. I didn't need to search the grounds to know that Beau was nowhere near, nor was anyone else who could or would help me. I was alone. I had no weapons, no plan and no energy to devise one.

It was pointless.

"Defending your life is pointless?"

I opened my eyes in shock at the voice only to realize it was in my head, etching itself into my brain as if from a not-so-distant reality. A reality where Michael Moiré was taunting me, rioting me, in Ghazni, Afghanistan—the place I'd come to know as the real Hell, the same place I had somehow, miraculously, survived.

Hold onto that, he'd said, that very first night. *It just might save you when the world starts to turn on you.*

Digging my heels into the sand, I quit fighting back and, instead, let my body go limp. The soldier pulling me, Jax, reeled at the sudden dead weight, his first reaction being to jerk against my wrists to continue forward movement. As he did so, I twisted my forearms as hard as I could and pulled backwards, counteracting the move while I anchored myself against the ground. Sweat had built up on my forehead long ago; it fell in waves from the heat and the exertion.

Caught off-guard by my sudden revolt, Jax was forced to drop my hands and I fell to the sand, hard, my face smacking against a patch of stone and a thick layer of sand collected on the surface of my skin.

Before he could grab me again, I rolled over and got to my feet in order to face him. It took more strength than it should have.

And, only feet away, Jax seemed much older, taller and even stronger than I had originally pegged him for when I had first caught sight of him, at Sean's side. Luckily, he had no guns at his waist, but he did have a knife sheathed at his side, a knife he undoubtedly was well-trained with and would prove just as deadly as a gun to an experienced hand.

"Experience means nothing when you have drive."

"What's your plan, girl?" Jax said, his accent thick yet just distinguishable, his eyes easily catching mine as they rested on the knife for one brief second. "You are alone."

"So are you," I said, momentarily caught off-guard by the fact that I had just opened my mouth and challenged a soldier. Blood pumped fast beneath my skin, an adrenaline that I wasn't ready for, but that came nonetheless.

His eyebrows lifted a tiny degree. "You want a fight?" He reached his gloved hand down and unsheathed a knife, his eyes never leaving mine. So he saw the fear that flashed across my face. "You're scared. Good." Jax lifted the knife up to eye level. "You should be. You fight, you die. That is how this ends."

With that last syllable, the soldier erased the

distance between us in a matter of seconds and had his knife slashing at me in the next. I took the only avenue available—backwards—and lost my footing as the terrain sloped down into a ten-foot-wide grade amidst another of Zaranj's countless valleys. I couldn't catch myself as I flipped and rolled to the bottom, my arms cutting against several sharp patches of earth, until I finally crash-landed, again, on my face.

Spitting sand from my mouth, I looked up to see him standing over me, his lips curved into a tight smirk that was all too familiar.

You're weak. Vulnerable. But you have potential, Michael had told me, wearing the same look. *If only you knew how to pick and choose your battles.*

I felt the blood dripping from my lips as I raised myself onto my hands and knees with great difficulty. For some reason, my body wasn't responding to me as well it needed to. My arms were shaking, and I could hear Jax saying something to me, but it didn't register in my head. Something else did.

"Surely my brother must've taught you something? Come on. Fight back."

I wiped a hand across my mouth and studied the blood-and-dirt-crusted streak it left behind, feeling my emotions drain away at the thought of Michael, of Beau, of Sean, of Major Brian Venn.

Jax reached down and lifted me by the front of my shirt, tearing it slightly as I fought to wrestle my way free. When his fingers lost their grip, he kicked at my ankles, knocking my feet out from under me so that, when I fell, I landed square on my back. Instead of pain, the same frustration and anger I'd gotten accustomed to with Michael burned in its place.

Reaching behind me at the object pricking my right shoulder, I clutched a rock in my palm and whipped it at the soldier's face. It smacked him in the jaw, the hit catching him by surprise that I capitalized on, using his backward momentum to wrap my legs around the backs of his knees and pull as hard as I could from my vantage, bringing him down the same way he'd brought me down.

He recovered faster than I, however, and within seconds, Jax was back up on his feet, a nasty scowl on his face. I jumped up as well, several scrapes on my legs slowing me so that I had only milliseconds to dodge the knife he slashed at me, but I did and it missed my throat by a mere hair's length.

He didn't stop. Jax lunged forward again with a strength and a ferocity I couldn't match. The knife made contact with my body this time, slicing a six-inch gash across my abdomen that stopped me in my tracks. Jax used the opportunity to jerk me forward, wrapping his left arm around my neck and pulling me tight against his chest to the point that I was securely pinned, left with only the slightest room to inhale. I scratched at his arm that held me, but it didn't seem to faze him. He tightened it against my throat, and then I couldn't breathe.

I kicked back at him frantically, my body going into a shock-like state that made me want to flail every appendage I had, but I knew his stance was too firm to be broken. Jax would strangle me until I lost consciousness, then he would probably slit my throat or drag me to someone who would. It was over.

No. I couldn't accept that because, for the first time, I didn't want this. Next to the bullets I'd endured and coming as close to death as I had put myself on the beach in California, all of the moments I'd had with Beau and the memories I'd made with Sean overshadowed all of that and I realized, for the very first time, I didn't want to die.

"Hold onto that." The electrifying beat of Michael's voice and his words replaced the consistency of my own as I took my last breath. *"Defiance."*

I couldn't dismiss the panic, but I pushed it to the very back of my mind that was starting to become clouded. My vision blurred as I started to gasp, but just before my eyes could water, I focused on his free hand, the hand in which he held his knife—it was bloodied from where he'd cut me. I watched as a thin line of scarlet dripped from the tip of the knife, to its hilt, to the palm of his hand where it had already begun to pool, as if in slow motion.

Channeling every ounce of strength I had left in reserve, I locked my wrists together and slammed them forward against his hand—not the one holding mc against him as he may have anticipated, but the one that held the blood-soaked knife. With the speed and intensity of the blow, Jax lost control of the knife for one split second, which caused his other hand to loosen its grip on my throat enough for me to take a deep breath. As he tried to catch it before it fell, the surface of the blade and his hand were too slippery and the knife dug itself into the dirt at his feet with a resounding *thud.*

He didn't make a move for it as I expected, but just before he could tighten his grip on me again, I used my second breath to clamp my jaws down on his forearm and bite into the skin as hard as I could until I tasted blood. With searing pain in his eyes and on the tip of his tongue with the curses that followed, Jax was finally forced to release me entirely, but not before kicking me in the side.

As I rolled to the ground, I pressed my knees tightly together at the right time and place as I had done in Ghazni and then turned over and got to my feet all in one fluid motion that jarred my senses awake again. Jax had recovered also, his arm sporting a large ring of blood and teeth marks and his expression lit with shock, anger and frustration as he eyed the knife—his knife—that I now held tightly in the palm of my lowered right hand.

While I envisioned every sort of bitter word crossing his mind, I heard only two in mine.

"Do better."

This time when the soldier came at me, I moved forward instead of back, choosing to counter his moves as they came by recalling where his weaknesses were and applying my strengths like puzzle pieces clashing together. I had a weapon, a sharp and deadly one and he didn't, nor did he have every inch of his skin concealed and protected from the blade. I was injured, probably worse than I thought, but so was he. He was faster, stronger, more aggressive and more experienced in combat, but I was smaller and more agile.

When he lunged forward with ferocity, I evaded

him with patience that his emotionally clouded judgment didn't afford him. The more we danced, the angrier he became and the more his precision waned. And I finally understood what Michael had done to me as I saw the roles reversed.

At that moment, the image of my mother pleading for my father not to leave her and go off to the war that we were fighting, here and now, forced its way into the forefront of my brain that I fought equally hard to erase. When it went, so did my sadness.

"Do better."

Jax sent a fist at my jaw and clipped me in the nose instead, knocking me off my feet with a powerful force that left my butt bruised and my nose dripping a steady stream of red. I ignored the fact that I was now bleeding profusely between my stomach and my nose and spun to the side as he tried to stomp down on my chest, cutting him just below the knee as I rolled where he had just been standing and slid the knife across his tan skin as I went.

I saw tears slide down the same suntanned skin of a nineteen-year-old boy as he held the girl who had just found out she'd become an orphan a boy that had become a soldier and, in the process, lost the sense of compassion that left me now.

"Do better."

Jax didn't bat an eyelash at the finger-length scratch across his leg, instead choosing to rush me with his arms out to prevent any sort of evasion. It worked, and I fell to the ground as he fell on top of me, his thick hands pressing hard against my shoulders, pinning me.

"Do better." Michael's voice was a commanding shout that drowned out every emotion my heart begged me to feel, erasing every splinter of the pain that had created a web-like safety net around my conscience and kept me from losing myself in it all. For the first time, I fought back against so much more than a mere man threatening me.

I slashed my knife at his face, missing the skin by a pinprick but causing him to turn his head to the side to avoid it. At the same time, I drove my knee as hard as I could up into his groin and pushed his upper body so that, instead of ducking forward the way men tended to do after getting hit in their manhood and crushing me further into the ground, he lost his position and fell backwards and to the side. When my legs were finally freed, I kicked my left foot forward and smashed his chin with the toe of my boot. His head fell back against the dirt, and I lifted the knife in my hand, ready to finish what I had started. No hesitations, no remorse. I knew that if this man had been in my position, he wouldn't have given it a second thought.

Yet somehow, for some reason, I raised the knife to Jax's throat and then dropped it to the sand beside him.

I was on my knees, staring at the limp but alive body of the soldier when I felt the barrel of another's gun against the back of my head. It was relentless. There was no fight left in me when Sean pulled me to my feet, his silhouette enclosed by the shadow of another man, another soldier whose identity hardly mattered.

You see, Jax was someone's son, the fruit of a father's hard work and the source of some mother's pride, despite his misguidance with the organization. Sean was also misguided and loved by many, not only for his compassion but his consistency and the fact that he was a genuinely good person, most times. But the man standing behind me was nothing.

He was no one's father, just as I was no one's daughter and hadn't been for a long time.

DEATH AND DESTRUCTION

BOTH SEAN AND MAJOR Brian Venn's guns were trained on me when I heard the subtle *click* of a loaded pistol that was equally close.

"Drop it, Sean."

I bit my lip at the sound of his voice. It felt like days since I'd seen or heard Beau speak; his tone was devoid of emotion, save for one—authority. And I had every urge to run to him, but knew that to do so would spark something that couldn't be finished without shedding even more blood—blood that over half of the people in this standoff I was tied to.

"That's Leah, Sean," Beau said sternly. "Your family. I'm asking you to drop the gun and let her go."

Sean had his arm around mine, so that when he turned, I spun with him and caught sight of the new arrival—*arrivals*. To my relief, Beau was not alone, but stood shoulder to shoulder with Luke, who had an Ak-47 trained on Major Venn just as Beau's Colt was aimed at Sean beneath a mask of control that made him look deadly.

Sean evidently thought the same. He jerked his chin at Beau's gun and at Luke. "That sounds less like a request and more like an order. I wasn't aware that I answered to terrorists."

"You've been answering to terrorists, you just don't know it yet," Beau replied flatly. "I'm not your enemy, Sean. Neither is she. You do know that."

"Sean…" Major Venn started to say, speaking for the first time.

"You're right," Sean said, addressing only Beau as if they were the only two in the vicinity. "She's not my enemy." He released me and shifted the aim of his gun onto Beau, drawing Luke's aim onto him and Major Venn's onto Luke. Sean seemed highly unperturbed by the shift. "You are," he said, with a half-smile that reeked of everything but the Sean I knew.

Beau kept his eyes onto Sean's, though I could tell he was growing nervous. I took a step towards the encounter, trying to draw as little attention as possible. Beau clenched his jaw.

"What did you honestly expect to accomplish by coming here tonight, Moiré?" Sean continued, his eyes darkening the slightest bit. "Besides handing my cousin over to me, where she belongs. Thank you for that, by the way. I'll see to it that she gets treated like a decent human being rather than a punching bag and a sex toy for you and your gang," he said harshly, spitting on the ground in front of Beau.

"Stop it, Sean," I snapped, seeing the hard line of Beau's mouth that was thinning by the second.

"Look at her," Sean continued as if I hadn't

291

spoken. Keeping his gun forward, he wrapped his fingers around my wrist and pulled me in front of him. I knew that, with that one simple distraction, Beau or Luke could've put a bullet between his skull. And I could see plainly the frustration on Beau's face at having to stand back and take every insult Sean threw at him, knowing that he could end this, right now.

Sean seemed to know that, too.

"Bruises, scars, blood," he scoffed, gesturing at my body while fully utilizing the spotlight to inch farther away from his opponents, towards the fractured buildings that ran perpendicularly behind us and were smoking. "Is that what you call love? Security?"

"Your men have put their hands on your cousin more times than I ever have," Beau said brusquely. He gestured at the soldier, Jax, who was still lying on the ground, unconscious but covered in my blood. "Proof obviously means nothing to you, and you've clearly done a wonderful job of protecting her since she's been in your care."

"Every word that comes out of your mouth means nothing to me," Sean replied, equally as heated. He took another step back. "I did what I had to do to keep my family safe and I'll do whatever it takes to keep her away from the likes of you. Count on it."

"Then you can count on disappointment," Luke said abruptly as he matched Sean step for step, "because she's coming with us."

Sean spared him a brief, irritated look that lasted only a moment. Before Sean could rebut Luke's words, however, I jerked my arm out of his grip and took a step forward, drawing all of their attention.

"I can speak for myself," I snapped, glaring from one soldier to the next. "And I'll go where *I* decide."

Sean snickered at me; Luke grinned; Jax grunted from the ground as he came-to; Beau held a calculated expression as if he were trying to understand my motives, and didn't. Underneath, however, I could see the one thing that mattered from him—trust.

It was Major Brian Venn who moved first.

"Leah," he began, taking several steps towards me, gesturing at Beau and Luke. "You don't understand. These men—"

I backed up once but it was unnecessary. Beau was in front of me in an instant, having erased the distance between this man and me before anyone even had the chance to shift their guns, blocking me from his vision, but it was too late. I had seen his eyes, seen the look of desperation on his face that matched one of my only recollections of him. In my head, he was pleading for my mother to move on with her life as he had, evidently, moved on with his. I understood now. I'd just forgotten how real pain felt.

In all of my weeks with Michael, my time spent with Beau and his family, I'd come to believe that pain was a bruised leg and a bloody lip, a broken jaw and a twisted ankle and wounded pride. But I couldn't have been more wrong.

Beau took my place and faced him, and it wasn't until that moment that I stopped denying it, stopped running from the truth and acknowledged the fact that the man he faced was the same one who'd raised me until he'd decided that my mother and I weren't good enough. That he was the one who should've been there to see me graduate, to teach me which boys were right and which were wrong, to keep me safe from the world, this world, until I was ready.

Perhaps if my father had never left, Beau would have never found me and we wouldn't be standing here like this because it would have been the other way around. It *should* have been the other way around.

But it wasn't.

And before he or I could say another word, bullets rang through the air like gunshots falling from the sky and the moment ended the way it began—in complete and utter chaos.

A black helicopter with two gray stripes down the side and no other markings flew over us just then, spraying bullets as it went.

Sean backpedaled and reached the barracks building he'd been edging towards within seconds, Jax—who must've risen during the encounter—was close on his heels. Major Venn dove in the opposite direction, instead landing behind one of the stone barriers in front of the buildings that ran adjacent. I lost sight of Luke, but thought I had seen him take cover, too. The only ones who were out in the open and exposed were Beau and I, for he'd had enough time to make only one move.

Beau wove his hands around my back and ducked his head down over mine, shielding me from the gunfire that hit the earth like hail.

Miraculously, I realized that we hadn't been hit at the same time he did. Instead, the aim of the fire was at Sean, at Jax and at Major Brian Venn—all soldiers of D79. In the distance, I could see other helicopters similar to this one, all unmarked, that were firing down on Division soldiers that had taken cover a second too late. The smoke that had scattered and dispersed from the explosions was billowing now. Thick black clouds were forming over Zaranj.

"Beau!" Luke's voice was barely audible amidst the firefight. It came from behind us where he was shielded behind a guard tower, aggressively motioning for us to get the hell out of there.

Beau spun and took me by the hand, and we ran as fast as we could but it wasn't fast enough.

From above, a man inside the helicopter fired what must have been an RPG. Soldiers that had fled to the tower next to Luke jumped out of the window just as the missile made contact with the stone exterior. I caught sight of Luke's wide eyes before the building burst at its core, weakening the thirty-foot-tall structure until it caved in and toppled forward.

Beau released my hand and grabbed me by the forearm instead, using the full force of his upper body to shove me in the direction of Luke and out of the path of the crippling tower. My boot caught in the sand and I rolled several feet before I came to a stop just as the stone collided with the ground in one loud *boom*. Sand sprayed in my eyes but I kept them peeled, frantic to find Beau and make sure he hadn't just sacrificed himself for me.

Relief flooded through me when I lifted my head and saw him on his back beside me, his fingers touching my wrist the slightest bit.

Our eyes met and I could see him, see the pain in his eyes of what he'd gone through this night to fight to where we were now.

"Don't let me go," I said.

"I won't," he promised.

+   +   +

WYATT VENDELLE SAW EVERYTHING.

From where he stood, atop a particularly high mound of terrain directly opposite the main entrance-side of the military compound in Zaranj, Afghanistan, shielded from below, Vendelle saw buildings collapse and men die. He saw bombs burst and bullets rain down like a prelude to the storm that was quickly moving in.

Above all, he saw the beginning of victory amidst a necessary tragedy that the world would soon become aware, and that reminded him of the Japanese attack on Pearl Harbor in 1941.

Now, too, awakes the sleeping giant, he mused.

Vendelle had watched as the rogue unit Yankee Two walked into the trap set by Division-7-9, knowing full-well what the consequences of doing so, and the implications, would be. He did not, however, anticipate the level of destruction that would ensue.

That was an added bonus.

He'd watched as his men flooded in at the midnight hour and finished what Yankee Two had started. The helicopters that still soared over Zaranj were a deep shade of grey that had undoubtedly confused the soldiers below who, in their final moments, had deduced they were aid from The General.

How tragic. He smiled.

In particular, Vendelle had watched as Beau Moiré fought through soldier after soldier to find the woman everyone had come to know as his greatest weakness. Vendelle, however, saw only his strength.

Maybe that was why he'd called off the helicopter that was tasked with shooting down the younger Moiré, despite the threat he'd made to the man's older brother that he would be killed tonight. Maybe it was the stupidity that drew Beau into conflict after conflict, or the resiliency that continuously got him out of it.

Maybe it was the blood that coursed through Beau Moiré's veins that looked a little like Alexander.

Maybe it was something else entirely, or nothing at all.

Men with power need no justification, he reminded himself, before turning away from what remained of Zaranj—a place, like many others under the control of Division-7-9, he knew all too well.

BEAU LIFTED HIMSELF TO his feet once he

determined the area was clear, and I could see how much effort it took. I brushed the sand from my face and stood to my full height, which was several inches below his. But my vantage was just as terrible. The sight that lay before us was horrifying, and it sickened me to the core knowing that we, alone, had caused all of this.

Destruction. At almost every angle, buildings made of wood were burning and smoke clouds were thick from the tattered remains of stone encampments that had sparked the flames. Few structures had actually withstood the bombings, and the subsequent air raid that we still had no idea who had orchestrated had demolished the rest.

Death. Everywhere the eye could see, men in dessert-colored camouflage lay dead or dying. There were women, too, though they were few and far between here. Zaranj was known for its violence and volatile missions in the Middle East that called for male soldiers. But every so often, you could look and see the face of somebody's daughter among the men.

"It wasn't supposed to be like this."

I didn't need to look to my left to see the tortured look in Beau's eyes as he spoke. His voice was weighted down with every dead soldier in sight.

"This is war, boy."

Beau and I both jumped at the sound of the voice, which was close, yet distant. I started to move towards it, but Beau held his hand out to stop me. Up ahead, underneath the rubble of the guard tower that had fallen, I saw his tousled brown hair that was streaked with gray and, now, strands of red.

I pushed past Beau's hand and moved to stand over him. Major Brian Venn. Though I'd never actually believed this moment would come, it was something I alone had to face.

Knowing that didn't make it any easier.

"We used to wait for you." As I spoke, I stared past him because I couldn't meet his eyes with tears in mine. The world around us was chaos and fire but in that moment, my mind was somewhere else. Somewhere quiet, peaceful and sad. "She would take me by the hand and we would walk down to the shore. I'd run and splash in the waves until I lost all of my energy, and she would sit on the sand in the surf until she lost all of hers too—what little she did have. Then we would just sit there, and for a long time, I thought it was because she loved the sea, loved the crashing sound of the waves or the wind in her hair but it was none of that. She was just there. Waiting."

I could feel Beau's presence behind me, a safety net I didn't need. Bitterness washed through me like the Pacific Ocean, and with it came every emotion, every feeling I'd ever repressed.

"I stopped waiting but she never did, and I think that's what killed me the most, year after year," I said numbly. "No award or trophy or goal or accomplishment of mine could change the fact that she was always waiting for something I could never give her." I clenched my fists just then the way Beau always did to center himself, but it didn't work.

I shook my head, forcing the solid stream of tears from my lids and off of my face entirely. "And I just want to know if you ever stopped to think about that," I said with a note of finality and sadness that was fading by the second, the way it always did. "If it ever crossed your mind that you didn't just take away my father. You took away my mother, too."

For the first time since the encounter, I looked his way. To see if he would cry, or smirk, or if he was even still alive to do either.

Brian Venn was lying on his back, his face visibly pained as his lower body was being crushed beneath the rubble that he wasn't fighting against, but there was no other sign of any adverse pain. His lips were firm and unyielding. His eyes were a blank slate that had lost their emerald shine a long time ago. And that alone—the look of unfamiliarity, of numbness, is what told me that he was already gone. That my father had been gone for twelve years now. Somehow, I knew I should have expected that.

After all, I didn't expect to get answers, nor had I walked into this expecting him to say anything, really. I wasn't naïve enough to think that I could change who he was—whoever that may be—or that it would spark some sort of reconciliation for either of us for a story that was never meant to be ours.

But I couldn't say that I felt nothing when I turned away and left him for dead, shocking myself, Beau and Sergeant Sean Collins, who, I noticed, was standing several yards away, a troubled expression written all over his face. The only one who didn't seem shocked was the man on the ground who was dying all over again.

"Leah," Beau said. His tone was gentle but firm. "Your father will die if we walk away."

I nodded my head, but that didn't stop me from putting one foot in front of the other the way I should have for the last eighteen years.

The gun shot that followed, however, did.

BEAU WATCHED LEAH WALK away from her father without hesitation, thinking that she was quite possibly the strongest soldier he'd ever met. Unlike Beau, she'd said her piece—not even for him, but for herself—and had let that be enough. She didn't want revenge, or tears, or words or blood. She only wanted to be able to say what she'd been thinking since the day he'd left, to expunge that from her conscience, and move on with what little closure could allow her.

But Beau knew it was the wrong thing to do.

"Leah," he said, a pleading note to his voice as he tried to reach her. "Your father will die if we walk away."

She nodded and kept walking as if she understood, but she didn't. Not really.

Leah didn't know that she was choosing to throw away what Beau would've killed to have. That, despite all of his deception and the death he'd caused, the man underneath the stone was still her father, fifty-percent of the reason she existed in the first place, and he was alive after all these years that she thought he was dead. The memories of her mother alone were reason enough to give him the last chance that Beau believed he, or anyone, deserved.

But to do so would be to deprive Leah of the choice that was hers to make, and that's what made Beau hesitate.

And before he could act, the building adjacent to the one that had originally fallen and crushed Major Brian Venn shook with the weight of an explosive, rumbling the ground and severing what little chances Leah's father had at rescue or survival. The stone slab that pinched him beneath the pile of rubble fell the rest of the way, burying itself beneath the sand, taking everything, including his body, down with it with all of the harsh authority that belonged to the earth. Judge, jury and executioner.

Still, Leah didn't turn.

Sean, who Beau had noticed long before the encounter had ended, evidently felt the same incredulity that Beau was wrestling with, only amplified as it had been his family, too. He channeled all of the anger and frustration that was written all over his face and used it to fuel his body as he lifted the Five-Seven in his hand.

There was no time to run, and nowhere to run to. Beau didn't know whether Sean was aiming at Leah or at him. He didn't wait around to find out. Before Sean could even reach the trigger guard, Beau fired one decisive shot that knocked the gun out of his hands entirely.

Sean knelt to the ground as he slapped a hand over the wound left by the bullet that tore through the skin of his right shoulder, nicking his clavicle. Though he'd placed the bullet well with what little time he'd had, Beau cursed because he knew what he'd just done.

Sean lifted his head slowly, obviously stunned, and gave Beau a look that was sharper than a steeled edge as he clenched his teeth to suppress the pain. And from several yards ahead of him, Leah's expression was just as unfriendly because she hadn't seen Sean lift his gun in the first place, only witnessed Beau fire at her cousin.

Really can't win today.

"Let's go," Beau said as he stormed forward. After a brief pause, and a whole lot of guilt, Leah followed him reluctantly, leaving Sean still shell-shocked on his knees.

Whether she'd seen the gun at Sean's feet or simply decided to trust him, Beau wasn't sure.

He was just grateful that he didn't have to fight her, too.

LAST MAN STANDING

BEAU WAS HEADING BACK towards the place where we'd last seen Luke when the idea I'd had earlier hit me like the bullet that had just hit Sean— one that I was sure Beau fired out of necessity, but that still unsettled me, nonetheless.

"Wait," I said quickly, my breath shallow with a deep exhaustion. "I need to tell you something."

"Luke was with Wes. If we find him, we can find them and get out of here before anything else happens," Beau replied, facing forward as if he couldn't stand to look me in the eye. "And don't worry," he added solemnly. "It wasn't a critical shot."

"This isn't about that," I said, struggling to keep up. I jerked my hand out of his and stopped abruptly, hoping it would stop him, too. It didn't. Beau continued his forward movement until, finally, I snapped.

"Beau!" I shouted after him. At the strength of my volume, his pace slowed but didn't stop. Frustrated, I said, "Have you forgotten the reason we even came here tonight?"

This got his attention. Beau turned, a look of not only urgency, but exhaustion on his face that mirrored my own. "Leah, we went to the armory, it's too heavily guarded. Besides, every other structure in the base is crumbling. We're out of time."

"We never had any time," I said plainly. "But the armory isn't the only place where weapons are being held."

Beau frowned. I had his full attention now. "What do you mean?"

"When we first got into the base, Luke and I got separated and I hid behind one of the guard towers. Before he saw me, I heard Sean and his men talking over the radio to someone close by telling them that the plan was for the majority of soldiers to protect the head command center and for the military police to protect the armory with every ounce of firepower they had."

"I don't see where—?"

"You have to *have* firepower to use it, Beau," I said quickly, hoping he would see merit where I did. "If the armory is where the majority of their weapons are, they have to have an alternate place to store the ones they'd need to protect it. Think about it. The military police…"

Beau scanned the base for a long time before I saw the wheels in his head begin to turn my way. The real tell wasn't the argument I made but rather that, every twenty to thirty feet, amidst the rubble of the buildings that had toppled and sparked fire anywhere it could, one tall structure stood out after another.

"The guard towers," he said.

Somehow, most had withstood the blasts, making them the most industrial structures and the most logical place to store weapons and ammunition.

"You're right," Beau said, a renewed sense of urgency on his face. "That must be where they're keeping their lesser-defensive weapons. Semi-automatics, rifles, explosives. It wouldn't be much, but..."

"Something is better than nothing," I said, nodding, my breath steadying for the first time tonight though I knew it would be short lived.

Beau didn't have it in him to nod back at me, but I could see the approval written all over his face as he took my hand and we took off in a different direction, toward the closest standing structure in sight. It didn't take long to reach, but the amount of debris on the ground and the thick, black smoke in the air was increasing to the point that every step was unpredictable and, therefore, dangerous.

Luckily, the guard tower we came to was vacant.

Beau turned to tell me to wait here while he went to scope out the building, then hesitated. Surprisingly, instead of leaving me out here the way I knew his instinct told him to, Beau reached behind his back and pulled out a gun similar to his Colt.

"An SR22 Ruger," he said, and handed me the weapon. "Most of these buildings split off in the center and have two ladder chambers that run parallel up to the top. If there are any soldiers inside, that's where they'll be." I nodded. "First we clear the building, then we find the weapons. Do you know how to use that?"

I didn't, but I nodded.

"Are you ready?"

I was the farthest thing from ready, but again, I nodded. I could do this, right? How hard could it really be?

The old, weather-beaten door guarding the building was locked, requiring an access code that neither of us had. Beau kicked it down after two powerful swings that sent wood splintering on all sides. He had two hands on his gun when he walked through the entrance, so I copied the move, feeling ridiculous as I went, and veered right when he motioned for me to do so. The gun felt heavy in my hands, but I kept it up and somewhat straight, praying I didn't have to fumble for the trigger if a soldier did in fact approach me.

Empty. I rounded the bend Beau spoke of, inside what felt like an underground concrete bunker but was actually an above-ground stone structure that smelt so strongly of gunpowder it sent my senses flaring—but there was no one in sight. The farther I went, the more I noticed the walls were covered with ash and layered grains of sand, meaning the access point to the top must be close.

Behind another doorway, this one open, I reached the ladder that was mounted against the outer wall and looked up into the chamber that allowed what little light there was to flood in. It, too, was vacant.

"Beau?" My voice echoed off of the walls, but there was no reply. Had he mentioned where to go after this?

Having reached the end, where my choices were to either go up or back the way I'd come, I leaned back against the wall feeling terribly out of place. All of the physical strain and mental stress of being in this place fell over me just then. And for me, and my team, it had been a matter of hours. I couldn't imagine living like this—constantly surrounded by people who wanted to do you harm—the way soldiers did on a daily basis. The way Beau, and Justin and Wes did. The way Sean did, now, and my father had.

And despite what Luke had said and the way Beau made me feel, I couldn't help but agree with Sean that I wasn't a soldier. None of my actions tonight were done out of bravery, but necessity. I didn't have what it took to risk my life fearlessly, unselfishly and above all, willingly. So what was I still doing here?

I lowered my non-gun hand and smacked it back against the wall, frustrated and afraid and uncertain of what to do or where to go and how. I wasn't prepared for this, instead I'd been too occupied with finding Sean and figuring out Michael that I hadn't listened to a word that Beau or Wes had tried to tell me the day before—safety measures, emergency situations, escape tactics, offensive strategies. Nothing. The *hum* inside my head stopped, and that's when I heard the faint sound of voices.

I raised my gun back up with clumsy inaccuracy before I realized the voices were coming from behind me. I pressed my hand flat against the wall again, curious. A third chamber?

Adrenaline hit me as the two voices, neither of

which sounded like Beau, moved from hushed tones to heightened ones. And then, through the clarity, I did recognize them.

I sprinted back towards the entranceway, my boots smacking against the concrete loudly. When I rounded the final bend and reached where we'd originally split off, I took off this time towards the center where I was met by a door that was sealed shut. Rather than kid myself that I could knock it down with force the way Beau somehow had, I pounded on the door, instead.

Not seconds passed before the door flew open and I was met with an SR22 Ruger like the one I had awkwardly in my lowered left hand. Luke lowered his the moment he realized it was me.

"How many times am I going to almost kill you guys tonight?" he said, with an exasperated tone only Luke could manage. "And where did you come from? I've been searching for you since the last tower fell. Ironic, I know. Where's Beau?"

I glanced behind me, but the chamber was empty. "I don't know, he's in here somewhere. We came to find weapons, ammo."

"You and me both," Luke said, nodding towards the room ahead. I followed him in, and as soon as I passed through the doorway, I saw who he'd, evidently, been threatening before I'd arrived.

Standing in the farthest corner of the room, dressed not in desert camouflage, but D79 Ghazni-gray, was the soldier Kyle Dellis—the man who'd saved me not two days ago from a grimy old alleyway and men who were even grimier.

Luke raised his gun back up, aimed at Dellis' chest. "I found him just outside of this building. I had the same thought as you, that there had to be some place they were keeping defensive weapons besides the armory that is sealed off."

"Unfortunately," Dellis said calmly, "there are none here. As you can see." He gestured around the room, which had evidently been used as a weapons storage. The gunpowder smell and abandoned boxes of shells—useless without their corresponding weapons— was proof of that.

"But there were," Luke fired back, steadying his hand on the gun. "And you're going to tell me where they've been moved to."

"Wait."

Luke seemed surprised by my sudden interjection, but Kyle Dellis did not. I walked forward, against Luke's protests, and moved to stand before him. We were almost the same height, and he looked just as young as I'd remembered him to be. My inclination that the girl I'd saved that night was *not* his daughter was stronger than ever, but I let that go for now.

"Do you remember me?"

The soldier nodded.

"Why are you here and not in Ghazni?" I asked, more out of curiosity than strategy.

"I go where I'm needed," he replied, a knowing look in his eyes, "Mrs. Collins."

Interestingly enough, he said it humorously, not accusingly. As if he already knew who I really was. Had he known then, too?

Before I could fumble for a response, the door smacked back off its hinges as Beau burst through and into the room. He and Luke shared a nod, then he eyed the situation with distaste before he said, "Who is that?"

"He's a—"

"His name is Kyle," I said abruptly, my tone loud and sure. "Kyle Dellis. He's not from the organization. I know because he saved me." I turned to face Beau, Luke. I met their doubt with certainty. "When I was in Ghazni, I was attacked. Not," I said quickly, seeing the look on Beau's face, "by Michael. By others, soldiers who were from D79. He's the reason I'm even standing here right now."

"Leah," Beau began, but I shook my head.

"Trust me," I said desperately. "It's over. He doesn't know where the weapons are."

"Actually," Dellis said evenly, speaking to them for the first time, "I do."

"What?" Luke was not pleased. "You fucking said—"

"I said they're not here," Dellis corrected him, his tone leveled. "Half were taken some ways outside of the perimeter of the base, where a chopper was supposed to come for them that never did. The other half were taken to a compound within the city."

"Why?" Beau challenged, disbelief clear in his eyes. "And how do we know we can trust your word? That you aren't sending us into a trap?"

Dellis did not respond to Beau. Instead, he simply looked at me.

I thought back to the terrifying encounter that

311

seemed like far more than forty-eight hours ago, and seemed less terrifying the more I grew accustomed to fear. I thought of the look on the men's faces as they pushed me around and tore at my clothes, trying not to cringe at the memory, but to remember the way it made me feel. But mostly, I pictured the face of the little girl I'd saved by risking my own life—a sacrifice that Kyle Dellis had made sure didn't go unrepaid.

Regardless of whether or not the girl was his daughter. Regardless of where his true allegiance lay.

Whether it was a guardian angel watching over us or merely a spin of fate that had bolstered us both to action, lives were saved that night. And I could see in this man's eyes that the same could be said about this night. That, amidst all of the death surrounding us, neither of us had any desire to add any more names to the list.

But because trust was a fickle thing, Dellis looked to Luke, then Beau, and said, "Believe what you will. But on my honor, I swear to you that it is not a trap. Enough men have died tonight. Take what you came for and leave this place to mourn its loss with whatever dignity it has left."

Beau and Luke exchanged a long look that I didn't understand, before, finally, they conceded and motioned for me to come with them as they headed towards the door, fingers still locked on their triggers. We had no way of completely knowing whether Dellis' word was true or not but standing here bantering, threatening him or worse wouldn't change that.

However, before I turned away from him, I saw

the look in Kyle's eyes as he added one last remark that would haunt me long after we left the guard tower, this base and Zaranj itself.

"When you secure those weapons, Moiré, I hope you realize that they are a very small fraction of what awaits you in Ghazni," he said. "The past has an interesting way of mirroring what lies ahead."

Luke was already out of sight, but Beau paused at the door, and I watched his muscles tense even from where I stood, confused by not only the words, but the face and the dissatisfied voice that delivered them with an equal amount of caution and warning.

When Beau spoke, he reciprocated neither.

"You have no idea where I've come from," he said.

Standing in the farthest corner where we left him, Dellis frowned. With a softened reply, he said, "Do you?"

I was more than a little unnerved as we walked out of the guard tower, though I tried my best not to show it. Beau seemed eager to dismiss the soldier's words, and I was just as eager to rid my head of all of the consequences that came with them.

We made the last turn and pushed through the door to the outside world, and it took me a second to realize that the wind had picked up and the coarse sand that hit my skin was mixed with drops of rain. I looked up to find the darkened sky growing darker as the storm had moved closer.

If time hadn't stopped us, nature soon would.

THE SKY WAS SECONDS from unleashing a storm that, Beau realized, would bring harsh rain and winds strong enough to displace enough sand to bury them all alive. They had to get somewhere safe, and soon. *All of us.*

Beau turned to Luke. "Where's Wes?" he asked, a frown tilting his lips before he even finished the question as he already anticipated the response that followed.

The look on Luke's face confirmed it. "After the bombs went off, I ran after Leah alone," he replied, confusion setting in. "I thought Wes was with you."

Beau frowned deeply now and glanced across the base toward one particular section he and his team had yet to traverse, and with good reason. All the while thinking of Captain Hunter Blain's last few words.

"Find Wesley Marshall and bring me his head."

"I know where he is," Beau said, to Leah and Luke's surprise and subsequent satisfaction.

I just hope we're not too late, is what he, reluctantly, did not say.

LONG FORGOTTEN SON

WESLEY MARSHALL STUDIED THE scene in front of him with intense calculation that, as always, sent the rest of his mental capacity spinning in one thousand different directions. Staring ahead at the soldiers that gathered in front of the armory that was *not* his target, Wesley also saw the wounded man that was lying on his back approximately ten yards to his right, the building that was crumbling piece by piece to his left and the storm clouds that were billowing up above, drawing out the moisture in the air like a vacuum over all of Zaranj.

Wesley took a short breath and started towards the armory again, knowing that, along with the head command center and the communications and networking tower that had been disabled, it was directly aligned with another structure that few knew anything about. *That* was his target.

He paused behind stone rubble when the sound of voices entered his path. Reaching into the bag that was strapped across his back next to his combat AR,

Wesley retrieved a walkie talkie he'd taken from a Second Lieutenant—it was how the soldiers of D79 had resorted to communicating with each other since he had knocked out all other forms of communication at the start of the ambush—and clicked several buttons to the side, activating the device.

Wesley peered behind the rubble and adjusted his glasses, allowing him to spot the names and classification patch on each of the three soldiers' chests who were collaborating approximately thirty yards ahead. He sank back to the dirt and raised his hand with the device.

"B Unit, Frederick, Atweae and Edmonton, report to the southwestern quarter of the base to assist in apprehending the target Wesley D. Marshall," Wesley said, disguising his voice as best he could with a harsh, guttural tone that could have substituted for several commanding officers he knew to hold significance here.

The men shared a suspicious look, but Wesley also detected a hint of fear when one of them radioed back, "Request to know who gives this order, sir."

To which he replied, amplifying his tone, "When you and the rest of the insubordinate bastards in your unit have apprehended Marshall, the man who's continuously evaded you in your own territory, I'll be sure to deliver your request to The General himself, private."

The man who'd spoken, Edmonton, lowered his radio. His face was ghostly pale, though he was unconsciously nodding. He didn't wait for approval from his comrades, who seemed just as rattled.

"Yes, sir. On our way."

Wesley pocketed the walkie and watched the three men depart, their direction clear—the southwestern quarter of the base. Wesley smiled to himself and, after surveying the area quickly, got to his feet.

Though he still had the poorly drawn, lowly detailed map that he and Beau had devised of the base in his back pocket, Wesley knew from his own memory that the subterranean structure to which he'd been aiming would be less than a mile ahead, directly past the head command center, adjacent to the armory.

To most of the soldiers' knowledge, The Grand Triage that every commanding officer in Zaranj referred to included the H-Comm-Center (head command center), the Armory and the new Comm-Net (communications and networking tower). And while they were two-thirds right, Wesley Marshall knew just a little bit better.

One of the three had been constructed, after the American air raid that destroyed the City of Zaranj in 2017, as a decoy to prevent the same thing happening to the organization's base that was located less than five miles away from the partial dead-zone. And though he'd been transferred weeks before the air raid and months before the layout was quietly altered, Wes had caught wind of the organization's deception to even its own deceptive soldiers. It hadn't taken him long to figure out which building was the decoy.

The real trick was finding the true Comm-Net tower.

And in due time, Wesley had figured out that it wasn't a tower at all, but a tunnel designed in true D79 fashion. He'd also, in his years of research from afar, deduced that The Grand Triage, while believed to be a straight line, was actually a triangle—making its location quite simple.

After passing the head command center and veering off to his right, Wesley spotted the entrance to the organization's bunker that had been sealed off in case of emergency attacks like the one they had suffered tonight.

Wesley tried not to think of all the men and women who'd undoubtedly fled to this very location expecting to be able to retreat to safety, only to realize the deception moments before it was too late. But he did think of them, he thought of their lives before the explosion and the gunshots, thought of all the loved ones they'd left behind, and the silver jewel he always carried in his front right pocket but never wore—it had never belonged to him—suddenly felt colder than usual when he touched his fingertips to it.

Wesley never shied off the thought of his beloved whenever it came. In his mind, it was her way of reaching out to him, no matter how painful and destructive Laci's memory was to his psyche. The ring also served as a reminder.

A reminder that as long as he was unable to fight against that which he'd been a vital part of creating, every man, woman and child murdered by Division-7-9 was his fault.

Wesley retracted his hand from his pocket without realizing he'd placed it there and started forward again, this time, instead, with his hand on the stock of his rifle.

He moved with a lithe step towards the bunker that was marked by a lone metal door and a hollow stone corridor that slanted down where it met with the earth. The hairs on the back of his neck stood on end as he took the last step out into the open, away from cover, though he didn't precisely know why until he detected the shadowed presence behind him a fraction of a second too late.

Wesley spun but he didn't have enough time to efficiently retrieve the weapon off his back. Rya Ivrea stood with a pistol raised to eye-level aimed in his direction, and in that moment, Wesley knew that her shot would be the first, and also his last.

But it wasn't.

One deafeningly quiet bullet from the barrel of a silenced weapon hit Rya in the chest, off-centered and piercing straight through her before she could pull the trigger the rest of the way.

Wesley knew who'd fired the shot. Luke Marshall, his brother, would've aimed for her head—specifically straight between the eyes, as he'd been instructed. She was a small target and Justin or Matt, he mused, would've missed. Beau, the man who retained every ounce of guilt for every kill he made, would've chosen to disarm her first, aiming for her shoulder or perhaps her legs.

But Michael Moiré had shot straight through her heart.

Michael's right arm was extended to the perfect degree, strong and unwavering, with every muscle in his body tightened, though his eyes were on the sand the way they had been when he'd pulled the trigger. The way they remained when he walked away without explanation or even a second glance at Rya or Wesley himself.

Wesley watched him go with a familiar sadness that he didn't have time to recognize when Beau, Luke and Leah arrived only minutes later, concern written all over their faces.

Wesley turned, realizing that none of them could see Rya's lifeless form some little ways away in the sand, nor had they witnessed Michael depart after subduing the woman he, unashamedly and after all these years, loved. None of them knew what had just happened, nor would they ever know.

But Wesley knew.

He always did.

SECOND CHANCES

"WESLEY," BEAU SAID, A frown in eyes and on his lips. He had so many questions, but couldn't figure out which was most important or even how to frame it. Wes looked like he'd just seen a ghost, but Beau knew better than to pry at the man's thoughts.

Luckily, Wes saved him the trouble as he took a deep breath and explained, "When Matt and I first entered the base, we recognized immediately that the head command center was too heavily guarded. Instead, I hit their communications and networking tower with some C-4 that I brought for that very reason. That tower controlled their ability to converse with one another; it did not contain their Intel."

"Is that why the communicators haven't worked?" Leah asked, a puzzled look on her face that matched that of Beau and Luke.

"It is. I attempted to take out their network's abilities, but in doing so, it disabled ours as well. It was a necessary risk to keep them from coordinating with the rest of the organization."

"So those helicopters...they weren't D79's backup?"

Wes shook his head.

"Why separate from Matt?" Luke interjected. "We agreed to stay in teams of two for security reasons. That was *your* idea."

Wes nodded. "Before the bomb went off, I sent Matthew to find you, Beau, after hearing shots fire. Though I anticipated you, Luke, to become involved as well. And the truth is that I didn't need Matthew as much as you did, which is why I've been alone," he said simply. "I planted the bomb at an alternate location and caused the same effect. I know this terrain, the infrastructure and how to penetrate this base, I have since the very beginning. You know that, Beau."

Beau stared at the ground, but he nodded his head. "We met in Zaranj. I knew you'd been here for a while, but...how long?"

"Three years. I was stationed here for a little under thirty-six months, which," Wes glanced at Leah as he spoke, "my apologies, is slightly more time than the Sergeant of whom they have in charge of operations currently." Wes paused for a moment before he added, "Laci and I lived in the city before it was leveled."

Leah glanced away. "Sean's only here because of me," she said. "He doesn't know anything about this place or the organization, his actions tonight were proof of that."

"Precisely," Wes agreed. "The General is only using your cousin to get to you and, obviously, Beau.

But Sean is more of a distraction than a secret weapon. The real soldier in charge tonight was Blain."

"Was?" Leah said, confused. She looked directly at Beau just then, who purposely didn't meet her inquisition. "He's dead?"

"He is," Wes replied, his eyes on Beau. "I'm to understand he almost took Justin with him."

"Almost," Beau said quietly, though he, as well, was still reeling from the encounter. "I don't think he'll be a problem any longer."

"Most of Division's soldiers here are dead but we're naïve to think that more won't come," Luke insisted. "Reinforcements will arrive, and if that happens while we're still here..." He shook his head. "We should destroy this place before it can be rebuilt."

"We can destroy it, or we can commandeer it," Wes countered.

And then Beau understood. He locked eyes with Wes just then, an uncertain frown plastered across his face because he knew it was dangerous territory they were crossing into.

"This was your plan from the very beginning, wasn't it?" Beau glanced at the metal door several yards away, pieces falling together. "Net-Comm," he said. "You want to harness their Intel core."

"Yes," Wes admitted. "Think about it, Beau. You know as well as I that we can finish what we started here two years ago. But we have to act now. H-Comm is down and I can access the old Net-Comm if I can just get to it for five minutes."

"You know it's only half of the puzzle," Beau

said carefully. "For us to have enough evidence to take to someone who matters or, better yet, to be able to create the virus and destroy it from within…it would take both circuits, both Intel cores."

Wes nodded as if that changed nothing.

"This is risky," Beau challenged.

Without missing a beat, Wes replied, "Risky is our middle name, remember?"

The two of them stood there for several seconds, Wes wordlessly trying to convince Beau, who was more moved by a silent moment to think than anything else could've done to sway him. Wes was correct in that they had tried to do this very thing when they'd first found out about the deception of Division-7-9, two years ago. But it hadn't worked then, and Beau wasn't entirely sure it would work now.

To take Zaranj's Intel core, which was an advanced blueprint of the organization and its missions across the world, since its origin, meant that they would alert D79 of their motives. Not only that, but the core was designed with a duplicate that safeguarded against a hack—which is why they failed two years ago. To be able to operate the intelligence collectively, you needed the combined codes of both Intel cores.

One had been placed here, in the bunker beneath Zaranj, and the other was somewhere beneath the tunnels in Ghazni, Afghanistan. And to take one meant that they may lose the ability to capture the second once The General found out they were, in fact, after it.

It was a gamble but, then again, when wasn't it?

And the only reason Beau knew any of this was because he had been briefed by Wesley Marshall, precisely two years ago, about this very location. Wes knew what he was doing. He always had.

Still, this newest agenda didn't resonate well with him. Beau had begun to believe that perhaps the soldier, Kyle Dellis, was right after all. Perhaps the best move was the one that took them the farthest way away from this place, away from Zaranj, away from the damage they'd caused and the danger that was still present.

Finally, Beau conceded. "Alright, Wesley. We go in, we get what we need, we get out."

"Agreed."

"But only you and me." Beau turned to Luke, who didn't seem pleased. "Take Leah out of here." When she began to protest, Beau held up his hand and said, "You heard Dellis. There's a mass of weapons stockpiled just outside of the fence on the western side of the base. Find them, find Matt and Justin and get out. We'll meet you in the city as soon as we're done here to find the rest."

"No," Leah said, right on cuc. "I'm not leaving you."

Beau studied her expression, lit with frustration, and couldn't help but feel like he was betraying her, and it almost swayed him back. After all, not ten minutes before, he'd promised her he wouldn't let her go. How could he explain that this was beyond him, beyond both of them? That he, too, was uncomfortable separating from her again and that he would've much rather left this alone the way his gut was telling him to.

"Beau's right." Luke placed a reassuring hand on Leah's shoulder. "We can't do both without splitting up, and I'll be honest, I don't know jack-shit about whatever the hell you two convicts just said for the last sixty seconds, so I guess I'm on weapons detail. That means you're with me again, Lee Lee."

Beau breathed a subtle sigh of relief. He was grateful to Luke for many things, the first and foremost being his willingness to act for the good of the team, and the second being his ability to stand in and protect Leah when Beau had to do the same.

She lowered her chin, which Beau touched gently and tipped back up. "Leah," he began softly. "I—"

"Go," she said, surprising Beau again. She reached up and pressed a kiss against his lips and it reminded him of the kisses she'd placed on him the night before, of the passion, the trust and the love she'd already surrendered. How much more could he expect from her?

Though resistance was on the tip of her tongue, she said, "I'll hold you to your promise a little longer."

Beau smiled the slightest bit because it was all he could muster. He conceded that no amount of words could describe his feelings or his thoughts just then. Instead, he watched as Leah walked, away, with Luke firmly by her side.

"Ready?"

Beau turned back around to find Wes watching him with a look of sadness he was all too familiar with. There was no doubt that just being in Zaranj was painful for him. Beau realized he wasn't the only one who was ready to finish this and leave this place for good.

"I'm ready," he replied.

Wes nodded and took out a card that Beau didn't recognize. It had the shape of a credit card, but rather than swiping it against a scanner the way he anticipated, Wes placed it flat against the top-right side of the metal doorway in what appeared to be a random place. After several seconds of nothing, Beau frowned with confusion until, finally, three subtle *beeps* echoed from within, almost soundlessly.

"X1-2200," Wes said briefly.

Wes pushed, not pulled, against the door that folded inward with difficulty. Metal screeched against metal, telling him that the door was not regularly used. Beau wondered if the soldiers of Zaranj even knew of its existence, let alone the nature of its contents.

Then again, soldiers weren't supposed to ask questions.

The door led down into a chamber that was musty and dark. Wes traversed the stone steps cautiously, his fingertips resting on the gun slung across his back. Beau followed him where the stone met with cement block that eventually gave way to thick steel, all the while anticipating to meet with the barrel of a gun.

The bunker was empty.

Well, not exactly. Once they took the final step down, the bunker opened up into a room that could've been the seventh floor of the Pentagon.

On every wall was a computer screen and at knee level were towers that connected to the screens and each other with a web of wires, splitters and extensions. Despite the vacancy of the bunker, buttons and lights were blinking at every turn as if it were fully operational and connected to a wider network that set Beau's nerves to work.

"What exactly are we looking for?"

Wes had already moved toward a particular screen in the closest corner, eyes scanning for one drive. At the same time, Beau took it all in, the computers, the cords, the buzzing electricity that produced almost an audible *hum*. He touched the outline of the Colt clipped to the back of the inside of his pants, his nerves thinning by the second.

"Wes," Beau said, voice low. "This isn't just Intel storage, there's a signal here."

Wes had said that Zaranj's networks were down, Beau mused. *But, maybe not all of them.*

"I don't like this," Beau said. "There's too much traffic."

Wes was kneeling in front of the drive he'd honed in on. He was far too focused to acknowledge Beau's questioning, suspicious tone. Instead, he was left to let his mind wander.

If we took out their communications and networking capabilities, where would the traffic be coming from? Beau thought to himself. *The City of Zaranj used to have its own satellite signal, but all traces of electricity were wiped out after the United States came in with drone strikes and leveled it all. The only feasible location that had enough power to generate a trafficking signal this strong was...*

Ghazni.

"Welcome," a voice said as every screen before them changed, one by one, into a picture Beau recognized all too well. He stopped abruptly, his entire body froze and then instinct drove him to a mix of fear, anger and a twisted sense of obedience that brought back a tidal wave of memories he fought hard to subdue.

Beau had his gun out before the man's lips could smack together into another syllable, but it was no use. He and Wes were still alone in the chamber that echoed eerily. The only difference was the array of screens that had all come to life, depicting one face he hadn't seen in over two years, but that Beau couldn't forget even if he lived to be one thousand years old.

The man opened his mouth, and all of it came back at once.

"Welcome," The General said with a sardonic smile. "Here at last, my young soldiers return. Welcome *back* to Zaranj."

YANKEE

THE GENERAL OF DIVISION looked just as young for his age as he'd always had, Beau couldn't help but notice. His stern face was topped with thick silver hair that didn't look natural to the eye, nor was there a single strand of it out of place. His eyes were a steely gray that blinked almost as often as his lips smiled.

Wes backed away from the computer station he'd been crouched in front of, though not before slipping a subtle hand into his back pocket. He moved to stand next to Beau, who lowered his gun but didn't dare take his hands off of it.

An unnerving silenced followed.

"General Reeves," Wes said at last, nodding his head the slightest bit. "It's been a long time."

The General narrowed his eyes at Wes's use of his last name—a name that had all but been forgotten. Beau glanced sideways at Wes, wondering if there was any extent to the knowledge the man had. *Reeves,* he thought, the name sounding strange when paired with the mass murderer on the screen. Almost as strange as the fact that Wes had never mentioned it before.

"Not quite long enough, I see," The General replied, replacing his momentarily disgruntled expression in favor of a more neutral one. "No matter. I have a feeling it won't be an issue for me much longer."

Wes seemed unfazed by the threat, more so than Beau had ever seen before. "Forgive me, General, but you have been trying to catch me for a lot longer than two years," he said coolly. "Now, it appears, the tables are turning."

The General sat back in his chair, a twisted look of satisfaction on his face. It was a while before he said, "Are they?"

Wesley didn't play into The General's mind games, instead letting silence pervade the bunker, unnerving Beau until he couldn't take it any longer. His curiosity got the best of him.

"How did you reach us here?" Beau challenged.

The General shifted his gaze, as if noticing Beau for the first time, and gave him a look that a negligent father might have for a troubled son. "You are aware that you're trespassing in *my* military compound, dear boy. I'm afraid that means you play by my rules."

"In case you haven't taken inventory yet," Wes said, an edge to his tone, "you're considerably low on soldiers here."

"You really think the death of two hundred pawns rattles me, Mr. Marshall?" The General folded his hands on the mahogany desk in front of him. "Surely you've realized by now that victory, like defeat, requires sacrifice."

"And what happens once all of your *ever*-loyal soldiers get word of their *dispensability*?" Wes challenged, his voice rising the slightest bit in disgust. Now, Beau realized, the encounter was beginning to get to him. "How many men will fight for you then?"

The General leaned forward and said, "Shall I ask you the same question, Mr. Marshall?" He shifted his eyes onto Beau. "Or shall I ask the pawn himself?"

Beau's lips tilted down into a frown even before the words fully registered. When they did, he looked to Wes only to receive a partial glance out of the corner of his friend's eyes in return.

"What's he talking about, Wes?"

Wes ignored him. He took a step towards the screens depicting The General's face, but as Beau unwilling sank further and further into his thoughts, the more it seemed like a step away from him.

"Be cautious, Mr. Reeves," Wes said instead, "and think about who will lose the most with this next move."

"I can think of only one particular loss that matters," The General said, sporting an obviously fake look of inquisition as he locked eyes with Wes. His smile was feral.

"Jason," Wes said through his teeth.

"January 17, 2005."

Beau's eyes snapped up to the screens to find The General's eyes on him now. In them, he saw the taunt, saw the deception and the mind games that Beau knew him to be capable of. But he also saw a flicker, a sudden wavering, of a horrible truth that, after all these years, still evaded him.

And just before he could say that, or say anything at all, the screen changed, one by one, into a picture he *did* recognize.

It was his parents. Alexander and Diane Moiré, on the day of their wedding, in Santa Monica, California. The teenage couple was bright-eyed and smiling on the Pacific Coast. Diane, young and sweet in a billowing white dress and Alexander dressed up in an older version of Army dress attire, for he'd enlisted that summer. The date was etched into the bottom of the picture: September 10, 1994.

Beau took a step forward unwittingly, feeling small beneath the screens that taunted him with the people he'd never known, but loved all the same.

All too soon, the image changed into a black and white picture of Alexander Moiré amid several soldiers whom he'd evidently enlisted with. They were standing on the tarmac at the airport in Tehran, Iran, arm in arm—men you wouldn't think were of different ethnicity and culture by the way they were embracing one another. Alexander's teeth were bright white against the background, but his eyes weren't focused on the screen. They were staring just past it, undoubtedly at the camera-holder herself. At the bottom, it read, in a woman's neat lettering: Alex, Wyatt, Ray and Scott, February 3, 1995.

Beau felt hollow as he stared at Alexander, seeing only the light in his eyes, the playfulness in his body language and the smile on his face that somehow didn't match the one and only photo he'd had of his father.

The next one, however, did.

Beau's body tensed like a rock as the screen changed into a picture of soldiers he *did* recognize, all adorned with the charcoal-gray attire; the badge and insignia that Beau was all too familiar with, but had never actually been a part of.

Diane's neat lettering was replaced by stenciled military script, and at the bottom right corner it read: Delta V Unit, March, 1996.

Amidst the *Greymarks* was Alexander Moiré himself, a new patch that signified D-7-9 on his left breast pocket, and a steely-eyed look that resembled none of the earlier photos. In true Division fashion, Alex was reserved, statuesque and deadly. A combat AR was in his lowered left hand—his dominant one.

Beau's mind turned to Michael, who was right-handed—until he'd suffered nerve damage in his right and was forced to relearn the dominance to his left. Like his father. And, as if The General, or fate itself, had factored in that very response, the screens shifted into an image that weakened Beau until he couldn't stand upright anymore. He placed one hand against the desk beside him, but it did little to give him any sort of stability.

It was a crime report dated January 17, 2005, and was filed by the Pennsylvania State Police. Beside was an obituary, then another.

And then another.

Beau studied the third photo with a mixture of shock and disdain. For, though Michael hadn't died that night, seeing the picture of his brother brought back a wave of memories. Sights, sounds, and tears that had been lost with time, returned.

He was only five years old that night, but in the back of his mind, Beau saw it all over again and he remembered. The gun, the knife, the cold air that hit his skin as he was carried far away. The look on his uncle Raymond's face when he showed up, lost and scared with nothing to hold onto but Michael's icy hand, at the Roland family's doorstep. He had forgotten the way his brother's hand had been shaking, and Beau glanced down to realize the way his shook now.

One thin drop of water slid down Beau's face, but the confusion that hit him from the next set of photos dried the teardrops instantly.

It was a *USA Today* news report that he'd never seen before. The date was September 23, 1996. A step back in time from the previous one, though Beau didn't exactly know why.

A jet departing from Ghazni, Afghanistan at approximately 2:43pm Eastern time, expected to arrive in the U.S. the same evening, crashed down six miles off the coast of New Jersey. The local coast guard reported the cause of the crash due to uncharted, violent wind currents. No bodies were recovered, but the full passenger list was taken from the airport in Afghanistan. The death toll was complete with thirteen passengers; no survivors, nor conclusive wreckage. The jet was evidently carrying U.S. Army soldiers on leave, and we regret this loss as a devastating one. The tragedy, as it stands, was deemed an accident, and the Federal Bureau of Investigation has sought no further investigative necessity.

Among the dead, Beau noted: *Mr. and Mrs. Alexander Moiré, ages twenty-two and twenty-three. Wyatt Vendelle, age twenty-two. Scottran "Scott" Dellis, age twenty-*

six. Raymond Roland, age twenty-three.

With the report was a photo that mirrored one of the early ones, though the people in it were rigid, unsmiling and hardly recognizable compared with the casualness of the earlier image of them. It was the four military men—none of them locked arms now— and a woman, layered in thick clothing and had a guarded look in her emerald eyes that were visible to Beau despite the image's lack of color. In some distant memory, he could picture her eyes on him—watchful and protecting, always.

The image flashed once and disappeared, but Beau stared straight ahead as if it were burned into his eyes, his memory and the words of the report on the tip of his tongue as if he'd crafted them himself.

Beau didn't turn—he didn't think he could—but he directed his words at the man standing several feet behind him, his voice mimicking the emptiness he felt inside.

"You knew?"

"Yes."

The word was like a knife straight through his gut. Beau closed his eyes and said, fingers clenched as tightly together as possible, "I don't understand…I remember the night they died. It was…How is this…? Why didn't you tell me my parents died in a plane crash?"

"Because they didn't," Wes replied.

Beau's eyes snapped open just as quickly as they'd closed. This time, he did turn, and he didn't try to disguise his anger or confusion. "I just saw—"

"You saw a report from *USA Today* detailing

your parents' deaths in 1996," Wes said, his voice quiet and calm, "but it was false. You know how they died, Beau. You were there."

Beau turned his accusations back to the screen, to The General's face that it depicted now, his cold eyes watchful and slightly amused. "You did this," he said. "You created the false report. You tried to kill them off the way you did to us." The General, however, shook his head and smiled.

"They did," Wes said. He took a step forward, nodded his head at the screen and said, "Show it again."

When Beau returned his eyes to the image with reluctance, he studied the picture of the five persons just before they'd boarded the jet to return to the United States, the photo that accompanied the *USA Today* news report, with malice that was beginning to overflow. Searching for the evidence of a truth he didn't want to see, it didn't take Beau long to find it.

Beau moved from Diane's somber eyes to the place where she had a protective hand. Beneath all of the layers of clothing she'd worn to try and hide it from the world, the slightest bump was visible.

"She was pregnant," Beau said, still puzzled. "But not with me."

"With your brother." Wes inclined his head. "When she found out, your father was already in with Division. He was a *Greymark*, and a highly respected leader in his rank. They couldn't just leave without repercussion. But to stay would put them all in danger. So Diane devised a plan to fake her and Alex's deaths before the organization could find out she had a son on the way." Wes took a breath. "But they found out."

"Of course we did," The General said with a laugh. "I made a deal with Alexander that if he stayed, I would let his wife go freely. A fair exchange. But he rejected my generous offer and I knew then that there was a child. That was the only explanation. He was afraid of the child becoming just like him." The General leaned forward. "*Mine.*"

"You see, what Wesley isn't telling you is that your father knew what he was doing," The General continued. "He was one of my *most* loyal men, and he knew what he was—a murderer. Like we all are. The only sliver of a conscience your treasonous father ever had was in that his wife wanted better for her son." He smiled venomously. "Diane was always the key to Alex. Isn't it interesting how a woman can bring a man to his knees, Beau?"

An image of Leah inside of a cell Beau recognized as Ghazni, Afghanistan flashed up on the screen beneath The General's cold expression. Beau's pulse picked up and The General's smile widened because he knew it would.

"Wesley?"

The image disappeared and was replaced by a picture of Laci Green, Beau recognized. Wes's fiancée. Her hazel gray eyes were focused and her thick, almond-colored hair that was as straight as a pin was secured back in a ponytail while she worked. Laci had been a registered nurse in a hospital that specifically cared for U.S. military men and women. That's where she'd been the day Wesley Marshall walked through the doors with a wrist sprain and changed her whole world, right up until the day she'd died.

Or, rather, been murdered by the man on the screen the way his...

Beau felt a sudden pang of emptiness as it all came together at last. "You murdered them."

The General didn't respond right away, oddly enough. He didn't gloat or make the confession smugly. To Beau, that only confirmed that the worst of it all was true. That The General himself, however ugly and vicious and evil, felt remorse for his father's death. That Alexander had, at one time, fought for the man willingly.

"It doesn't matter," Beau said through his teeth, words feeling strange to his lips after so much of the battle having taken place inside of his own head. "My father left. He sought better for himself, his family. The reason doesn't matter."

"Of course it matters," The General replied. "The original team Yankee. Ironically, your father didn't leave because he disproved of my methods, child. Alexander was just as ruthless as I am. No, your father left because he thought he could shield you from me, from my organization and my way of life. And he was *dead* wrong."

Beau shook his head to try and rid it of the words, the images and the truth that his father had fallen into the same trap he had, but none of it would stop.

Yankee Two.

Yankee.

Beau knew that Alexander had been a soldier. He also knew that he had been murdered. He just didn't know what kind, and why.

"Even in his death, Alex tried to shield you from me," The General spoke this time without remorse. "Haven't you noticed that not a single photo from either of your parents' alleged deaths includes the existence of a second son? Only Michael. That was your mother's doing, of course. A home-birth, no school or medical records on file, nothing to reveal she'd fucked up and gotten herself pregnant again." The General laughed again. "Beau Moiré, the soldier who was never meant to exist. What better weapon than a man you can build up from scratch."

Beau shook his head but the pounding didn't go away. Suddenly, Gabriel Schrader's words back in Kandahar made sense.

So it is true, after all. You really don't know who you are.

You're nothing.

As if he were inside Beau's head, The General capitalized on that very thought. "Your father helped me build this Division, Beau. And then he gave me an identity-less soldier to finish what he started. You were born to be a part of this. Stop fighting it and just accept the fact that, despite what your mother wanted, your father would be proud of what you've become. What you were always meant to be."

"Your father was a good man," Wes interjected, though his voice was still quiet. "He and your mother wanted nothing more than to protect you, and they died doing so. They faked their deaths and ran from the organization for eight years until they were killed for real in 2005 in Pennsylvania by the monster you see on the screen."

Wes took a step forward. "The child they wanted was Michael, it wasn't you. You were the one thing The General never anticipated, Beau, and that's why you're the only one he desperately wants to kill. An unpredictable pawn is a dangerous one—"

"I am not," Beau said through his teeth, "a pawn."

A smile broke out on The General's face. Beau caught it out of the corner of his eye.

Wes's desperate expression didn't change. "Don't do this again, Beau. Don't let this man, this Division, get to you, get inside your head and take you back to where you started. You still don't know the full story—"

"And you do?" Beau challenged, his anger suddenly flaring, anger that was now aimed at Wes, at his brother by every means but blood, his best friend and the one whose lies hurt him the most. "You know The General's name, his background, my parents and how they died and you never once felt the need to divulge any of this *so why don't you tell me why*. And better yet, how! How, Wes? How the fuck do you know all of this?"

Wes stared at Beau but didn't respond. At that, The General's crooked smile widened. His folded hands were just as taunting as his eyes that knew precisely how far they'd penetrated. Silence pervaded the bunker; a deafening, deadly silence that pressed and pressed.

"Ah, the million-dollar question, at last," The General said, making Beau's skin crawl until he couldn't stand there and take the pressing anymore. "The true price of loyalty revealed."

And then he stopped trying. Beau's fingers tightened into fists and he spun with his Colt raised and shot straight through the screen that depicted The General's face in what would've been a kill shot. The bullet rebounding back against the cement wall where it shot forward again, smashing two more screens. The signal must have shorted out, for the rest of the screens crashed into static images and sounds as well, drawing empty silence to the room at last.

Beau didn't quit. He spun one final time towards Wes, gun raised eye level, and said, "Answer me! *How do you know?*"

Wes opened his mouth but the words that followed weren't his.

"Because I told him."

DESTINED

MICHAEL MOIRE STEPPED DOWN from the last of the stairs leading into the bunker below Zaranj. "I told him everything," Michael said, his dark eyes intense, "you were never supposed to know."

"Why?" Beau said through gritted teeth.

"Because you're nothing like Alexander. You're weak." Michael exhaled mockingly. "And because Wesley has been on my side since the very beginning. Honestly, I'm ashamed you never put the pieces together yourself. After all, it was quite obvious that someone was handing over all your dirty little secrets. You just assumed, after all these years, you've grown predictable. And you're not wrong."

Michael's words hit every pressure point they were meant to, and Beau struggled for words, for emotions, for something to say or give in return, but there was nothing.

"I've told you once already, *al-sagheer*, that I know how easily it is to pick you apart," Michael added, his hands folded behind his back the way they'd been throughout the entire exchange. Careless

343

and at ease. "Unfortunately, you've forced my hand in doing just that."

"I've never done anything to you," Beau whispered, lifting his head for the first time to lock eyes with his older brother. "I kept my promise that I would fight for you. You, Michael, were the one who decided that that didn't matter to you anymore, not me!"

"Do you remember the night they died?" Michael said abruptly, his stance firm and his eyes hard and unwavering. "Because I do. I remember the music, and the smell of the oven and the cookies and gunpowder from the gun we were cleaning. I remember the way they looked at one another, as if the world was at peace and always would be. I remember thinking that I was safe.

"But I think the thing I remember the most, aside from father's pleas and mother's screams that you'll never hear because you were too busy drooling on the carpet, was the look she gave me just before our mother died," Michael said. "Not worry or fear or concern for me, no, it was all about you." In a rare moment, Michael purposely allowed emotion to cloud his expression, and Beau felt every ounce of it. "In her final moment, she still fought to keep you a secret from them. You, Beau, were all our parents ever cared about. You were the one thing that D79 hadn't touched.

"Of course, once they found out about you, that's all The General cared about, and it became the quest that ultimately killed Raymond, as well, when the organization eventually did come for us."

"What do you mean?" Beau challenged. "The organization didn't touch us until we'd already sworn our lives away to the Army."

"You really think that." Michael posed it like a question, but the look on his face and the way he shook his head said otherwise. "You really are so gallant, aren't you? So, trusting and naïve."

"Stop playing games with me."

Michael smirked. "All right. You want to know the truth, Beau? The truth is that our father was a D79 mutt right up until the day he died and our mother was a broken angel who tried to save him from himself, yet they somehow managed to drag us down with them. D79 is in our blood, it followed us all our lives, through military school, through the military itself; it's no coincidence The General sought us out. He's known us our entire lives, Beau."

"Raymond would've—"

"Raymond tried as best he could to prepare us for the inevitable," Michael said with every ounce of bitterness he could throw into the words. "But he was never foolish enough to think we wouldn't end up exactly where we did. Even Alyson knew we weren't safe, nor were her own children, why do you think she lost her strength against the cancer? Because in her mind…it was only a matter of time."

Beau shook his head.

"The only one who didn't see this coming was you."

Michael studied Beau up and down, a disgusted look on his face that reeked of disappointment, shame and a little bit of something else. There was always something else. "You're the prodigal son Alexander never had," Michael said, his voice level and calm again. "I suggest you man up and deal with that before it kills you, too."

Michael turned away and, at the same time, Beau shifted the aim of his gun onto his brother for the second time in less than forty-eight hours. And, once again, he was ready to pull the trigger. There was so much new information in his head that Beau had yet to separate what was fact from fiction, but he knew nothing he deduced could change the fact that Michael Moiré was, and would always be, his enemy.

Michael paused, but that wasn't what stopped Beau. He glanced to his right to find Wes's rifle trained on him and that's when everything changed.

"I'm sorry, Beau," Wesley offered, but it hardly registered. In his mind, Beau heard only one thing. One voice.

His own.

"Thank you. For your wisdom, your guidance, your trust. I know you think me irrational and reckless—you've always told me so, even without directly saying it. I want you to know that you have my trust and my respect. If it weren't for you, I would have died many times over and I know that. For standing with me, in possibly the worst of times, I just want to say thank you."

Wes didn't turn back around, didn't face him. By the low set of his friend's shoulders, Beau could sense an unexplained contriteness. For what, however, he had no idea.

"Don't thank me," Wes responded finally, his voice quiet. "When all of this is over…just remember that I was always your friend."

Beau felt his heart sink into his stomach. How many times that could possibly occur in such a short span of time, he didn't know. Beau held his gun where it was, even though his body had gone numb long before then, and he remained like that until the chamber was empty and he was alone with the crashing waves of thought that wouldn't stop probing at him. They spun and spun in his head until it was just too much and he sank to his knees because he couldn't stand and didn't know how.

After everything, he didn't know how to get back up this time.

He didn't know how he'd find the strength to make it out of the bunker, out of Zaranj, and out of the endless desert that taunted him every step of the way.

He didn't know how he'd face Leah, or Justin or Matt. Or Luke. Or himself, who he didn't even know anymore.

Without Wes, Beau realized he didn't know much of anything.

In fact, all Beau knew at that moment was that Wesley Marshall had just chosen a side. And for the first time, it wasn't his.

FROM THE ASHES

EVERY INCH OF MY vision burned red and orange with the bright, bursting flames that consumed the U.S. Army base and the thick, billowing smoke that attempted to create a blanket of cover. Seeing it, no matter how far away I was, made me feel like I, too, was on fire. Like the heat was only inches away instead of a mile, like the smoke was dancing from my skin instead of the rubble and remains of Zaranj.

We hadn't found the weapons that Kyle Dellis had promised were somewhere out here, on the outskirts of the base. Somehow, I never actually believed we would. How much more could we take from this place?

Thunder cracked on the horizon, startling me as it sounded an awful lot like a gunshot. I looked up and felt the fat drops of rain fall into my eyes, my nose, my mouth and across my skin, which was partly revealed through the ripped clothing I still wore, and this time I felt the rain just as I'd felt the fire. They mixed and somehow made more sense than anything I'd encountered this night. Nature, as Sean always said, was steady, consistent.

Matt was tending to Justin—who had regained consciousness—a distance off, for Luke and I had agreed to do one final sweep of the area in case we'd overlooked the weapons. It was funny how they left me alone now, as if they thought me capable of holding my own. I didn't know how to tell them they were wrong. After all, how could they possibly know that with this new strength in this new beginning, I didn't even recognize myself.

So, I was alone to feel all of the emptiness that should've been replaced by sadness, by tragedy. I glanced at the gate that had allowed us to pass so easily through and cause all of this, hoping to see a light in the darkness, to find Beau and Wes cresting the mounds to join us. But it was only the light of flames visible. A constant mirage of misconception.

My skin pricked, but not because of the fire or the rain or the sullenness of the moment.

I felt his presence behind me, and I knew I should have been scared. We were enemies now, that much should've been brutally clear. Whether it was because of the encounter we'd had that ended poorly, the way I let my father die right in front of his eyes, the fact that Beau had shot him and I'd walked away then, too, or just the simple knowledge that we'd chosen different sides—if they were still that definitive. But my feelings were so messed up, my head a twisted jumble that I didn't know what was what. Enemy, friend, criminal, hero?

Nothing made sense anymore. Nothing but fire, and rain.

"So that's it? You find out your father is alive and then you do absolutely nothing when he's killed for real? You walk away like nothing's happened, nothing's changed?"

I didn't turn, instead continuing to stare out across the desert into the inferno that seemed to burn every last of my feelings away. The mist dampened the flames, but it didn't matter. Everything, everyone. They were all dead.

My tone, likewise, was dead. "Nothing has changed, Sean."

"He's your fucking father!"

"My father left me," I said, as I turned to face him at last. "Twelve years ago. He cut me out of his life and took away my choice." Sean stood a few feet from me, his uniform torn and bloodied from the fight, a poorly constructed tourniquet bandaged his right shoulder. I almost wanted to run to him, to care for his wounds and give him a breath of life.

Almost.

We were different people now.

"My mother never loved me," I said to Sean, my voice simple. "She only ever loved him and now they're both gone, together. All my life, choices have been made for me, Sean. My father chose to cut me out of his life, my mother chose to end hers, you chose to take me in and the world so far has chosen to punish me every second for that. Not anymore. For once in my life, I *do* have a choice. And I choose retribution."

In my mind, it was simple. In reality, I knew it wasn't.

Sean shook his head as he scoffed. His brown hair was thick with dirt and singed on the edges. "Retribution?" His expression was a mix between anger, disbelief, disgust and more anger. Sean was all fire. "Do you really think your mother would have wanted it this way? You think she'd be proud of you?"

To be honest, I hadn't thought about that and I didn't think about it now.

I didn't scream at him for hiding this from me for however how long he knew. I didn't break down at the twisted irony in the fact that my mother ended her life thinking she'd be joining her husband in whatever afterlife awaited them, or at least so that she didn't have to wake up every day breathing without half of her heart, when in reality he'd been alive all this time. I didn't cry, didn't scream hate at the sky that carelessly added thunder and rain to the mix or even look up to acknowledge Sean's twisted remarks meant to cut me deeper than the truth already had— more than he, or I, could've ever foreseen.

I shrugged my shoulders because there was nothing left for me to say. We were different people now.

Right?

Sean continued to shake his head. His eyes flitted past me and he stared at the crumbling walls in the center of Zaranj that had, so far, withstood much of the rest of the base's destruction.

Minutes passed; Sean continued to stand there, wordlessly shaking his head as if he expected that to change something in me. It didn't. It couldn't. And I couldn't explain to him why.

When he finally figured that out, Sean spoke with a rigid voice of disgust, his tone fused with a deep hatred that pierced through every last layer of protection surrounding my heart.

"I don't even know you anymore, you heartless little bitch," he spat at me. "You're right where you belong, and you'll get *exactly* what you deserve. I hope you like your choice."

I stared straight ahead, not meeting his gaze as he eyed me one last time and then walked away. I closed my eyes, expecting tears to squeeze out of them and slide down my cheeks to join the torrential downpour, but none came. I didn't cry. I didn't even want to.

And this was the problem. The number one question that I was too afraid to justify with an answer. Was I still here for Sean? Or had it stopped being about him a long time ago?

Maybe Sean was right, after all. Maybe I had changed, into what I'd always tried to protect myself from. A stranger, a killer, a vacuum for hope and love and life. Someone who didn't grow from their grief, but rather succumbed to it. Maybe I'd become so empty and emotionless and bad that nothing could faze me anymore. Maybe I was selfish, heartless, soulless, and alone inside of my body, behind the wall I'd spent eighteen years building and only three months knocking down. Maybe the wounds beneath the band aids hadn't had enough time to heal before I'd been forced to rip them off.

Unfortunately, that was the one thing for which I still had *absolutely* no control.

Time.

EPILOGUE

"And without loyalty, war never ends.

Like my father Alexander and Uncle Raymond before me,
I fear that the coming war will demand the utmost and
test the limits of mankind. To nationality, to brotherhood,
to God and to family.
After realizing that our story is a mirror of what happened
to those who first attempted to fight this war, I fear for
the future and what is to come. What *will* come.
I fear that pieces have been set in motion from long ago,
seeds of absolution and inevitability that spell chaos and
death that has been in the cards for mankind since the
beginning. Not tyranny, no.
Something far worse that neither Wesley nor Beau nor
General Jason Reeves himself could ever predict or
prepare for.
Worst of all, I fear that Beau will succumb to it.
As I have.

D79 was only the beginning.

June 2, 2018
One month after The Breach
Location: Ghazni
Entry: six

THE PRICE OF LOYALTY

Washington D.C.
August 8, 2020

IT WAS RAINING OUTSIDE. But that wasn't what made the mood glum or what had sucked all the life out of the air at what seemed like a random time on a random day in August. This day, however, would not be so easily forgotten.

Special Agent Thomas Lawton watched the casket lower, the ceremony convene and the cries from the deceased's family ensue for what felt like hours, but had only been a short amount of time.

Time, Lawton mused, though he wasn't particularly certain what was ironic about that. Perhaps it was the fact that he'd attended many funerals with the man who was now buried six feet beneath the earth that Lawton, precariously, stood above.

You get sick, after a while, Derek Vince had told him, in 2001. *You get bloody fucking tired of losing people that sometimes you lose yourself.*

Lawton remembered 9/11 like it was yesterday.

He had been there, in New York City, where the Twin Towers had been struck by jihadists that, at the time, had no idea what sort of ripple effect would happen. Or maybe they did know. Those bastards.

Maybe they knew that, a little over eighteen years later, America would be at war with the Middle East when the fight should've been against terrorism itself. Unfortunately, Lawton reminded himself, terrorism was an idea, and a contagious one that had the potential, as it did, to light the world on fire from time to time.

It couldn't be snuffed out with drone strikes or boots on the ground—no matter how much either of those felt good in temporarily quenching the thirst for blood. Neither, he admitted, was diplomacy any sort of hope for resolution, particularly when neither culture nor religion or people could come together and acknowledge that any similarities existed amidst a world of differences that divided them in the first place.

Not when planes crashed into buildings.

Lawton couldn't help but feel like Derek Vince, retired USMC and Special Agent for as long as he'd been in the business, was his plane.

Long after most of the funeral procession had departed, Lawton found himself seated on a bench several yards away. He tried to convince himself that it was because he was somehow trying to piece together the man's untimely death to save his own skin, or that it was because he didn't have anything to go home to and so staying would give him an excuse not to face the solitude.

But the truth was that Derek Vince, however brash, had been his friend. He owed him a few more minutes.

Lawton's mind, as it always did these days, wandered back to the case at hand—the one he felt compelled to finish even more now, if not for his friend, but for the fear that came with the knowledge that words weren't just words on a page anymore. Words were actions, actions that had put Vince here in the first place, and could very well put Lawton himself here soon, too.

Lawton glanced at the gravestone and pictured a different name on that stone and wondered if the case of Beau Moiré, Justin Roland and Wesley Marshall was worth the picture in his head.

As dusk began to fall on Washington, D.C., Lawton felt the woman's presence before she spoke. Who was she to think she could sneak up on an FBI agent?

Oh, right.

"My condolences, Mr. Lawton."

Lawton didn't turn. "Thomas," he reminded her.

"Thomas." The woman paused for a second longer than normal. "He was your friend?"

"More of a mentor, really." Lawton breathed in the scent of her, his nose picking up a strong hint of dust. "If I may, what cellar does the CIA have you digging in now, Ms. Vienne?"

If she was surprised that Lawton had tapped her files or called her out on it, she didn't show it. Savanna Vienne took a step forward so that her thin frame was parallel with the bench on which Lawton's slouched figure was perched. In his peripherals, he noticed the way her knee bent to the perfect degree beneath the black skirt she wore over sheer panty hose that poorly matched the circumstance.

That she was trying to seduce him, and had been trying since the very first encounter, was evident. Whether it was working or not…

"I asked you a question last time," Savanna said abruptly, catching his boyish brain off guard yet again.

"You asked me if I like him, him meaning Democratic Nominee for President Tyler Millerton." Lawton turned to give the woman his full attention. "Have you come to acquire a different response?"

"I've come to tell you that you're wrong."

Savanna locked eyes with Lawton as if the façade she'd been maintaining meant nothing to her now. Lawton took a moment, as he'd been trained, to ponder what hidden agenda she was seeking by making such a statement, but the sheer boldness of it stopped him from being able to form a proper conclusion.

"Wrong, Ms. Vienne?"

"Wrong."

"How so?"

Savanna smiled, causing the skin surrounding her lips to wrinkle in a way that a twenty-year-old's would not. Lawton got the feeling her age wasn't the only thing she was trying to cover up.

Not that cover-ups were all that shocking for a CIA agent.

"Ask your friend, Thomas."

Lawton followed to where her gaze rested on

Vince's gravestone. The indecency of the accusation made him suddenly angry.

"You're telling me Tyler Millerton is responsible for murdering this man?"

"Murder?" After a brief pause, she feigned surprise. "I was under the impression your friend died of a heart attack."

"You of anyone should know that impressions can be deceptive," Lawton replied coolly. He was growing tired of the banter, the games. Besides, Lawton realized that he had already revealed too much.

She's good.

But Lawton didn't want to play anymore. Not when the stakes had become so high and people were dying all over again. Not when he'd put too many lives at risk already. He glanced at the gravestone one last time, got to his feet and turned to depart.

"Be careful, Thomas. They're watching you."

Lawton paused and gripped the hat in his lowered left hand tightly between his fingers. Finally, he looked up and placed it atop his head. "I know."

"Then you already know what the answers you are searching for entail." Savanna Vienne stepped to meet him, her eyes intense, voice low. She reached out and touched his wrist before he could return it to his side. Her fingers were warm despite the cool air.

Lawton lowered his eyes and couldn't help but notice the way her fingers, all of them, were bare.

Lawton took a breath and made a decision.

With barely a sound, he asked, "How far does this go?"

A light entered Savanna's eyes, if only for a moment. But the one brief flash told Lawton that she understood—and had for a while. It appeared she had been waiting for *him* to understand.

But Lawton didn't want to. He didn't want to acknowledge that perhaps this woman had an agenda aligned with his. He didn't want to realize that the case he was following could lead to secrets, lies and more death. He also didn't want to believe that perhaps the CIA was just as much at fault for this weirdness as the FBI—that alone spelled dire consequences.

But above all, Thomas Lawton did not want to accept the extent of corruption that came with Savanna's next words.

As smooth as a loving wife planting a kiss on her husband's cheek, she leaned in and pressed her lips against his skin. But just before the contact was made, her whispered words hit him first.

"All the way."

Savanna Vienne retracted her touch, like a withering goodbye, and walked away without looking over her shoulder.

Lawton, though not shocked by her words as much as that she'd spoken them to him, after all of the allusion, sat back down on the bench beside the graveyard.

He wasn't sitting long before the phone in his right pocket began to ring. Without shifting his thoughts, Lawton lifted the device to see who was calling.

Out of the frying pan…

"What is it, John?"

"Mr. Lawton, finally. I've been trying to reach you for hours, sir. I mean uh, Thomas." The man's young voice was quick, rushed. He backpedaled suddenly. "Oh, right, Mr. Vince's funeral…"

"Over. What is it?"

John Lansford got straight to the point. "Do you remember the files we discussed weeks ago? The personal files of Moiré, Marshall and Roland and their lives before they joined the U.S. Army?"

"Yes?"

"Remember how you and I agreed that they all cut off on the same day. August 18, 2016."

"Yes?"

"And we agreed that, despite our efforts to recover them, the files were deleted from the National Archives?"

"Is this a 'true' or 'false' quiz, John? Have I passed?"

Like a seasoned partner, Lansford ignored the quip. "Yet, despite all of that, we wondered why *all* the files, why the very existence of these men, wasn't erased entirely to avoid this kind of disparity."

Lawton paused. "Go on."

"That's just the thing. The files *were* lost, Thomas. All records *were* erased entirely. *Wesley Marshall brought them back.*"

Lawton leveled his stare as his mind went back to work. "Where did you find record of that?"

Lansford didn't skip a beat. "I have a contact I've been conversing with," he said offhandedly. "The point is that Marshall hacked into the CIA and reinstated files for Moiré, Roland and himself. *He placed the cutoff date as August 18, 2016. Intentionally two years before the three went Absent Without Leave.*"

"You're telling me that this man, Marshall, recovered information that had previously been erased by…himself?" Lawton tried to soften his skepticism. "And only *half* of the information?"

"The files weren't deleted by Marshall, my contact confirmed they were erased by an advanced technological communications circuit in the Middle East," Lansford recited. "What if Marshall brought them back so that we, or someone like us, Mr. Lawton, could see the holes, pick apart the discrepancy? What if he was pointing to that cutoff date as a hint of some sort?"

"You're telling me," Lawton reiterated, "that this man, Wesley Douglass Marshall, a twenty-year-old, recovered information that had previously been erased by *an advanced technological communications circuit in the Middle East* for himself and two other ex-soldiers who are also *on the run* from the United States government while they were in the U.S. Army? And no one at all sought to question that?"

"Code 3394:6 of the National Archives' database states that all information and/or intelligence breaches during a time of war are to be investigated solely by the federal government, and can only be approved for release by said government. Which ironically includes organizations such as the Central Intelligence Agency. They didn't have to make anything public, sir. Not even their own involvement.

The law protects them."

"How do you even—?"

"I don't think our government is the only thing these soldiers are running from, Mr. Lawton," Lansford continued, making his final pitch. "Like you, I immediately assumed that perhaps Marshall, Moiré and Roland were held hostage in Afghanistan. But their trafficking across the country is too frequent. They were working for someone, doing something. So, I dug further, and I picked up a power grid from a friend in the Foreign Affairs Department—"

"—You seem to have a lot of friends, John—"

"Tell me, where were the fugitives stationed again, collectively?"

Lawton racked his brain before he replied, "Zaranj, Sheberghan, Tehran and Ghazni."

"All of which have been pulling enough power to generate the entire American west coast." Lansford took a mandatorily dramatic pause. "That doesn't sound like typical military practices to me, sir."

"It sounds like an advanced technological communications circuit in the Middle East?"

"I have reason to believe so, yes."

"Our people have been there." Lawton looked up at the sky as if the answers would suddenly appear out of nowhere to back up his skepticism.

None did.

He sighed. "As detailed and well-researched as all this sounds, John, I can't help but believe that, if there were a terrorist operation occurring at any or all of these sites, our people would've recognized it and shut it down."

"What if they are our people," Jonathon Lansford said.

Lawton opened his mouth to respond, but words got lost in his throat.

Lansford seized the opportunity to continue. "What if the military bases we've established in each of those areas is run by terrorists using our faces, our military, our men and women to carry out their plans? What if Moiré and Marshall and Roland are running from the very same people we're *also* fighting against."

Lawton removed the hat from his head slowly.

"What if we're not enemies after all, sir?" Lansford said with finality. "What if we're allies?"

Something inside of Lawton's mind clicked just then, the way it obviously had for John Lansford, for Savanna Vienne and, perhaps, Derek Vince—before it was too late. He eyed the etched stone again. What else had Vince known? What more was there to know?

Was the United States Army compromised?

Had Lansford, a man who'd been working for the Federal Bureau of Investigation for less than a year, really figured that out?

The kid's got talent, not to mention charisma, Vince had said. *You could use someone with a different view from you, Lawton.*

It's all about perspective.

Trust no one but yourself, your experience and Jonathon Lansford.

And was there a glaring possibility that it didn't just end there? That, perhaps, the U.S. Army was just the tip of the iceberg?

Clearly Savanna Vienne, a top operative for the CIA, thought so.

How far does this go?

All the way.

Lawton took a breath and recounted the words in his head once more, playing it all back to him, fitting all the pieces together, and this time he allowed the meaning to hit him full force without the slightest bit of a safety net that he'd allowed himself in 2001.

All the way.

The hat gripped between his hands fell to the earth. Because, despite all the holes that remained, Lawton couldn't reject that maybe Savanna's warning, Vince's hints and Lansford's argument all added up into one deadly truth, with deadly implications.

It was September 11th again, and the planes were coming.

What if we're not enemies after all? What if we're allies?

The young man, however, forgot to ask one vital question.

Allies against *who?*

Zaranj, Afghanistan

BEAU HADN'T SLEPT IN over three days, and he didn't dare try to change that now.

The sky had poured out all its fury, soaking the

earth and drenching the sand so that he was forced to trudge through it like it was thickening mortar. The clouds had settled hours ago, dispersing as if to avoid the reckoning that morning would bring—leaving the horizon an endless sequence of varying degrees of darkness. The ones closest to the city of Zaranj were beginning to brighten.

He wasn't sure how far he'd walked, or how long it would be before he reached the city, or if he'd even accomplish the feat by morning. To be honest, it didn't matter. He was in no hurry to race back and tell the others what had happened. Tell them about Wes. About Michael. About the truth behind Beau's past.

Somehow, it didn't shock him that Michael knew more than he'd let on. Michael was always smarter than him, which was part of the reason why Beau had blindly fallen in line behind his brother all those years when he should've realized where that sense of blind loyalty would lead.

Wes was different.

Luke. What would he say when Beau told him his own brother was a traitor to their cause? Would he also turn away from Beau and decide to abandon him entirely? Did family outweigh the years of friendship they all shared?

He didn't know.

Beau's muscles shook from the consistent movement and the fatigue that he just couldn't shake. He stopped pacing forward for one brief second to let his body catch up, but doing so made it worse. He tried to let himself down easy, but the weight of the hour and the injuries he'd sustained made it hard not to crash to the sand the way he did just then.

Lying on the ground, the moisture in the sand soaking through his clothes felt unusually cold against his skin. Like water among the wreckage of the plain that had never crashed down on the east coast.

Beau closed his eyes and counted to ten.

It didn't go away. It never really did.

How could he believe that his parents could've died before ever making it back to America? How could one picture and a few dozen words stand a chance against the distant sensations, the fragile jumble of memories he had of that snowy night in Pennsylvania? Deep down Beau remembered the soft, subtle humming of his mother. Like a ringing in his ears that never quite made it out of his head, he could hear the melody of her voice from time to time.

The same couldn't be said about his father. No matter how hard he tried to picture the man outside of the photos, beyond the grey charcoal uniform, there was just nothing.

Nothing but the gun in his lowered right hand, his father's own weapon, that he'd taken from Michael many years ago.

You're nothing like Alexander.

You're nothing.

Beau realized for the first time that the voice in the back of his head, the one that never seemed to let up, was Michael's voice. It had always been his voice.

Beau put one unsteady foot beneath him and used it to stand. He wasn't going to stay here and die. Not with his brother's voice inside of his head egging him on.

It wasn't even about proving it wrong anymore. Or maybe it was. Either way, Beau knew that it would chip away at him, little by little, if he stayed in one spot and allowed the voice to do so. So he walked away with all the rigid grace of the soldier he was, but only after the damage was done and he felt it in his heart that the words were truer than he could've ever been willing to admit to himself.

Despite the fact that he had no memory of his father, Beau knew one important thing.

He was nothing like Alexander.

Beau dropped the 1911 Colt in the outline of his body in the sand and didn't turn back for it. Whether it was a weight lifted off him or an anchor that would eventually pull him under, Beau didn't know that either. He just kept walking, and when the voice came back, like it always did, igniting a fire inside of his mind, he walked with his head tilted down.

Because he was afraid that, if he looked up at anything, he'd see it burst into flames.

The outline of Zaranj was visible in the distance. Beau leaned against the fractured remains of a building, watching the sky as it consumed the darkness, replacing it with a warm glow of orange. The aura was peaceful and restorative, but not to Beau.

Somewhere along the way, he'd grown angry.

One day you'll find yourself questioning it, you'll search to the ends of the earth for the answer because that's what you do, what you've always done. But it is inside of you, it is everything good in you. Honesty, purity, peace. The drive, the passionate fire to fight for those whom you love. I don't challenge you to accept it—you're not ready, not yet. I only ask that you remember it. Because one day, it will be tested and it will be the key to discovering your purpose in life.

Remember the reason you fight.

Beau pulled his knuckles in tight against his palms and slammed his right fist back against the wooden siding.

"You're going to need those fists when the real fight begins."

Even as tired as he was and off-balance as his stance, Beau spun at the sound of the stranger's voice. His fingers reached for the gun that was always in the small of his back, but when his fingers touched air after he remembered he'd discarded his failsafe weapon, Beau held his knife out instead thinking he was at least going to put up a fight.

The man was standing less than three yards away, a smile on his face and a pistol in his hand. *Damn.*

"Drop your weapon."

"You first," Beau said.

The man smirked. "As tempting as it would be to see your skill with that knife." He dropped the gun to the sand like it was nothing to him, his expression still bearing amusement that furthered Beau's adrenaline, anger and suspicion. He noticed. "Relax. I'm not going to fight you."

"Like you could win?"

The mysterious man's smile widened, and it jolted something in Beau's head. He remembered that smile, the face. But where?

"Careful, my boy," the man said calmly.

"Confidence can often be mistaken for arrogance."
He stepped out of where he was shadowed by the
glow of the morning sun and Beau took note of the
man's appearance instantly. He was shorter than him,
with broad shoulders and a smart face. His hair was
pitch black with strands of gray that stood out
between the strands. His face, however, seemed
young. There was an energy about him that radiated
strength to a cause that remained unknown. He was
dressed in charcoal grey.

He seemed to study Beau just as much without
even lowering his eyes. "But you're not arrogant at all,
are you, boy? You're just angry."

"Stop calling me boy."

"Alright, Beau. What shall I call you? Enemy?
Ally?"

Beau narrowed his eyes and lowered his knife
but didn't sheath it. He trusted this man almost as
much as he trusted a pierced lung to supply breath. "I
don't know who you are or why you're following me,
but I suggest you turn around. I'm not who you think
I am."

"Of course you're not." The man laughed. "And
I'd be willing to bet you're not who *you* think you are,
either."

Beau shook his head. He was tired of the mind
games, of the joke that everyone seemed to be in on
these days. Quite frankly, Beau was sick and fucking
tired of everyone telling him who he was not.

Eyeing the man one last time, Beau turned and
started to walk again; he kept the knife close, counting
his steps and listening for the sound that would

follow. He was ready for it.

He wasn't ready for the words that took its place.

"Alexander Moiré was my best friend."

Beau paused, then shook his head. "I doubt it."

"Alex was murdered, as was your mother, Diane, when you were five years old and your brother Michael was eight, because of an organization called Division-7-9, currently based in the underground tunnels of Ghazni, Afghanistan—I place I assume that you, Beau, are very familiar with."

Beau did stop this time. He turned and gave the man a very simple stare—suspicion. "Who are you?"

"My name is Wyatt Vendelle."

His breath caught as he recognized the face to match that of the picture on the screen in the NetComm bunker. *Wyatt Vendelle.*

"You're supposed to be dead," Beau said, frowning. Vendelle merely smiled as if to say *so are you.* Fair enough, he thought.

"What do you want?"

The friendly face vanished, and Beau recognized an end to the façade that he wasn't in the mood for anyway.

"You think you're alone in all of this, but you're not." Vendelle took one calculated step forward. "I was a soldier for Division-7-9 when your father served them. When he left, I left. He couldn't evade Division when they came for him, and for that I am sorry."

Beau stared straight ahead, unmoving.

"But I did. I've been in the shadows for a long

time. Watching. Waiting." The man kept his voice low, but his tone was far from neutral. "But I am here now, and I'm going to get what I came back for. Something tells me, Beau, that you and I share a common interest."

Beau lifted his eyes to find Vendelle's smile returned. It was a cold smile that matched his words.

"Blood," he said. "Together, we can get it. Together, Beau, you and I can destroy Division, can topple the coward who calls himself The General once and for all. Together, we can end this war."

Beau felt his breathing slow even when his pulse began to pick up. The fire in Vendelle's words sparked something in him that, no matter how hard he tried to smother it, burned as blue as the sky.

"No more games, no more running and no more deaths. Isn't that what you want most? To protect the ones you love?"

Remember the reason you fight.

No. What he wanted most was freedom. Freedom to do as he pleased, go where he wished, without fear of losing himself and his loved ones anymore. Freedom to be who he wanted to be, not who the organization had turned him into. To be with Leah, somewhere safe where colors didn't remind of him of blood or fire or pain. Beau wanted safety, security. Simplicity. Peace.

At least, he *used* to. But now?

Remember the reason you fight.

With a shock, he realized that Raymond had been right, all those weeks ago, on a plane ride he would never return from. Raymond had known Beau like no other had. His words from that night, from the beginning of the crack that had begun to split his family, his team, flowed through Beau's head at that moment, outshining the time when Ray had told him to remember the reason to fight.

No, you don't know what you want, why you fight. You never have.

Vendelle's hand remained extended in the morning light. Like a chance to flip to a new page, a new beginning—one that promised a different ending.

"Why should I trust you?" Beau said.

Wyatt Vendelle lifted his left hand. In it was Beau's 1911 Colt. "What do you have to lose?"

Beau lowered his head and clenched his fists. He thought of his mother, murdered in cold blood because of something she had never been in control of. He thought of his father, a man who he'd always sought to embody, not realizing he was embodying the very essence of all that drove him mad with rage.

Nothing. He had nothing to lose. Not anymore. He let go of his prejudices, his guard, the voices in his head that always held him back. Michael. Raymond. The soft voice of his mother's careful hums, her safety and her protective layer of a love that was long lost.

No, Ray. I don't know.

But I will find out.

Beau thrust his hand out and took the weapon into his hand once again. It felt different this time. Or, maybe, *he* was different.

Because in his head, Beau finally pictured justice that matched the tattoo that had become his defining mark. Beau saw a way out of the bloodbath, a beginning that started with retribution and ended with peace—peace for himself, for his family, for the country he longed to protect and the people who deserved every definition of the word.

But first, he would fight. He would do whatever it took to make sure that no more innocent lives were destroyed. Zaranj would be an example, not only to the organization but to Beau and his team, that the price already been paid.

War, then peace.

Meanwhile, with a patient smile, Wyatt Vendelle had something a little different in mind.

✦

ABOUT THE AUTHOR

Amber Renee, the only daughter in a family of seven, grew up in the mountains of West Virginia before moving to Tionesta, Pennsylvania, where she attended school and began work on *Spin of Fate*, the first book in her breakout series, Pawns. Published a little under two years later, *Price of Loyalty* is the second installment in the Pawns series. Amber now has an undergraduate degree from the University of Pittsburgh, and is pursuing a graduate degree at Syracuse University—all while simultaneously planning a wedding, learning a second language and working to complete the action-packed series. As always, she is grateful to God, and family for keeping her passion and drive alive, and to her readers for tagging along on this heart-racing adventure. Stay tuned for the final installment, *Soldier of War and Peace,* coming soon.